"Have a seat in the waiting room," she called out. "I'll be with you shortly."

Her voice carried a slight lilt. Not nearly as pronounced as his Irish nanny, but still detectable. The sound conjured thoughts of his youth, of playing hide-and-seek and hot-and-cold. He couldn't remember the last time he'd had fun.

Lantern light painted the woman in a golden glow. Dark hair coiled at the nap of her neck. She wore a serviceable gown of gray with an apron tied at her waist. She was of average height with a slender waist that tapered to generous hips. Curves in all the right places, his schoolmate Donald Marcum would have said. Donald also had several missing teeth, courtesy of an angry husband who didn't appreciate having his wife's attributes so verbally categorized.

She handed the patient a glass swirling with murky liquid. "Drink this, Mr. Pardue. It will help with the pain and there's also something in it to stimulate faster healing."

Anson stiffened. Images surfaced of a crate of empty tonic bottles shoved beneath the bed. Of his wife Alice lying on the mattress, cold and lifeless. No one would die of drinking a charlatan's brew again. Not while he drew breath.

Praise for Donna Dalton

I am immediately intrigued by the young woman with healing abilities who is trying to find her place in the world.

Check out Donna's other historical romances available from The Wild Rose Press, Inc.:

Magic in Her Eyes, The Gifted, Volume One
The Cavalry Wife
The Rebel Wife
Irish Destiny
Irish Charm
Seven Swans Bride
The Gift
Loving Byrne

Magic in Her Touch

by

Donna Dalton

The Gifted, Volume 2

This is a work of fiction. Names, characters, places, and incidents are either the product of the author's imagination or are used fictitiously, and any resemblance to actual persons living or dead, business establishments, events, or locales, is entirely coincidental.

Magic in Her Touch

Cover Art by *Debbie Taylor*

The Wild Rose Press, Inc.
PO Box 708
Adams Basin, NY 14410-0708
Visit us at www.thewildrosepress.com

Publishing History
First American Rose Edition, 2018
Print ISBN 978-1-5092-2294-0
Digital ISBN 978-1-5092-2295-7

The Gifted, Book 2
Published in the United States of America

Dedication

I dedicate this book to my friend and co-worker Juanita Hobson. Her support and delight in my books has been quite uplifting.

Acknowledgements

I want to thank Alida Berman for her candid and insightful critiques, and my faithful critique partner Mary Ann Clark. I couldn't do this without you.

Chapter One

Indian Territories
September 1877

If the mountain wouldn't come to her, then she would go to the mountain.

Moira unpinned her apron and draped it on a wall peg. The starch held the cotton stiff and crisp even after hours of wear. Her simple day dress likewise showed little signs of creasing. Quiet days like today barely produced a pucker much less a wrinkle. While she didn't wish ill health on anyone, there surely had to be someone suffering who needed her help.

She penned a quick note to Mrs. Lidle. The elderly widow had left earlier that morning to visit her convalescing sister. She didn't want her companion to worry if she returned to find the place empty. Mrs. Lidle had agreed to stay at the office and act as assistant and chaperone without any compensation other than meals and a room. While the woman did little more than greet visitors, Moira was grateful for her kindness. And relieved. It was shocking enough that an unmarried young lady had assumed the position a man usually held—she didn't need to throw dirt in society's face by living alone.

She slung a thin wool cloak around her shoulders and snagged the physician's handbag from the table.

The black leather had been burnished to a soft, marbled gray over the years. Even the oak handle had been worn smooth and slick. The bag had served Doctor Troutman and the people of Mineral well. She hoped to do the same with a little luck and a lot of perseverance.

Her heels clicked on the floorboards, sounding like a clock in the wee hours of the morning when every tick stoked sleep's rebellion. On the other side of the hallway, the waiting room stood silent and empty with chairs lined in precise formation, awaiting patients. It had been that way since her arrival a month ago. Only a handful of folks had ventured inside, those desperate to ease the ache of a decaying tooth or the spasms of a tiresome cough…or men merely curious about the young lady who had come to administer to the sick. Those were few and far between and wouldn't put coins in her purse. Nor would it fulfill her pledge.

The matron of Seaton House orphanage had asked her to stand in as healer when the beloved town physician had unexpectedly passed on. The people of Mineral were important to Mrs. Campbell; therefore, they were important to her. She would do everything in her power to honor her mentor's request—to please the one person who had offered shelter and understanding when no one else would.

She tugged open the door and stepped onto the boardwalk. The late afternoon sun painted the main thoroughfare in broad orange strokes. Carts and wagons trundled past, their wheels clattering on the dirt-packed roadway. People rushed about, eager to complete their tasks before darkness set in, which it did in a hurry once the sun disappeared behind the towering mountain peak to the west. Established nearly fifty years ago, the mining community of Mineral sprawled at the foot of the Shoehorn. While mining operations still managed to unearth pockets of silver, the railroad coming through had been the chief boost to the town's population and economy.

Residential homes spread out to the south, tucked away from the dust and noise of the bustling business district. The smaller single-story dwellings of the merchant class stood as a buffer to the more ornate two-story homes of the wealthier citizens. She wouldn't find many open doors in either community. Not yet. Given time and proof of her abilities, they would come around. They had to. Failure was not an option.

She turned to the north where false-fronted stores paraded down each side of the street. Some advertised their wares behind large glass-plated windows. Mrs. Stone's millinery and dress shop had an exquisite display of hats and bonnets. A green felt cap adorned with white tulle and a dainty feather had caught her eye. But it would have to remain in the window until she had more than just lint lining her pockets.

Cool air swirled around her, and she clasped her cloak tighter. It wouldn't be long before winter descended and brought with it the ills of cold weather. She had to earn the people's trust. Fast. Else she risked returning to Seaton House in dishonor. For that matter, she might not be able to return at all. Mrs. Campbell was expected back any day now with a new batch of orphans. There may not be any room for her at the orphanage.

An approaching man edged to one side and tipped his hat. "Morning, Miss Devlin."

He wore a plain tweed suit, faded yet crisply

pressed. His beard and mustache were clean and neatly trimmed. Hair tonic glistened in his smoothed-down, short-cropped hair. He was as tidy with his appearance as the poet William Allingham was with words. However, instead of his usual bay rum scent, Mr. Cavendish smelled of apples. The sweet aroma triggered a mouth-watering vision of a barrel overflowing with freshly picked fruit. John Cavendish and his wife owned the general store in the next block, a quaint little shop that sold everything from pickles to pick axes to plows. In addition to the savory apples, she had discovered several boxes of glass bottles tucked high on a shelf, the perfect vessels for her potions.

She put on her most engaging smile, the one she used to calm fretful children and reassure anxious parents. "And a good morning to you, Mr. Cavendish. How is the missus? And young Peter?"

"They are doing w-we…" He shoved a handkerchief to his nose and sneezed—a loud honking noise that would make a goose proud. He frowned and wiped a snout glowing with rawness. "Pardon me. This morning my eyes started watering, and my throat turned raw. Now I'm sneezing. Didn't expect the winter sickness to start so soon."

His skin appeared normal, no tautness or flushing with fever. This was no winter sickness. She wagged her head. "I suspect you are merely suffering from hay fever. Weeds tend to sow their spores this time of year. When you breathe in the tainted air, your nose and eyes sometimes react to the particles."

His face crinkled. "Hay fever, you say?"

"It's not as grave as it sounds." She fished in her medical bag and extracted a blue tinted bottle. "I have something that will help ease those symptoms if you are of a mind to try it."

He eyed the bottle as if she held a snake. "What it is?"

"Just a tonic made from nettle leaves. It's quite harmless." She uncorked the bottle, drizzled a drop onto her finger, and plucked the droplet into her mouth. She smiled. "You see. Perfectly safe."

"I don't know... I'm not one for taking unfamiliar remedies."

Perhaps appealing to the businessman inside him would help. She stoppered the bottle and held it out to him. "Try it. Free of charge. Take one spoonful when you rise and one just before going to bed. If the tonic doesn't lessen your suffering, then you're not out anything except your time."

He hesitated, his mouth twitching as he considered her proposal. After a few seconds, his shoulders went up in a shrug. "I suppose it wouldn't hurt to try. It's quite frustrating when you stop constantly to sneeze while assisting customers."

"I imagine it would be." She handed him the bottle. "Twice a day should remedy the problem."

"Thank you, Miss Devlin. If this works, you will be a Godsend."

She nodded and resumed her trek down the boardwalk. One down. Two hundred to go. Giving away her wares wouldn't fill her purse, but a little goodwill and word of mouth could prompt more clients to seek her services. *Paying* clients.

Just ahead, a tall, slender man dressed in a somber suit of black slowed his approach. Color fled from his face. He clutched a Bible against his chest and muttered something under his breath. His Adams apple bobbed above the white necktie strapping his collar. He looked like a criminal about to face a hangman's noose.

"Good afternoon, Reverend Turnage," she called out in her most cheerful voice. Robins after a spring rain couldn't chirp any happier.

The pastor of Trinity Presbyterian Church made the sign of the cross over his chest and left the boardwalk for the other side of the road. Contrary man. As Granny Tate would have said, if you threw him into a river, he'd float upstream. He wouldn't call her a Godsend. Nor would he be visiting her any time soon, even if the grim reaper came rapping on his door.

She'd encountered many like him over the years. Religious zealots who considered anything abnormal to be spawned of Satan. A pang stabbed her heart. She'd lost a lot at their hands. First her mother, and then her beloved granny. If it hadn't been for Mrs. Campbell and Meredith Booth, those fanatics would have snuffed out her life too.

She shook off the maudlin thoughts. She had a job to do and dwelling on the past wouldn't get it done.

As she started forward, a low grumble tumbled through the town. The boardwalk began to wobble and shake. She glared at the distant peak. Dingled miners. One day, their blasting was going to cause more than just rattling and annoyed eardrums.

The rumbling got louder, the shaking more violent. Her feet threatened to go out from under her. She spread her arms for balance, pulse tripping. This was no blast tremor.

It was an earthquake.

The boards rattled and pitched beneath her. Dust

boiled up from the street. A cart mule fought his owner's hold. A horse yanked free from the hitching rail and bolted down the street, whinnying and kicking up its heels. On the next block, a large display window fell to the ground amid a shatter of glass. A loud screeching noise blasted the air as the sign over Mr. Cavendish's store swung loose and dangled precariously from one end. All along the street, shop doors flung open and people staggered outside, their faces stamped with terror.

After a few minutes, the shaking diminished. The grumbling slowed and then ground to a silent halt. Moira drew in several calming breaths. Her childhood home in the hills of Tennessee had growled with tremors from time to time. Nothing like this teeth-rattling shockwave.

People milled about, dazed and confused, calling to one another. A woman emerged from a nearby shop and braced against the door jamb. Blood oozed from a gash on her temple. It was the schoolmistress, one of the few people who had visited the office. Miss Neagle had come in seeking relief from a monthly flow that sent her crawling to bed with debilitating cramping. She appeared to need help once again.

Moira rushed to the woman and grasped a slender elbow. "Let me help you, Miss Neagle."

Glazed blue eyes rounded on her. "I-I was trying to get to the door when something fell from a shelf. It struck me on the head. Everything went black for a moment."

Moira steered the injured woman to the edge of the boardwalk. "Sit. Let me have a look at you."

Miss Neagle wobbled to the landing, and Moira

fished a clean cloth from the physician's bag. She dabbed gently at the gash. It wasn't very large, maybe an inch long at most. And shallow. The bleeding had already started to slow. Was there any damage underneath? While the schoolmistress's coloring was pasty, her pupils were the same size and reacting to the sunlight. A good sign. Granny Tate had told her the eyes were the window to the body and would show any injury lurking inside. Miss Neagle's wound seemed to be contained to the outside.

Moira dabbed blood from the schoolmistress's forehead. "How are you feeling? Still dizzy? Any queasiness?"

"I'm feeling a little better. Not as woozy as before. And no queasiness."

Good. Miss Neagle would recover just fine. Moira handed her the cloth. "Keep this pressed against your head just below the temple. There's a small gash. It's not serious, but I want you to stay here until the bleeding fully stops and you can stand without any dizziness."

"Will it need stitching?"

"I don't think so. It ought to heal fine on its own. You will probably have a headache for a day or two. Come and see me if it starts to bleed again or if the pain worsens."

Miss Neagle gave her a wan smile. "Thank you, Miss Devlin. You are just what the folks in this town need, even if they don't know it."

Moira merely smiled and pushed to her feet. Did anyone else need her help…even if, as Miss Neagle said, they didn't know it?

All along the street, people collected in pockets,

some frowning and pointing at the destruction, others sifting through the debris. A tearful child clung to his mother's hand. Another had buried his head in wide skirts. It would be a while before frayed nerves mended.

A horse-drawn wagon appeared at the far end of town, kicking up dust as it hurtled down the street. People shouted and scampered out of the way. Moira frowned. Only something grave would cause such a reckless and dangerous careening through a crowded town.

As the wagon drew closer, the driver became more distinct. A substantial beard stretched to the man's third shirt button and was an unusual mixture of red and brown. A few weeks ago, Claude Gunderson had brought his son into the office for the extraction of a stubborn baby tooth. It had taken quite a bit of sweet-talking to convince the boy to surrender his hairy anchor. The child finally let go and left with a gaping smile and a piece of peppermint.

The wagon rattled to a stop in front of her. "Miss Devlin," Claude said over a rushed breath. "You're needed at the sawmill straight away. The quake toppled lumber onto some workers. One of 'em is hurt right bad."

Her stomach tumbled. While she wanted to help those suffering, this was not what she had in mind. Now she had an abundance of patients to treat, any number of which could require *special* handling. Mrs. Campbell's oft repeated admonition scuttled in her head.

Be careful what you wish for. What you think you want may be more than you can handle.

****

Moira gripped the edge of the wagon seat as the horses galloped down Main Street. They raced past the Empire Hotel, past the livery, and past the saloons and brothels where even the drunks had left their whiskey and cards to survey the destruction. The quake had spared no one.

Buildings gave way to open space and to Dancer's Creek threading its way along the base of the Shoehorn. Gunderson reined the horses to the left and onto a well-worn path that paralleled the waterway. The crystalline water rushed along, undisturbed by the recent upheaval. A good thing. Disruption of the town's main water source would only worsen the disaster left in the earthquake's wake.

A large millhouse surrounded by a hodge-podge of open-sided sheds loomed ahead. The usually busy sawmill was eerily still. Nothing moved in or around the front of the building.

Gunderson guided the horses to the rear of the mill. Toppled boards littered the yard. Others balanced dangerously on listing stacks. Men surged around the piles, pulling out planks and shouting to one another. A battlefield after a barrage of cannon fire couldn't look more chaotic.

Gunderson tugged on the reins, and the two draft horses plunged to a prancing stop. Moira footed the cleat and clambered to the ground. The sun sat a hand's width from the top of the Shoehorn. Not much of the day left. They had about an hour of light before darkness intruded. She would have to work fast.

She shaded her eyes with a hand and scanned the swarming yard. "Where are the injured workers?"

Gunderson pointed to a large mound that looked as if someone had up-ended a box of oversized matches. "Over there. On the other side of that stack."

Clutching her medical bag and a handful of skirt, she raced around the heap. On the other side, three patients were lined up, waiting for treatment. The closest was a young man sitting with his knees bent and holding a bloodied rag to his head. She squatted next to him. His eyes were clear, his pupils equal and reacting to sunlight. No head injury. Good.

"I'm Miss Devlin from the doctor's office. I'm here to help. What's your name, young man?"

"John. John Smith. Most folks call me Johnny."

"Very well, Johnny. Would you please remove your hand, so I can have a look at your head?"

He hesitated, his brow furrowing. While his hesitation pinched, she couldn't let it interfere with her task. "It's all right. I only want to examine you. I won't do anything without your permission."

He nodded and lowered the rag. Blood leaked from a deep slash splitting the skin just above his ear. The red ooze clumped in his hair and slithered down his neck. Unlike Miss Neagle, this wound would require medical attention.

"You have a good-sized gash that will need stitching. I can do that at my office if you'd like. Are you hurt anywhere else? Any nausea or light-headedness?" At his shake, she pushed his hand back to the wound. "Keep that cloth pressed tightly to your head for now. I'm going to check these other workers."

She shifted to the next patient. While pain twisted his face, she recognized his bulbous nose and pock-marked skin. Hank Jones had come into the office several weeks ago, seeking help for an obstinate cough. He sat with his back against a wood barrel, his left arm clutched across his chest.

"Is it your arm that's hurting, Mr. Jones? Or your chest?" Arm would be preferable. Chest injuries could be quite dangerous, considering the precious organs protected beneath frail ribs.

Hank grimaced. "Arm. Feels like it's broke."

Nothing life-threatening, then. At least not at this point. His shirt sleeve was intact with no tears or blood stains. If fractured, the bone ends had not broken through the skin. A blessing for Mr. Jones. There would be no open wound to go septic.

"If it's all right with you, I'd like to examine your arm. Check for any fractures. I promise to be gentle." At his nod, she reached out and began prodding his lower arm with her fingertips. The bones were solid. No breaks. She moved her examination upward. Her fingers met a bulge halfway between elbow and shoulder. The man moaned.

"You're right…it is broken." She pulled her hands back. "The break will heal faster if the bone is properly reset and a splint applied. I can do that at my office and give you something for the pain, if you'd like."

He heaved a resigned sigh. "I can't be out of work waiting for this thing to mend. Mouths to feed, you know. Your tonic worked on my cough, so I reckon it'd be all right if you patched up my arm."

"Same for me," Johnny said. "I'd like you to stitch up my head. I can't afford to be out of work either."

"Perfect. When things settle down, I'll have someone help you to my office. Just relax for now."

She scooted over to the third patient. He lay prone

on the ground, eyes closed, chest rising and falling in quick, shallow draws. Unlike the other two coverall clad men, he wore a tailored tweed suit and shiny brogans. Definitely not a worker.

A soldier from the nearby army fort knelt beside him. Private Greene often visited the orphanage, bringing treats and town gossip. While beloved by everyone at Seaton House, he wasn't privy to the special abilities of the inhabitants. Mrs. Campbell only allowed a select few *normals* into the fold.

"Where is he injured, Private?"

Greene shook his head. "I'm not sure, Miss Devlin. Mr. Pardue was awake for a while, moaning and mumbling. He only just drifted off."

Not a good sign. "Is this Ben Pardue, the mill foreman?"

"Yes'm. We were picking out lumber for a requisition when the quake struck. I was on the other side of the yard, so I didn't see him get hit. One of the workers said they found him under a pile of boards."

She dropped to her knees beside the unconscious man. There were no visible gashes or bruising. No blood staining his clothes or the ground around him. Yet his skin color was fading, his lips and fingertips turning blue. An internal bleed could cause such symptoms and would quickly turn fatal if not stemmed. However, stopping the bleed would require something no one should observe.

She turned her gaze to Claude Gunderson. "All three of these men will need to be treated at my office. If you and Private Greene could assist Johnny and Mr. Jones to the wagon, I'll stay here with Ben until you return."

"Certainly, Miss Devlin." Claude motioned Private Greene. "You help Johnny. I'll take Hank."

Together, they helped the less critically injured workers to their feet. As the foursome disappeared around the stack, she made a quick survey of the yard. No one seemed to be paying her any mind. Most were digging through the wreckage and restacking fallen lumber. It was the perfect time to employ her gift.

She unbuttoned Mr. Pardue's jacket, vest, and then his shirt, exposing his chest and upper stomach—the core of the body. His skin was pale and dotted with sweat. His breaths were slowing. She had to work fast, else death could descend.

She closed her eyes and rubbed her hands together in a brisk motion. The noise in the yard diminished until all she heard was the rapid thud of her heart. The sharp odor of cut wood retreated. The breeze batting her face abated. The only sensation she felt was the energy building inside her like a swirling whirlpool.

A ball of heat formed beneath her ribs. It pulsed and bucked, fighting for release. It was time. She gave the ball a mental push. A current of heat streamed down her arms and pooled in her palms. Her skin tingled. Her fingers twitched. It was like submerging her hands in a tub of warm water after being chilled by the snow. Soothing, yet not without pain.

Ignoring the ache, she placed her hands on Mr. Pardue, just below his breastbone. Energy leapt from her and gushed into him. His muscles shuddered beneath her fingertips. He moaned but remained still.

She guided the probing stream along his spine and up to his head. Everything was white and warm…normal. She moved down his throat to his heart.

Still beating—a little unevenly, but that was to be expected when there wasn't as much blood to move through the vessels.

His lungs were clear, drawing and expelling air with no whistling or rattling. She slowed over his ribs. The curved bones swathing his back glowed red and throbbed. Most likely the place where he'd been struck. She shifted her search to the liver. It was cold and oozing. *There you are.*

She drew in a deep breath and concentrated on sending pulsing waves of heat into the injury. The coldness warmed. The blackness lightened to gray and turned white. The seeping slowed and then stopped. She'd stemmed the bleed, but the liver still throbbed with rawness. Her healing only had the power to start the mending. It would be up to Mr. Pardue to do the rest.

A shout broke through the veil surrounding her. She withdrew her hands, trembling now from the aftereffects of using her gift. She would have to take care for the next few hours. Deep healing sapped her own ability to heal. Any injury to her person could be deadly.

Mr. Pardue moaned, and his eyelids fluttered open. Pink flooded into his cheeks and lips. His breathing evened out. He tried to sit up, but she stopped him with a hand to his shoulder.

"Keep still, Mr. Pardue. You have an internal injury. Moving may make it worse."

Frown lines scored his face. "I remember the ground shaking, and I crouched beside a pile of lumber. The stack shifted, and boards started tumbling off. One of them struck me on the back." He reached for his side. "What the devil… My pain. It's gone. What did you do?"

Dingles. Perhaps she should have stopped just shy of fully repairing his bleed. Unfortunately, the sawmill foreman was too far gone for that. Anything less than a total heal would have resulted in his death. She'd have to do a little zig-zagging to keep him off the scent.

She reached out and pulled the folds of his shirt together. "I didn't do anything except examine you for injuries. There's bruising on your back and your stomach is rigid…all indications of a possible internal injury. The shock is concealing the pain right now. However, once the numbness wears off, you will feel the ache. A lot of it. I'd like you to come to my office where I can apply a constrictive bandage and give you something for the pain."

He cocked his head and eyed her like a schoolboy puzzling over a tricky math calculation. "You're that healer from the orphanage. The one who took over for Doc Troutman."

Here it comes. The colorful epithets. The rejection. She forced a nod. "I am."

"Hank told me about you. Said your tonic cured his cough. And Fuller said you fixed his boy's broke finger as good as new."

"I did."

"Well I reckon that's good enough for me."

Relief swamped her. She would take good enough any day.

Footfalls thumped the ground, and then Claude Gunderson and Private Greene rounded the stack of lumber. The lanky soldier pulled up, his eyes going wide as wagon wheels.

"Glory be. I coulda swore Mr. Pardue was on death's door. Miss Devlin, you must be an angel."

Chapter Two

The stationhouse was no bigger than a two-stall barn. The door had been propped open, most likely to catch a breeze since the builder failed to fabricate any windows. The wallboards were faded and pocked. Several roof shingles hung at odd angles near the apex. In comparison, the antiquated train station in Philadelphia looked like the *Taj Mahal*. If this was any example of the rest of the town, his life of comfort and luxury would soon be nothing more than a cherished memory.

A train attendant approached, toting a traveling trunk as if it weighed no more than a sack of feathers. Muscles bulged beneath the cotton shirt, evidence of the man's fitness. "Here's yo' baggage, Doctor. Where does you want it?"

Anson motioned to the stationhouse. "Just set it over there near the door. I'll send someone to fetch it after I am settled in town."

The dark-skinned man grunted a response and rolled the trunk off his shoulder and onto the platform. Anson nestled his bowler hat onto his head. Now to take care of his own *settling*, whatever form that may take.

He traded the platform for a narrow lane leading toward a potpourri of buildings spread out at the foot of a towering mountain. The Shoehorn, Mrs. Wentworth had called the mount in her letters. Situated in the heart of the Indian Territories, the mountain and an army garrison protected the small mining town of Mineral from bad weather and bad men. For the unforetold future, this fortification would be his home.

The last slice of sun glimmered just over the mountain peak. Dusk would soon be upon them. He'd best hurry with his task, else he'd be fumbling around in the dark, a stranger in a strange town. Not a healthy situation to be in.

Dust billowed around his brogans, ruining the shine the bootblack had painstakingly worked into the leather. During the rainy season, the rutted lane would be nothing but mud. As would the wide thoroughfare that loomed ahead. There were no cobbles, no street lamps, or bricked walkways. Just rolling boardwalks that stretched along either side of a dirt-packed street. The town looked like a beggar needing a hand-out. He fisted the handle of his medical bag. He couldn't turn back now. He'd given his word, and he wouldn't betray Alice's memory by breaking it.

He footed the plank walkway to the right. False-fronted buildings lined the street, their windows glowing with muddied lantern light. There were only a handful of people going about their business. A woman stood near a shattered window, sweeping shards of glass into a pile. Farther down, two men toiled at straightening a store placard that dangled from one end. The place was in worse shape than he first thought. Beggarly didn't begin to describe it.

A man toting a lantern rushed toward him, his face pleated with worry. Anson held up a hand. "Pardon me, sir. If you could spare a moment… I'm looking for Dr.

Troutman's office."

The man slowed and glanced at the medical bag. "Are you a doctor?"

"I am. I have come to assume Dr. Troutman's practice at the behest of Mr. and Mrs. Wentworth."

"Good. We can sure use your help. Especially after a day like today."

"Why? What happened?"

"An earthquake is what happened. Shook the town right hard. Some folks were injured by falling rubble. The worst ones were taken to Doc Troutman's office so Miss Devlin can tend to them."

"Miss Devlin? Who is she?"

A shout echoed down the street. The man looked in that direction and frowned. He began shuffling backward. "Don't have time to explain. The doctor's office is back that way, first building on the left after you cross Stationhouse Lane. Good-day to you, Doc. Welcome to Mineral."

The man raced off, lantern swinging wildly at his side. Anson wheeled around and headed back the way he'd come. Earthquake. What next? An erupting volcano? He wouldn't discount such a calamity in this land of bleakness.

He crossed over Stationhouse Lane and bounded onto the walkway on the other side. The first building to the left was a two-story wood plank structure with a shingle hanging over the door that read, *Troutman MD – Surgeon and General Prac*. That would need to be changed as soon as possible. Let the people of Mineral know there was a new doctor in town.

He twisted the knob and pushed inside. A bell perched over the door clanged obnoxiously at the intrusion. He grimaced. Noisome creature. Yet another thing he would have replaced.

He stepped into the foyer and closed the door behind him. The brisk aroma of soap mixed with a hint of vinegar assailed him. Not the carbolic acid he was accustomed to smelling, but any disinfectant was better than none.

To his right was a brightly lit parlor with chairs lining the walls. Two men sat quietly, one with his head swathed in bandages. The other had his arm cradled in a sling. Cripes. He didn't expect to be seeing patients on his first day in town. Yet that was the life of a physician, big city or not.

On the other side of the foyer, an open doorway led into another well-lit room where a man sat on an examination table. A band of white sheathed his upper torso. A woman stood beside him with her back to the doorway.

"Have a seat in the waiting room," she called out. "I'll be with you shortly."

Her voice carried a slight lilt. Not nearly as pronounced as his Irish nanny, but still detectable. The sound conjured thoughts of his youth, of playing hide-and-seek and hot-and-cold. He couldn't remember the last time he'd had fun.

Lantern light painted the woman in a golden glow. Dark hair coiled at the nap of her neck. She wore a serviceable gown of gray with an apron tied at her waist. She was of average height with a slender waist that tapered to generous hips. Curves in all the right places, his schoolmate Donald Marcum would have said. Donald also had several missing teeth, courtesy of an angry husband who didn't appreciate having his wife's attributes so verbally categorized.

She handed the man a glass swirling with murky liquid. "Drink this, Mr. Pardue. It will help with the pain, and there's also something in it to stimulate faster healing."

Anson stiffened. Images surfaced of a crate of empty tonic bottles shoved beneath the bed. Of Alice lying on the mattress, cold and lifeless. No one would die of drinking a charlatan's brew again. Not while he drew breath.

He pounced into the room. "Don't drink that."

The woman whirled around. She had a pert nose and full lips. The faint kiss of sunshine tainted her silky skin. While beautiful in an exotic sort of way, he preferred his women more refined. Not this bold raven with ebony eyes spitting fire and outrage.

"Excuse me?" Incredulity stained her voice. "Who are you? And why are you interfering with my patient?"

He thumped his medical bag onto the sideboard. "I am Dr. Anson Locke, the new town physician. These are *my* patients now. I won't allow you to administer snake oil or any other poisonous concoction to them."

Red blossomed in her cheeks and rushed to her ears. She cupped those wide hips, her left hand notably absent of a wedding ring. "My potions are not poisonous, nor do they contain snake oil."

The man sitting on the table wagged his head. "Miss Devlin wouldn't give me anything harmful. She's good and kind and has a gentle touch. Her doctoring didn't hurt a' tall."

Footfalls thudded in the foyer and sling-arm man filled the doorway. "Mr. Pardue is right. Miss Devlin set my broke arm quick and clean as you please with almost no pain. She's a real prize, she is."

So, this was the mysterious Miss Devlin. She possessed more medical skills than a nurse, yet she looked far too young to be a certified physician. Not to mention being a woman. Very few females in his experience entertained the notion of being a doctor, much less accepted as one. "Are you a physician? Did you apprentice under Dr. Troutman?"

She shook her head. "I'm a simple healer. I was asked to care for the people of Mineral when Dr. Troutman passed on."

Faint clock gongs drifted in from the foyer. The mournful peals sounded like a funeral dirge. Anson squared himself. There would be no deaths. Not on his watch.

He crossed to the examination table. Mr. Pardue sat straight, no slouching or guarding. His eyes were clear, his coloring normal. His chest rose and fell in regular intervals. He appeared hale as a horse.

Anson held out a hand. "May I have a look, sir?" At Pardue's nod, he set two fingers on a thick wrist. A steady, even pulse throbbed under his fingertips. Quite normal. He moved his inspection to the bandages swathing the man's back and pressed lightly. Pardue grimaced.

"How bad is the pain?"

"Not too bad. It's starting to ache again, but Miss Devlin said that would happen once the shock wore off."

"Shock?"

Miss Devlin shuffled closer. A burn scar ribboned across the back of her neck and dipped beneath her collar. It appeared to be an old injury, the blemish a translucent white while the skin around it was a healthy shade of cream. How had she come to have such an injury? Were there any other scars hidden beneath her humble veneer? The physician in him itched to trace the mark, to soothe any lingering pain. The rational part warned to keep his distance.

She picked up a white cotton shirt draped across the end of the table. "We had an earthquake earlier that sent stacks of lumber in the mill yard toppling over. Some boards struck Mr. Pardue's back, bruising ribs and perhaps his liver. I applied that constrictive bandage to keep him as immobile as possible until the injuries can heal."

The proper treatment for blunt trauma to the body. Except for...he pointed to the glass clutched in Mr. Pardue's hand. "And that?"

"A mixture of white willow bark and milk thistle. Perfectly safe, I assure you."

That's what all the snake oil peddlers claimed. "Be that as it may, your services as healer are no longer required. You may gather your things and leave. I shall administer medical care to the people of this town from now on."

The man on the table glowered at him. "Here now. There's no cause to be dismissing Miss Devlin out of hand. She's done a wonderful job taking over from Doc Troutman. No reason the two of you can't work together for the good of the folks in Mineral. The town is growing. We could use more than one doctor."

He could think of a thousand reasons why they shouldn't work together, the least of which she was uncertified. "Physicians are sworn to do no harm, Mr. Pardue. Those potions she dispenses are unproven and could be deadly. I won't have them peddled in my office."

"Miss Devlin brought me back from the dead. I trust her…and her potions."

Anson swallowed back the colorful rejoinder hopping on his tongue. Returning fire would only fuel the man's misplaced chivalry.

Mr. Pardue wasn't as inhibited. He hefted the glass to his mouth and proceeded to consume the swill in one continuous, noisome gulp. Once done, he lowered the glass and swiped a hand across his mouth. "There. I say Miss Devlin stays."

"Yeah, us too," came a chorus from the doorway.

Narrowed eyes dared him to disagree. Anson fisted his hands at his sides. If these men were any example of the pulse of the town, there would be an uproar if he forced the charlatan to leave. Best to let her dig her own grave.

The front door squealed open, bell jangling. The twosome shielding the doorway moved aside, providing a view of the foyer. A man toting a young boy stepped inside. Two other men and a woman trailed behind him. Great. More patients. It appeared he would have to swallow his outrage for a while longer, no matter how unappetizing.

"Miss Devlin, you and I will discuss our working arrangements later. For now, there are patients to attend to."

As he slipped out of his jacket, a throbbing gathered at his temple. His simple act of atonement was turning into an inoperable tumor.

****

Moira pulled open the front door and stepped to the

side. Lantern light splashed a golden streak across the boardwalk and into the darkened street. Nightfall had descended during the hours they had been seeing patients. Weary bones cried out for the soft bed in her chambers over the office. But sleep would have to wait. There were chores yet to be done, one of them not so appealing.

"Thank you, Miss Devlin," came a voice behind her. "The missus and I are grateful for your help. We'll pay for Luke's doctoring soon as we get the summer corn harvested."

She forced a smile through her exhaustion. "There's no hurry, Mr. Johnson. Pay when you are able. All you need to do right now is focus on your son. Try to keep him as still as possible for the next week or two. I know that won't be easy with a five-year-old, but the less he moves that arm, the faster the injury will heal."

Little Luke Johnson had dislocated his shoulder after falling from a tree during the earthquake. Dr. Locke had repositioned the bone while she had fashioned a sling to keep the boy's arm immobile. They had worked well together, like tightly-fit grindstones milling patients quickly and efficiently. Hopefully that seamless collaboration and the sawmill workers' enthusiastic endorsement would tip the scales to her advantage and the good doctor would consider keeping her on. Hopefully.

The door closed behind the Johnsons, and silence descended. The waiting room was finally empty after holding nearly two dozen visitors…more people than she'd seen in a month. While exhilarating, treating a constant stream of patients had sapped her strength. Her mind, however, had no such difficulty. It raced with thoughts of her life's latest complication.

He stood by the sideboard in the examination room, cleansing a piece of medical equipment with carbolic acid, an innovative new antiseptic. Dr. Locke was everything she wasn't. Well educated, as demonstrated by his fancy speech and advanced medical skills. And wealthy. His tailored suit and precisely barbered hair spoke of affluence and class. She couldn't find fault with his bedside manner either. He treated each patient, young and old, male and female, with respect and patience. The townsfolk were sure to welcome him with open arms. That didn't bode well for her, a woman of modest means and schooling.

With a heavy heart, she gathered the lantern from the waiting room and headed down the hall. She was evading the elephant in the office, but she needed time alone to think. When first asked to step in as town healer, she had balked at the idea. If anyone found out about her special skill, she could be labeled a witch and run out of town...or worse. She rubbed the scar at the back of her neck. It had happened before. But Mrs. Campbell had convinced her it was time to stop hiding and start living. This job was a chance to prove to herself that she could survive on her own without fear of discovery. Oddly, now that she'd had a taste of life outside of Seaton House, she wanted more of it.

All she had to do was convince a well-dressed mule to drink.

She stopped just inside the doorway to the storage room. Broken glass littered the floor. Blue, brown, and amber...a rainbow of destruction. The quake had rattled the bottles off the shelves and destroyed her precious stock. Was her life always to be filled with misfortune?

For every step forward, it seemed something cropped up forcing her two steps back.

She huffed out a growl and snagged a bucket from the corner. Sniveling was for cowards. She had never given up before. She wasn't about to start now.

She rolled her skirts into a pad against the glass shards and knelt. Using care, she plucked pieces of glass from the floor and tossed them into the bucket. Over the noisome clanging, the sound of footsteps thumped behind her.

"We need to talk, Miss Devlin."

The elephant had trumpeted. She glanced over her shoulder and into a gaze that ran over her, evaluating and assessing. Her arms prickled with gooseflesh. There was no denying the force of his presence. The wise thing to do would be to pack her belongings and leave. No one had ever called her wise.

She sat back on her haunches. "I know you don't want me to stay, Dr. Locke. But I was asked by someone I respect and admire to serve the people of Mineral. I would like to honor that request by continuing in my current capacity as healer and herbalist."

"With *whatever* those bottles contained."

His sarcastic tone sliced into her. She ignored the jab. She wouldn't give him the satisfaction of knowing how much his mistrust pinched. "Yes. With my herbs and medicinal potions." He didn't need to know about her gift. It would only fuel his quest to send her packing.

"Their medicinal value remains to be seen."

Stubborn as the day is long. She tossed a piece of glass into the bucket. "What made you want to become a physician, Dr. Locke?"

"Pardon?"

"Why medicine? Why not become a lawyer or a banker? You clearly have the intelligence, education, and the financial wherewithal to be anything you want. Why a doctor? It's not the most glamorous or well-paying of occupations."

Floorboards protested under the shuffle of feet. "I simply want to help those in need of medical aid."

"As do I, especially the children. They are so innocent and vulnerable. They need our help the most."

"You were uncommonly good with little Luke Johnson. He sat quieter than I've ever seen a child sit before. Most squirm and shriek like banshees while being treated."

His tone was softer this time, more respectful. She couldn't stop from looking back at him. His gaze met hers, curious and definitely more attentive. He had the bluest eyes she'd ever seen, dark and deep, like the ocean depths. His chin sported the faintest hint of a beard, in contrast to his perfectly barbered hair. He was slim and trim, his tweed suit only slightly rumpled from travel. He was a most attractive man. A man who would please a woman in many wonderful ways. Her body seemed to notice. Pleasing heat gathered under her ribs and spread into her belly. She smothered a groan. She should have better control of herself. Wanton behavior would not be tolerated. Not by her, and for certain, not by a Puritan like him.

She swung around and snatched up a chunk of glass. A jagged edge jabbed her finger. Pain bolted up her arm. She jerked back with a yelp. Blood bubbled on the tip of her index finger. Her stomach vaulted into a round of summersaults. Had her healing power restored itself? If not, the bleed could go on for hours.

Footfalls thudded closer. "You've cut yourself. Let me have a look."

The last thing she needed was to have him notice her oddity, either profuse bleeding or abnormally rapid healing. She hunched over, hiding her hand from him. She wrapped her finger with the apron tied at her waist. The barest hint of blood streaked the white. Good. Her powers had returned.

"It's just a little cut. Nothing to be concerned about."

"I can apply a bandage if you'd like. It's difficult to treat yourself one-handed."

Allowing him to touch her would be akin to poking a hornet nest. Control over her body already hung by a thread. A very thin thread. "A bandage is unnecessary. The bleeding has already stopped."

"So quickly?"

"Yes. A shallow cut, as I said." She gathered her feet under her and pushed upright. He was closer than she thought. His heat and the heady aroma of cologne cloaked her. Bay rum with a hint of lemon. Her head reeled. Her mouth went dry. She'd been hornet stung.

She took a step back and busied herself with shaking glass shards out of her skirts and into the bucket. He mustn't see her inappropriate reactions to him. It would only confirm his doubts about her suitability to remain as his associate.

"Are you all right, Miss Devlin? You look a little shaky."

The man was far too observant. She squared herself against his scrutiny. "I'm perfectly fine. As you were saying, little Luke sat quietly because he understood I only wanted to help him. That's all I want to do. Help people...in any capacity I can."

His hand shot out, and he seized the only surviving jar of potion from the shelf. Pink flushed his face. "How can you claim to want to help people? These potions are untested and if administered incorrectly can cause debilitation or even death."

What caused him to be so caustic and unbending? The few doctors she had come across had encouraged her holistic remedies, especially when modern medicines failed. She hefted her chin. "I am well-schooled in their use, and centuries of administering them have proven their worth. Are you not a man of science, Dr. Locke? Can you not admit there could be valid medicinal purposes for them?"

"You, my dear Miss Devlin, are far too young to have been properly educated in the art of medicine. It takes decades to learn such things. I'm still learning myself."

True. While she had absorbed every ounce of knowledge Granny Tate had to impart, she was learning new things every day. Like adding gunpowder to a plaster of crushed sheep sorrel leaves. According to the blacksmith in Willoughby, the mixture sloughed off obstinate skin blemishes quicker than a ripened tomato rotted. Unfortunately, the sociable smithy was one of the few people who would share such tidbits with her.

The distant bay of a wolf filtered through the square of window. A shudder coursed through her. If she couldn't convince Dr. Locke to allow her to stay, she would be out on her own, exposed, and at the mercy of sharp-fanged strangers.

"Give me two months to prove myself. You can inspect every ingredient that goes into every potion. You can observe their effects. Test them for yourself. If after that time, you or the folks of Mineral decide I am doing more harm than good, I will pack my things and leave."

"Absolutely not."

"Why? As you saw earlier, I am a very capable assistant. There was nary a hiccup in our collaboration. In addition, I could take care of the minor treatments by myself. That would allow you free time to study the latest developments in medicine."

The skin covering his jaw twitched. He opened his mouth to reply. She didn't give him a chance to spew any more venom.

"You heard Mr. Pardue and the other workers. They have confidence in my abilities…while you, a newcomer, will have to earn it. You have everything to gain by keeping me on."

He finally let go a grunt that could have meant anything. "I will give you one month. Not a day more."

Relief flooded her. "Thank you, Doctor. You won't regret your decision.

He leaned forward, eyes narrowing. "Know that I will be watching you, Miss Devlin. Closely."

Chapter Three

Anson stepped onto the porch landing and shucked off his hat. The stiff brim dug into his palm. He itched to do an about-face and retreat. But he couldn't. He had an obligation to fulfill...no matter how distasteful.

A wreath festooned with colorful ribbons and wildflowers decorated the plain wood door. Images sprouted of a grand ballroom drowning in flowers and streamers and people. A bride in a pale blue gown held court over the multitude, her head swathed in a coronet of roses and gossamer white ribbons. Alice flitted from perch to perch, trilling her happiness like a finch greeting the springtime.

It was the last time he saw her smile.

He shoved a hand into his pocket and fisted the small box inside. A chair by the hearth and the latest discoveries in the *New England Journal of Medicine* would be a much more enjoyable evening. But this visit had to be endured. He couldn't avoid them forever.

He dragged in a calming breath and knuckled the door. After a few moments of silence, footfalls clicked on the other side and the door swung open. A stouter, more mature version of the bride from the image appeared in the opening. Milky blue eyes widened, and a squeal of delight that would rupture even the sturdiest of tympanic membranes blasted over him.

"Anson. Oh, my sweet Lord in Heaven. You're

here."

Arms enveloped him, squeezing as if he were the only tree standing in the middle of an avalanche. He fought for a breath and was inundated with the cloying scent of lavender and vanilla. His head reeled. Alice had worn the same fragrance. Had bathed in the stuff, much to his nose's dismay.

He shifted, and Mrs. Wentworth thankfully eased her death grip. She leaned back, hands locked like talons on his arms. She was clingier than he remembered. And older. Her upswept hair was more white than blonde. Even her eyebrows were streaks of snow across her brow. Bags cradled her eyes, and folds of skin ringed her neck. The past few years hadn't been kind to her.

"Did you just arrive, Anson?" She craned her neck to peek around him. "The four o'clock from Guthrie must have been delayed. It's usually the last train run of the day."

He peeled out of her grasp and held his hat in front of him, a buffer from any further invasions. He liked people. He just preferred them in their own space.

"There was no delay. After arriving at the train station, I went to the doctor's office where I discovered an abundance of patients injured by the earthquake. I only just finished treating the last of them before coming here. Are you and Mr. Wentworth all right? Did you hurt yourself in the quake?" She didn't appear to be injured. Her eyes were clear. Her skin tone normal. She stood solidly on both feet, no swaying or favoring.

She gave a dramatic shudder. "The house shook like a railcar on an uneven track. I thought the walls were going to fall in on us. But everything stayed intact, thank the Lord. Stanley and I were unharmed."

"I'm glad to hear it. Many folks weren't so fortunate."

"I'm sure you patched them up good as new." She stepped back and motioned to the hallway behind her. "Please come in. Stanley is in the parlor having an after-dinner drink. You can join him and tell us all about your trip."

After the day he'd had, a mind-numbing glass of whiskey sounded quite enticing. But that would mean investing time in drink and chit-chat. He wanted this task over and done with as soon as possible.

He followed Mrs. Wentworth down the hall and into a small parlor. A painting of a young lady garbed in a sea of blue ruffles hung over the mantel. Her pale eyes drilled into him, condemning him for his failure.

Despite the heat in the room, a cold sweat popped over his skin. His chest tightened, and breathing became an effort. He forced his focus onto the hearth where a hearty fire popped and crackled. Odd for such mild weather. Yet the skeleton of a man huddled in a chair in front of the fireplace explained the need for warmth.

His face was sunken, his eyes rimmed with black circles. A lounging jacket sagged on gaunt shoulders. The past few years had been even crueler to Alice's father.

"Look, Stanley," Mrs. Wentworth crooned. "It's Anson. He's finally arrived."

The hairless skull turned, and a smile broke through the bony edifice. Mr. Wentworth fumbled for the cane propped against the chair arm. He pushed to his feet, wobbling like a newborn calf. "Anson, my boy.

It's good to see you."

Anson crossed the floor in three quick strides. He extended a hand, more to keep the man from falling than to offer a greeting. "It's good to see you too, sir. Please, don't get up on my account."

A bony hand clasped his and held for the requiem three seconds before releasing. Friendly, yet reserved. The reception he'd expected.

"Welcome to Mineral, son. It's good to have you here. Sorry we're not dressed for company."

"It's not a problem. I should have sent a note earlier, but things were quite chaotic at the office."

A claw claimed his elbow, fingers digging in. "Anson was helping folks who were injured in the quake. Such dedication. We're so glad you agreed to come. Mineral desperately needs a good doctor."

"I'm happy to be here." He motioned to the other chair facing the hearth. "May I sit, sir? It's been a long day. My legs aren't as young as they used to be." While he didn't want to stay any longer than necessary, getting Mr. Wentworth back into the safety of protective padding took precedence. Not to mention unfettering his arm from needy talons.

Wrinkles deepened on an already craggy face. "Don't I know it. By all means, my boy, have a seat."

As Mr. Wentworth settled back onto the chair, Anson eased out of Mrs. Wentworth's grasp and took the other one. His rear sank into the padded cushion and kept going. Something hard jabbed his left buttock. Definitely not in the best of condition. Nor was the rest of the room. The curtains were faded and showed signs of moth damage. The rug had a worn streak across the middle. Perhaps the mining business wasn't as prosperous as Mrs. Wentworth's letters proclaimed.

"Pour us a drink, Edeline. From the brandy Anson sent for Christmas."

Anson dismissed the offer with a wave. "No thank you, sir. I'm off for bed soon. Brandy will only keep me awake." It had been a long day. Full of hard work and mental turmoil. It would take that entire bottle of brandy and then some to shut off the prattle raging in his head.

"Oh toosh. One drink won't hurt."

"I agree. You could use a drink, Anson. You're looking a little pale." Footfalls shushed across the carpet. "Brandy will put some pink back in your cheeks."

Who was the doctor here? The clink of glass echoed from the sideboard. Then came the soft gurgle of liquid. His mouth watered. Perhaps she was right. He could use a drink.

"What changed your mind about coming to Mineral?" Mrs. Wentworth tossed over her shoulder as she poured. "You sounded so uncertain in your letters."

He'd been foundering in uncertainty for years. Alice's death had cannonballed into his life, destroying everything he knew and loved. Nothing seemed to matter anymore. Not his comfortable brownstone in Hamilton Village. Not his favorite foods. Not even his medical practice served to cheer him. He'd been a ship without a rudder. When his inattentiveness had almost killed a patient, he'd decided it was time for a change. The vacated medical practice in Mineral offered a lifeline, and he grabbed onto it.

"As you can imagine…" He glanced up at Alice's portrait. "Philadelphia holds far too many sad and regretful memories."

Mr. Wentworth nodded, his milky eyes watering. "Indeed."

Damn. The last thing he wanted was to cause the man pain. He shifted for a more comfortable position in the chair and only received another stab for his efforts.

"Moving to Mineral offered the opportunity to start anew…to honor Alice's memory without all the pain."

Lips cracked with dryness turned up in a knowing smile. Had Mr. Wentworth discovered a way to deal with his loss? He hoped so. The man deserved some ease in what appeared to be the last few years of his life.

Footfalls shuffled behind him and then Mrs. Wentworth was there, setting a pair of brandy-filled glasses on the table nestled between the two hearth chairs. Her gaze settled on the portrait. "Alice would understand your decision to leave Philadelphia. Mineral was her home for many years. She treasured her life here. She would be happy knowing you were recuperating with her friends and family."

Treasure. The reason he'd come. He fished the box from his pocket and held it out to Mrs. Wentworth. "I thought you might want this returned to you. Alice said it was a family heirloom."

She accepted the box and slid off the lid. Tears swam in her eyes. She traced a finger over the precious contents. "This necklace has been in our family for decades. I gave it to Alice on her sixteenth birthday. She said wearing it made her feel like a princess."

And he'd beheaded that princess. Well, not literally. But he might as well have. He snagged the glass from the table and took a hearty swallow. Fire bathed his tongue and coursed down his throat. It collected in a numbing pool in his stomach. Yet the spirit did little to deaden the ache piercing his heart. His incompetence as a husband had brought pain to these wonderful people, pain they didn't deserve. He had taken away their only daughter, their only joy. He owed them a lifetime of recompense.

"You don't have to return this, Anson. You can keep it. To remember her by."

His collection of memories would stagger Hercules. "No. It's a precious treasure. One you should have. Not me."

"As you wish. But I'm sure Alice would understand if you wanted to keep it."

He tossed back the rest of the brandy and set the glass on the table. He'd had enough. Of futile spirits and bleak talk. He pushed to his feet. "Thank you for the brandy, but it's getting late. I should be going. Tomorrow promises to be another busy day."

"You're welcome to stay here with us," Mrs. Wentworth said. "There's plenty of room."

"Thank you for the offer, but I've already sent my belongings to the boarding house just down from the office. Mrs. Gilliam's, I believe it's called. Miss Devlin recommended the place." As much as he wanted the charlatan gone, he didn't have the heart to evict her or her chaperone from the apartments over the office. From the look of Miss Devlin's outdated gown and worn shoes, she didn't have the funds to board elsewhere.

Mrs. Wentworth's mouth turned down as if she'd sampled something distasteful. She crossed arms over her bosom and gave a shudder worthy of the famous actress, Charlotte Cushman. "You shouldn't have anything to do with that healer woman. She's trouble. Send her on her way as soon as possible."

"That's my intention. However, she appears to have the support of a good number of the townsfolk. I must tread lightly with her dismissal. I want to earn people's trust; not offend it."

"You watch yourself, Anson. The devil lives in her. She comes from that orphanage of evil children. Witches, all of them."

Witches? Now that was going a little too far. Fanatical allegations of witchcraft had died out with the Puritans. Had Alice's death affected this heartbroken mother more than he thought? Was her mind, like her husband's body, on the decay? It wasn't out of the realm of possibilities with an emotion as powerful as grief.

****

Moira opened her eyes to pale sunlight dribbling through the curtains. Her head thrummed, and her body ached. Bedsheets snaked around her legs. Sleep had been elusive as a coin in shifting sand. She had one month to prove herself. Not a long period of time considering the folks in Mineral had only just begun warming to the notion of a lady healer. But she wasn't about to give up. She wanted this job, needed it, and nothing was going to stand in her way…not even her own misgivings.

That Dr. Locke would be watching her every move added to her unease. Not only was he a most handsome man, he was quite observant. Nothing missed that highly trained and penetrating gaze. She would have to take extra care to avoid prodding his suspicions—be as unremarkable as a noon shadow.

With a grunt, she flipped aside the bedcovers and rolled off the bed. It was past time to be up and about. Knowing her ill luck, Dr. Locke was already in the office and elbow-deep in some important task. He would frown at her idleness.

She slipped on worn but comfortable shoes and donned a simple work dress, one of two that hung in the wardrobe. After pinning on a clean apron, she secured her hair into a serviceable bun. A quick check in the mirror said she was as presentable as she would get. Hopefully the hawk-eyed doctor wouldn't notice the shadows cradling her eyes. He didn't need to know how much his presence affected her sleep. It would only encourage more hammering at her resolve.

Halfway down the staircase, the tinkle of the doorbell drifted up from the hallway. A patient? It was early, but then illness didn't carry a pocket watch.

She made for the entrance and found Evan Smithers standing in the doorway. Worry lines pocked the boy's face. Was his mother having more troubles? Annabelle Smithers had come into the office a few weeks ago, seeking ease from the strain of a late term pregnancy. White willow bark for a soothing tea and a good dose of reassurance should have lessened her pains.

Grubby fingers twisted a threadbare cap. "You gotta come, Miss Devlin. Ma's been trying to have the baby all night, and it won't come. Pa sent me to get you."

The mule tied to the hitching rail just outside the open doorway brayed as if punctuating the urgency. Moira clasped the boy's shoulder and squeezed.

"There's no need to fret, Evan. Everything is going to be all right. Is that your mule?" At his nod, she gave him a nudge. "Ride down to the livery and have Mr. Gunderson ready two mounts. One for Dr. Locke, and Dolly for me. We will meet you there shortly."

Evan grunted an agreement and slapped on his cap. He wheeled around in a squelch of shabby boot leather and made for his mule. As he vaulted onto the animal's back, Moira pushed the door closed and hurried down the hallway. A million thoughts clanged in her head. Granny Tate had once told her about a woman whose baby refused to enter the birthing canal. The mother languished for days in agony until the rotting infant took both their lives. She prayed nothing like that happened to Annabelle.

Just as she reached the storage room door, a tall figure stepped into her path. She pulled up with a gasp and avoided a collision by a mere hair's breadth. Her knees wobbled, and she reached out to steady herself. Her hand curled around a bared arm lightly dusted with fine hairs. He'd rolled up his sleeves for whatever task he'd been about. Her mouth went dry as a summer pond.

"Whoa, there. What's the hurry?"

She released his arm and retreated a step. "Pardon me, Doctor. I didn't see you coming into the hall."

"No. It's my fault. I shouldn't have charged through the doorway like that." He cocked his head to the side and peered down at her with those arresting eyes. "Are you all right? You're looking a little bland this morning."

Bland? What did he expect after the sentencing he'd handed down? Sunshine and roses? She pushed back a stray tendril tickling her forehead. "I'm perfectly fine. Just in a hurry is all."

"Were you rushing because there's a patient to see? I thought I heard a bell ding."

"You did hear the bell, and we do have a patient. But she's not here. Evan Smithers just rode in to get us. Says his mother is in prolonged labor and not doing well. I sent the boy to the livery to have our horses readied. The Smithers live about ten miles outside of town. We should make haste."

"*Our* horses?"

"Mrs. Smithers trusts me. I have been helping her through these last few weeks of her term. I want to be there for the birthing."

He opened his mouth as if to say more, then snapped his lips shut with a grunt. "Very well. Give me a moment to ready my medical bag."

"Perfect. I'll ready mine as well."

He followed her into the storage room. "There's no need to bring a bag. I will have everything that is needed."

Dingled man. Childbirth could be tricky. He couldn't be prepared for *every* consequence. She scooped a tin from the shelf and held it out. "Do you have this?"

"What is it?"

"Tallow. For lubrication should the lower end of the birthing canal not stretch enough or dries up. Considering how long she has been in labor, it's a possibility."

"Interesting. I hadn't thought of using lubrication."

Of course he hadn't. He was a man. She stuffed the tin into her medical bag and reached for a sealed jar sitting at the back of the shelf. Shredded roots jangled against the glass.

"And that?" he asked.

"Angelica root. For stimulating contractions."

"Absolutely not. I have not had a chance to evaluate its efficacy. This is much too dangerous a situation to be experimenting with medications."

"But—"

"No buts. We had an agreement. Remember?"

How could she forget? She set the jar back on the shelf. "Yes, Doctor."

"Is that all?"

"Yes, that's all."

"Good. I'll get my bag and meet you on the boardwalk."

She waited for him to leave and then grabbed the jar from the shelf. Experimenting her tush. She knew what the root could do. Annabelle might need it. She would risk Dr. Locke's wrath if it saved a life.

Footfalls shuffled in the hall. She jammed the jar into her bag and snapped the latch closed. She turned, heart jumping like a March hare.

The figure in the doorway barely reached halfway up the frame and had gray hair and wrinkles. Moira let go the breath she'd captured in her lungs.

"Good morning, Mrs. Lidle. I'm glad you came downstairs. Dr. Locke and I have been called out on a medical crisis. I don't know how long we'll be. You'll need to greet any patients that come in and advise them of the wait."

"Very well. I can attend to some mending for Eliza. She's still too weak to sit for long periods of time, much less have the strength for sewing." Mrs. Lidle's sister's recuperation from a potent lung illness was taking longer than normal. Moira made a mental note to go by and check on the woman when she had a free moment. Whenever that might be.

She left the storage room and joined Dr. Locke on the boardwalk. His gaze raked over her, but he remained silent. A Christmas gift in September.

She pointed down the street. "Gunderson's livery is about four blocks down on the other side of the street."

"Yes, I recall seeing the signboard yesterday when I arrived." He fell into step beside her. "What can you tell me about Mrs. Smithers' pregnancy?"

"I know she has had difficulty with lower back pains these last few months."

"Did you palpate for the child? Was it moving about?"

"The last I treated her was two weeks ago. The babe was active, though it was still high in her belly. Odd for so late in her term."

"A possible breech birth, then. Why would this woman wait so long to send for a doctor?" Concern and frustration spiked his tone. "She could be hemorrhaging severely by now."

"She's had two successful births with no complications. I imagine she thought this one would be no different."

Fingers curled around her elbow. "Well, she thought incorrectly." He herded her across the street toward the stable where Mr. Gunderson held the reins of two saddled horses. "Mount up, Miss Devlin. We must hurry if we want to save both mother and babe."

Chapter Four

A small cabin loomed ahead, smoke leaking from the chimney. It had one window and a crude, leather-hinged door. The rough-hewn logs were faded and pocked. Moss coated the chinking. The sun had bleached the thatch roof to a milky gray. It looked much like her childhood home in Tennessee. While meager and lacking amenities, the one room shack held her happiest memories. Loving arms cradling her, laughter, and stories told by the fire. That was before trouble came traipsing up the mountainside. Before a religious posse came looking for retribution. Before she, her mother, and her grandmother had to flee for their lives.

Moira reined in her sorrow and her mount. Now was not the time to be clouding her mind with the past. She needed to focus on the impending birth, else her inattention could cause Annabelle or her babe to suffer.

The cabin door squealed open and a coverall-clad man stepped onto the stoop. A short-cropped beard of black swathed his jaw He bounced a toddler in his arms, his mouth as pinched as the whimpering child's.

"Miss Devlin. Thank God, you're here."

Dr. Locke dismounted and turned to assist her. He might be a curmudgeon about her healing potions, but he was still a gentleman. Once on the ground, she shrugged out of his grasp and rushed toward the cabin.

"We came as quick as we could, Mr. Smithers." She pulled up at the edge of a wooden landing outside the door. "How is Annabelle faring? Has she delivered the babe?"

"No babe yet. The bleeding has slowed, but her strength is nearly gone. She can hardly hold her head off the pillow. I'm a 'feared she and the baby ain't gonna make it."

A sharply indrawn breath pulled her attention to Evan. Color had fled from the boy's face. Tears swam in his eyes. He needed a distraction. Moira motioned to the fenced enclosure. "Evan, would you put our horses in the corral with your mule? Then come and take your little sister out into the yard to play? That would be a great help to everyone."

Evan nodded, the worry easing from his eyes. "Yes'm. Whatever you need, I'll do it."

As the boy gathered the horses, Locke joined her at the landing. "I'm Dr. Locke, Mr. Smithers. I've taken over Dr. Troutman's practice in town. Miss Devlin and I will do everything we can to help your wife and baby."

Mr. Smithers backed out of the doorway. "It's good to have you, Doctor. Come on in. Annabelle is in the back bedroom."

Dr. Locke motioned for her to precede him. She plunged across the weathered boards and through the door opening. Braided rag runners ran the length of a large, living chamber. At one end, a small table and several chairs sat next to an ancient cooking stove. At the other end, a pair of rocking chairs faced a stone fireplace. Other than a few toy blocks scattered about, the place was neat and tidy. A hat tip to Mr. Smithers for keeping order during a difficult time.

Moira made a beeline for the only other doorway leading out of the room. A lantern sitting on a bureau poured golden light over the woman lying in the bed. Cotton sheets tented the bulge at her midsection. Her eyes were closed; her skin as pale as the bedsheets. If not for the slight rise and fall of her chest, she could pass for a body ready for burial.

Moira squared herself. Not today. Not if she could help it.

Dr. Locke surged past her and stopped next to the bed. He gave Annabelle a quick appraisal and began shrugging out of his jacket. "We'll need a basin of hot water and some lye soap, Mr. Smithers. And all the clean towels you have on hand."

"Already have water heating on the stove like Miss Devlin told us to do if things started going bad. Soap and clean towels are on the bureau, though I already used a few whilst trying to stop the bleeding."

Dr. Locke tossed his jacket across the chair pulled near the head of the bed. "Very good. Bring the water then." His gaze flicked to her. "Roll back the bedsheets, Miss Devlin. I'd like to do a quick exam. See if the babe has breached the canal."

She moved to the other side of the bed and rolled down the sheets. A large slash of red stained the white nightgown and coated the mound of towels packed between pale thighs. Annabelle had lost a lot of blood. Hopefully she still had enough flowing through her veins to keep her alive.

Eyelids fluttered open, and a worried gaze flicked from her to Dr. Locke and back. "Miss Devlin. What's going on? W-who is he?"

Moira rested a hand on the woman's trembling shoulder. "It's all right, Annabelle. This is Dr. Locke. He's here to help."

Footfalls shushed into the room. Mr. Smithers had traded the toddler for a white porcelain basin. "Here's that hot water, Doc. Where do you want it?"

Dr. Locke reached over and pulled open drawer to the bedside table. He stowed away the Bible that had been resting on top. "Right here will do."

Smithers set the basin on the cleared table and then stood there, staring down at his wife, swaying like a sailor on shore leave. Gray tinted his sun-browned skin. Even the stoutest of men fainted during the birthing process.

Moira caught his arm and nudged him toward the door. "Annabelle is going to be just fine, Mr. Smithers. I promise. Why don't you go outside with the children? We'll call if we need anything more."

He hesitated, mouth sagging, and then gave a brief nod. As the anxious husband left the room, Dr. Locke fished an apron from his bag and tied it around his waist. He gathered soap and a towel from the bureau and returned to the bed.

His expression intent, he rolled up his sleeves and plunged his hands and arms into the basin of water. He soaped every inch of exposed skin. Even his fingernails got a good scrubbing. He clearly knew the benefits of good sanitation.

She watched his ablutions, unable to look away. He had slender fingers. Long. Trained to touch, feel, and examine. They would be magical on a woman's body. Moira laced her hands together in a pious fold in front of her. Now was not the time to let her mind wander to sinful places.

Dr. Locke dried his hands on a towel and hung it over the chair back. He peered down at Annabelle, his fierce expression softening. "I'm going to examine you now, Mrs. Smithers. I need to see if the baby has entered the birthing canal. I'll be as gentle as I can, but it may be uncomfortable."

Annabelle nodded and bit down on her bottom lip. Such a brave, young woman. Childbirth was hard enough, but to have to go through the process with a stranger…a man…not something she would care to endure either.

Dr. Locke shifted to the end of the bed and leaned over. He slid a hand under the soiled gown. Annabelle stiffened, and a moan poured from her lips.

Moira unfurled her hands and reached for a quivering shoulder. "Easy, Annabelle. Just breathe. In through your nose and out through your mouth. In and out. Deep and slow. Yes, that's it."

Granny Tate had taught her the most effective way to help patients bear serious pain was to have them concentrate on their breathing. Let the task soothe the mind and the body. The pain would fade. And it did. The stiffness retreated from Annabelle's shoulders and face. Her trembling subsided. She would be ready to face whatever was to come.

Dr. Locke withdrew his hand and stepped away from the bed. His tense expression said whatever he'd found, it wasn't good.

She rounded the bed and leaned in, keeping her voice low. "What is it, Doctor? What did you find?"

"It's just as I suspected. The baby is breech."

Not what Annabelle needed. "Can you turn it?"

"It's too far down the birth canal for that. I'm going to have to assist the child out."

"Won't that be painful? Annabelle is already frail from losing so much blood. Manhandling could send her over the edge."

He wiped his hand on the apron, leaving a jarring streak of red across the white. "I'm afraid we don't have any other recourse. Both mother and child will die if I don't."

"Do you have anything we can give her for the pain?"

"I would administer chloroform, but the uterine contractions aren't as strong or as close together as they need to be. She hasn't had a contraction since we arrived. Chloroform will only stifle them more."

She had a remedy, but he wasn't going to like it. She squared herself against the impending storm. "I have something in my bag that will help. An infusion of pigeon grass tea will strengthen her labors."

Thunderclouds gathered on his face. "You brought your wares? When I expressly forbade them?"

"Can you save Annabelle or the baby if her labors don't resume?" At his deepening scowl, she continued. "No. So at least give this a try."

She didn't wait for his reply. Annabelle and her unborn child took precedence over his absurd notions. She went into the kitchen, found a clean mug, and filled it with water from the steaming kettle. She returned to the bedroom and fished a sack of pulverized pigeon grass from her bag.

Dr. Locke stood at the end of the bed, his piercing gaze following her every move. Contrary man. He should open his eyes. He might see things more clearly.

She spooned a generous helping of powdered herb into the mug and stirred until it dissolved. She crossed to the bed and slid her free hand under Annabelle's head.

"Sit up, Annabelle. I've made you a special tea. It will help bring back your labors so we can get that baby delivered."

The woman wobbled upright, and Moira held the mug to her lips. "Drink all of it, Annabelle. I know you're tired, but this will help. I promise. Your suffering will be over soon, and you'll be holding your baby."

Annabelle sipped at the tea. Some leaked from her mouth and trickled down her chin, but she managed to down a goodly amount. Moira smiled and assisted her back to the pillow. "Good. Very good, Annabelle."

"How long before this brew does whatever it's going to do?"

He didn't say "kill the patient," but she knew what he inferred. She set the empty mug next to the basin and picked up a towel. She dabbed tea from Annabelle's chin. "Her labor should resume in about ten minutes. While we wait, I'm going to get her out of that soiled gown. There's a clean one on the bureau, if you would be so kind as to get it for me."

She half expected him to turn tail and run. In her experience, most men avoided unpalatable duties. Surprisingly, he retrieved the gown and proceeded to help her get Annabelle out of the blood-stained garment and into the clean one. She tried not to marvel at how nimbly his fingers performed the task.

As she plumped the pillow behind Annabelle, a pained grimace sliced the woman's face. She grabbed for her belly and gave a low moan.

Dr. Locke rested a hand on the baby bulge, now visibly rippling beneath the thin material of the gown. Surprise lifted his eyebrows. The pigeon grass had done its duty. Moira corralled a smile. No sense rubbing her success in his face. Annabelle's well-being required her and Dr. Locke to work together in harmony. They were only halfway through what promised to be a long process.

"Well done, Miss Devlin," he said. "It appears your concoction has affected a resumption of contractions."

A compliment. Would miracles never cease.

"We should prepare for delivery." He reached for his medical bag. "While I gather my things, please help Mrs. Smithers to sit and position her legs bent at the knees. Once that is done, bring the lantern to the end of the bed and hold it overhead. I'll need as much light as I can get."

After helping Annabelle into the requested position, Moira gathered the lantern and moved to his side. She held the lantern over the bed, ensuring as much light as possible poured over the patient. "Is that good, Doctor? Do I need to hold it higher?"

"No. That's perfect." He peered across the bed at Annabelle. "I'm afraid your baby is breech, Mrs. Smithers. It's coming feet first which is why you are having so much trouble with the birth. I'm going to have to reach in and guide the child out. The process will be painful, but there's no way around it. Do you understand?"

Annabelle nodded and fisted the edges of the mattress. Dr. Locke leaned forward and slid a hand into the birth canal. A pained shriek clawed the air. Moira clasped Annabelle's ankle with her free hand, sending sympathy and reassurance through her fingertips.

Dr. Locke worked steadily and patiently, encouraging Annabelle when her will to go on receded. After what seemed like an eternity, he gave a steady tug, and a slime-coated infant slid onto the pad of towels. It was a girl. A very blue and lifeless girl.

He snipped the umbilical cord with a pair of scissors and made a quick knot. "Take the child, Miss Devlin. Clear the mucous from her nose and mouth and then rub her down with a towel. Brisk, but gentle strokes. She should begin breathing on her own."

Moira set the lantern on the floor and gathered the child in a towel. She cleared the nose and mouth and began scrubbing the tiny torso. As much as she wanted to probe the lifeless infant, she didn't dare. Dr. Locke was too close and far too observant for the use of her gift.

The child began squirming, her little legs and arms twitching. After a few seconds, she let go a squealing wail. Moira sagged with relief. The child would live. So would her mother. Annabelle rested against the pillows, face pale, but eyes sparkling with joy as she watched her newborn daughter.

Moira wrapped the baby in a clean towel and settled her into Annabelle's arms. The little girl had pinked up nicely. Her little mouth puckered, instinctively seeking to suckle.

"She's lovely, Annabelle. What are you going to call her?"

Annabelle looked up at Dr. Locke standing at the bedside table, hands submerged in the basin of water. "Do you have a wife, Doctor?"

His shoulders went rigid, his washing stilled. Something flickered across his face. Pain? Guilt?

"My wife passed on several years ago."

"I'm so sorry for your loss. What was her name?"

"Alice."

"That's a lovely name." Annabelle jiggled the bundle in her arms. "That's what I'll call my baby girl…if that's all right with you, Doctor?"

He snagged a clean towel from the chair. "If that's what you want to name her, it's fine by me."

Those stiff shoulders and rigid tone didn't say fine at all. Was his wife a sore spot? There was a story there. Oddly, she wanted to hear it.

Moira patted Annabelle's arm. "You get some rest now, Annabelle. I'll come back in a week or so to see how you and little Alice are doing."

"We *both* will," Dr. Locke added.

Satisfaction for a job well done leaked from her like blood from a sliced vein. After all they had done to save Annabelle and her child, she hadn't gained one ounce of his trust.

Was she fighting a losing battle?

****

The ride back to town was slower and much more relaxed. It would have been the perfect time to take in the scenery. Yet the untamed backwoods with its thickets and meadows and stark cliffs rising in the distance did little to hold his interest. The woman riding ahead claimed his attention.

Wisps of dark hair had escaped her pins and danced around her head like woodland fairies. She rode sidesaddle as befitted a young lady, yet an improper swathe of skin showed above her boots where her skirts had bunched. Despite his attempts to remain unaffected, he found himself spellbound.

The physical attraction was understandable. He'd been celibate for more than two years…his desires tamed by work, exhaustion, and a good dose of guilt. Miss Devlin called to him like a siren to a sailor. Any red-blooded male would find her charms difficult to resist. But he couldn't give in. Lusting for her would only complicate an already prickly truce.

Miss Devlin had no formal instruction in medicine, however she had an uncanny sense of healing…and of people. She'd put Mrs. Smithers at ease with a simple touch and an encouraging word. Her herbs had provided the needed stimulus for the resumption of uterine contractions. He didn't want to admire her or her herbal remedies. It went against everything he held sacred. But he couldn't muster a trace of contempt.

His mount slowed and dipped its head, stretching for the creek meandering close to the pathway. Poor creature must be thirsty. He loosened the reins and let the horse have its drink.

"Hold up a moment, Miss Devlin," he called out.

She reined her horse to a stop and peered over her shoulder, those ebony eyes washing over him like a tidal wave. "Is there a problem?"

"It appears my mount requires a drink. We pushed them rather hard on the ride out. We have the time to allow a brief respite." And one for themselves as well. He was drained. Mentally and physically. If the slouch to Miss Devlin's shoulders was any indication, she could also use a rest.

Images surfaced of her spread out on a blanket, slopes and curves laid out like a feast. Sunlight would dance over her creamy skin. Blood quickened in his groin. He swallowed back a groan and pointed to the creek. Perhaps talking about the mundane would take his mind off the exotic.

"I've never seen such crystal-clear water. It looks almost like glass."

"That's Dancer's Creek. It flows from deep within the Shoehorn. The water stays cold most of the year, even on the hottest of summer days."

"Very refreshing, I'm sure."

"Would you like to sample a taste? As you say, we have the time."

Perhaps a good dose of chilly water would help tame the heat smoldering inside him. "Yes, I believe I would. It's been hours since my morning coffee."

He swung his leg over the saddle and dismounted. He started for Miss Devlin's mount, but she had already slid to the ground quicker than a startled rabbit dove into a burrow. Was he so irascible that she couldn't abide his merest touch? The thought sliced like a scalpel through tender flesh.

"Go ahead and have your drink." She flipped up the saddle bag flap and traded her riding gloves for a pair of leather gloves. "I'm going to forage in that meadow over there."

Before he could respond, she untied a large burlap sack from her saddle and plunged into the tall grasses flanking the path. Curiosity trampled his thirst. He lurched after her. "What are you foraging for?"

She didn't slow, merely kept pushing ahead, her backside swaying in delightful wiggles as she maneuvered through the sawgrass grabbing at her skirts. Thirst turned to hunger. The urge to have her poured through him. He fisted his hands, fighting for control.

A slender finger slashed the air. "I saw a patch of stinging nettle growing over there just off the path as we rode by. I need to replenish my supply of potions that were destroyed by the quake."

He pushed aside a rather pesky vine that wanted to mate with his trousers. Another tried to lynch his arm. Perhaps he should have stayed with the horses and enjoyed his drink. For more reasons than one.

She stopped and tugged on the leather gloves, fingers disappearing into the thick leather. Those clever appendages would play havoc on a man's body. Teasing. Provoking. Binding him with her charms.

He halted beside her, panting—more from wrestling with his desires than from the exertion. "Why…the stout gloves?"

She prodded a tall, wiry weed topped with small, brown flowers. "Because the leaves and stems have tiny hairs that when touched causes a stinging sensation. Hence the name stinging nettle."

An apt appellation. And probably why his legs smarted beneath his trousers. It almost overrode the fire burning in his loins. Almost. "What medicinal purpose does this nettle serve?"

"There are many. The stinging barbs can help lessen the pains of rheumatism and gout. The leaves can be boiled to produce teas and tinctures that will ease a variety of ills…hay fever, asthma, hives. This time of year is particularly bad for folks with aversions to ragweed. I need to harvest a substantial quantity to keep up with the demand."

The potion sounded innocuous, possibly even

helpful. But fishing expeditions required diligence and carefully aimed tosses. "What other ingredients are added to these nettle tonics?"

"Just fresh water and a pinch of sugar to tame the acidity." She plucked a leaf and held it in her outstretched palm. "See, it's an ordinary leaf. Green and supple. But the things it can do are almost... well, magical."

"Where did you learn about these herbs and what they can do?"

"From my mother who learned from her mother who learned from her mother. The knowledge has been handed down in my family for centuries."

A process similar to his medical apprenticeship. He had been taught by his mentor who had learned from his. It was a familiar connection, and it made her skills seem somewhat more believable.

She stripped leaves and flower buds from the plant and stuffed them into her bag. "And where did you receive your medical training? A university?"

"Not at first. I apprenticed under William Giles, a well-respected physician in Philadelphia, for several years. Dr. Giles recognized my potential and urged me to attend the Philadelphia School of Medicine where I would learn more modern techniques. I owe him for all he did to further my career."

Owed the good doctor for that and much, much more. After his mother's death, he'd lost his way and raced full tilt toward mental and physical destruction. It wasn't until he began apprenticing under Dr. Giles that he was able to shake off his demons. He lost a wonderful mentor and a great friend when the elderly doctor drew his last breath.

"And after medical school?"

Her question prodded him back to the present. "A fellow graduate and I opened a practice on the west side of the city. John and I did fairly well for a pair of physicians straight out of medical school."

"If your practice was doing so well, why leave it to come out here? Mineral is a far cry from the luxuries in Philadelphia."

Who was doing the fishing here? As she moved through the nettle patch, plucking leaves and tucking them into her burlap bag, he considered his answer. He rarely opened up about that painful part of his past. And on the occasions when he did, the memories haunted him for days.

He bent and scooped up a rock, fisting it like an anchor. "As I said, my wife passed on several years ago. Since then, her parents have been hounding me to visit. They wrote recently advising of Dr. Troutman's death and begged me to take over his practice. It seemed the right thing to do." For them and for him.

"Her parents live in Mineral?"

"Yes. Edeline and Stanley Wentworth. Do you know them?"

A shadow darted across her face, a hummingbird flitting from danger. It disappeared as quickly as it surfaced. She jammed a fist full of nettle leaves into the bag. "Everyone around these parts know the Wentworths. They own the Shoehorn Silver Mine. I didn't make the connection earlier when you mentioned your wife's name. How did the two of you meet?"

Rock points bit into his palm. "She was living with her grandparents in Philadelphia the same time that I apprenticed with Dr. Giles. As the Wentworth's family physician and friend, he was often invited for dinner, and I would accompany him. What started as a social relationship grew to more." More for him. Not for her. If only he had opened his eyes, he would have seen the reluctance, the stilted laughter, the failure to meet his gaze. Yet, he plowed ahead, oblivious. A wife with connections to upper society could open many doors.

"I can see how difficult her death was for you."

He should take better care. Little good would come from exposing his emotions to the open air. "The grief has mostly receded. I try to remember the good times and not focus on the bad."

"A sound plan, yet not always so easy to shoulder."

Sadness tainted her tone. Was she plagued with painful memories as well? Oddly, he wanted to hear every detail.

She pulled a short length of twine from her pocket and tied it around the neck of the sack. "I'm sure you had many remarkable memories, especially with the Wentworths as in-laws. Edeline Wentworth is known for her lavish dinner parties."

"Many of our clients treated us to lavish dinners as compensation for our services."

She laughed, but the sound rang hollow. "How fortunate you were. I'm lucky to get a sack of potatoes for my services. I remember one farmwoman offered me her old rooster in payment…provided I could catch it."

"Did you? Catch it?"

"Heavens no. That scrappy fellow dodged me for nearly an hour. I finally gave up and trudged home with scratches and sore feet for my efforts."

A picture emerged of her chasing a bandy rooster,

ebony hair flying behind her like a sail, and skirts hiked to her knees. A chuckle escaped his lips. He stopped with a grunt of surprise. When had he last laughed? With true good humor and ease that made the sound seem so relaxed? Years, if ever. And that shocked him. What was it about this woman that made him come out his shell?

Chapter Five

The mid-day sun painted the two-story farm house with a welcoming glow. Seaton House Home for Children. This was home. This was safety and unconditional love. After enduring several days of Dr. Locke's scowls and constant scrutiny, she needed some cheerfulness.

A bearded man wearing faded coveralls rounded the side of the house. Retired from ministering the Lord's word to a flock in Kentucky, Joseph Hoggard had become the groundskeeper and spiritual mentor for the orphanage. He dispensed Bible verses and advice with equal amounts of compassion and wisdom. Not to mention bits of peppermint tucked in his pocket for soothing scraped knees and wounded egos.

Moira unhooked her leg from the side-saddle and slid to the ground. "Good morning, Mr. Hoggard. How is everyone? Meredith sent a note saying you had all survived the earthquake just fine, but I had to make sure."

"No need to worry. The only casualties were a few cracked windows and some frayed nerves. Other than that, everyone is doing fine, just like Mrs. Booth said. How about you, Miss Moira? How are things at the doctor's office? I heard some folks were injured during the quake. I pray everyone is all right."

"Some were hurt, yes. But they are all recovering

nicely."

He gave her a wink. "Thanks to your wonderful gift of healing no doubt."

Mr. Pardue might agree, if he knew the true reason for his miraculous recovery. The sawmill foreman had returned to work after only a week of recuperation. A miracle from Heaven, many had said. She was no angel, but she did thank God for a gift that saved lives.

She tucked her riding gloves into the saddle pouch and retrieved a burlap sack. "Is Mrs. Campbell around? I need to speak with her."

"She's out back with the children. They're taking advantage of the temperate weather and having lessons under the old oak."

"It is a nice day for that. Won't be long before cold weather keeps everyone indoors."

He held out his hand. "Let me see to your horse while you visit. Miss Dolly looks like she could use a handful of oats."

She handed over the reins. Dolly would be well cared for and would probably gain another layer of belly fat. Mr. Hoggard treated his animal friends just as kindly as he did his human flock, if not better.

At the back of the house, five children ringed a woman sitting on a stool beneath a tall oak tree. Salt and pepper colored hair framed a face that radiated with love and encouragement. Moira fingered the pendant dangling from a silver chain around her neck. St. Sophia, patron mother of orphans. Mildred Campbell had given her the necklace on her sixteenth birthday. It was a reminder that she would always be watched over. Always be loved.

"Good, Timmy. Very good." Mrs. Campbell held a

turnip, balanced in her palm. "Now one more time. Try to hold it concealed for a little longer. Concentrate."

The turnip shimmered and then disappeared in a flash of blue light. Moira counted off the seconds. At twenty, the turnip reappeared in Miss Campbell's hand. Moira smiled. Timmy was progressing well with his talent. Before she left to take over the medical practice in town, he'd only been able to keep objects cloaked for a few seconds.

Seaton House wasn't an ordinary orphanage. Mildred Campbell rescued children with special talents from all over the country. She helped them learn to control their gifts so they could assimilate back into society. It was a special place full of special people.

A squeal rent the air and a pink ball of ruffles rushed toward her. Arms trapped her legs. "Moira. You're back. It's so good to see you."

She brushed fingers over soft red ringlets. "Good morning, Anna. It's good to see you. I've missed you. All of you."

"We missed you, too." The girl tilted her head back, a twinkle sparking her green eyes. "'Specially Gabe. He's been moping around like a dog that lost his last bone."

Thirteen-year-old Gabe Hunt had a *tendre* for her. He was sweet, but a bit over-zealous. He had used his special skills to send her possets of flowers or an apple fresh from the orchard. He'd once sent her a pie pilfered from the pie safe. It was a bit disconcerting to see objects floating across the ground of their own accord. But that was life at Seaton House.

A woman bulging with child and holding the hand of a toddler approached the group. Meredith Booth. Her savior. Five years ago, Meredith and her husband had saved her from a posse of angry vigilantes and brought her to Seaton House. She owed Meredith and Mrs. Campbell a huge debt.

Meredith sent her daughter to play with the other children and joined her under the tree. "Moira. It's lovely to see you. What brings you out here? Didn't you receive my note?"

"I received it, but I had to come see for myself. I also wanted to harvest some Angelica root. Much of my stock was ruined during the quake, and I need to replace it."

"As you can see, everyone is doing fine." Meredith laced her arm with Moira's. "Come. I'll walk with you to the garden."

Moira fell into step beside her friend, following a well-worn path leading to the barn. "How's the baby? Is everything progressing as expected?"

Meredith settled a hand on her belly. "The little jackrabbit kicks and rolls constantly. I think he's eager to get out and take on the world."

"He was unusually difficult to examine. Never would lie still." Moira had probed Meredith's belly when complications cropped up early in her pregnancy. She'd discovered the little wick that told the baby's gender.

"The child isn't the only one eager to get out. Preston must be beside himself with impatience."

Meredith laughed. "Indeed. He won't leave my side for more than an hour. I'm lucky to have these few minutes to myself. So, tell me about yourself. How is everything going in town? Are folks coming to see you for medical care?"

"Some have. I think I earned more of their trust after helping with the quake victims. All was well until...well, until Dr. Locke arrived." Just saying his name brought forth images of a gaze that drilled into her very core.

"Dr. Locke?" Meredith asked. "Who is he?"

"He just arrived from Pennsylvania. He was asked by the Wentworths to come and take over Dr. Troutman's practice. He was married to their daughter, Alice."

They reached the fenced area at the side of the barn. Moira pushed open the gate and stepped into the garden. Rows of late summer vegetables stood in precise formation. Off to one side, closest to the barn where they were protected from harsh weather, were the herbs she had planted in early spring. The cold-tolerant ones were still doing well. Those that required more warmth were withering...the perfect time for harvesting.

Meredith trailed her through the gate and leaned against the side of the barn. Protective hands cradled her belly. "I remember hearing about Alice. She moved to Pennsylvania to live with her grandparents. She never liked living here in Mineral. To uncivilized for her tastes. She met a man, a doctor if I recall, and they married. After a year, she became pregnant. Both she and the baby died during the birth."

The unexpected deaths of his wife and child explained some of Dr. Locke's behavior. Some, but not all. "How sad. The Wentworths must have been devastated."

"They were. Alice was their only child. Mrs. Wentworth took her death especially hard. She locked herself in her bedroom for weeks and refused to come out."

Moira rolled her skirts into a pad and sank to her knees near a mounded hill of dirt. "I can understand such grief. No mother should have to bury her child. Least of all her only child."

"Indeed."

Tall lanky plants spiked the mound. *Angelica.* A versatile herb, good for curing a myriad of ailments when used properly. Deadly when not. Meredith was wise to keep her distance, else she could harm her unborn child.

Moira plucked a stalk out of the ground, roots and all, and stuffed it into the burlap bag. The dried seed pods would produce new plants come next spring.

"Alice's death appears to have affected everyone close to her," she said. "Dr. Locke left a prosperous medical practice in Philadelphia. I suspect he needed to get away from all the reminders."

"Will he allow you to continue to work at the office?"

That was the question of the century. "I don't know. He calls my potions snake oils. He's almost fanatical about their evil. He's given me a month to prove myself. A month. I barely got my foot in the door with the townsfolk in the month before he arrived." She yanked another stalk from the mound, sending dirt clods flying.

"That's unfortunate."

Very unfortunate. She sank back on her haunches, her energy uprooted. "I want to stay, Meredith. For Mrs. Campbell. For the people of Mineral." She couldn't keep despair from muddying her voice. "For myself."

"Then you should do all you can to make that happen."

"I wish it were that simple. As if his distrust isn't enough, I find myself attracted to him. If I have any hope of staying on, I must squash those feelings. I get the impression the last thing Dr. Locke wants is a romantic entanglement, especially with someone like me. I don't even come close to his standards of acceptance."

Meredith pushed away from the barn, clucking like an agitated hen. Her forehead bunched with furrows. "Don't you dare put yourself down, Moira Devlin. You are kind and caring and loyal to those you care about. You would make any man a wonderful wife."

She laughed but without any humor. "I doubt the starchy Dr. Locke would want me as a wife. Once he finds out about my ability to heal, he'll toss me out on my backside without a second thought."

Meredith's expression softened. "If I may offer some advice…?"

She owed Meredith her life. Anything her friend had to say was worth listening to. She brushed dirt from her hands and pushed to her feet. "Certainly. I always take great stock in your advice. You and Mrs. Campbell mean the world to me."

"And you mean the world to us. We want you to be happy, Moira. Don't let anything get in the way of that. If you want something, go after it, without fear or restraint. Whether it's to continue with your healing or finding the love of a good man, don't give up on your dreams."

"I'm not sure Dr. Locke will believe in me, even if

the proof smacks him in the face."

"Is he a good man?"

Deep down, she knew he was. He behaved irascibly only because of his desire to protect people from harm. She understood that. She would stand up against an army of evil to keep her patients safe.

"I can see by that wistful expression he is. Don't let a chance at something amazing slip away."

"What if he isn't ready or interested in finding love again? I could ruin my chances of staying at the practice."

"Don't try to be something you are not. Shutting down your feelings will only make things worse. If Dr. Locke is half as perceptive as you say, he will pick up on your charade quicker than a duck pounces on a June bug."

"Indeed."

Meredith smiled. "You'll know soon enough if you and Dr. Locke are meant to be. Once you cross over the threshold to love and passion, nothing will break that bond. Not your misgivings. Not his. Believe me, I know about such things."

"But you and Preston are perfect together."

"We are now. However, we had a long road to travel and many obstacles to overcome to get where we are. But that's a story for another time. I can only hope my advice will make your journey to happiness much shorter and a lot less taxing."

She always thought her happiness would come from administering to those in need as her mother and grandmother had…without the need for a man in her life. What if she was wrong? Was she letting fear get in the way of the chance at something wonderful?

****

The bureau drawer wedged halfway open. Anson tugged harder. The ornery thing wouldn't budge. Not one inch. Damnation. Had the woman put an enchantment on the furniture too?

He wriggled and pulled. The drawer refused to cooperate. It looked up at him with a half-gapped grin. Infernal oak.

Giving a growl of frustration, he leaned back and leveraged all his weight into the effort. The stuck drawer screeched open, sounding like a banshee screaming for a victim. He stiffened and listened. Only a soft snoring drifted in from the bedroom across the hallway. Lucky for him, Miss Devlin's companion slept like the dead.

He poked under the neatly folded stacks. Nothing but handkerchiefs and women's underthings. Simple cotton garments. She wasn't a frilly woman. Not in clothing. Not in life. Yet she exuded grace and refinement. It poured from her like perfume from a rose, captivating any who drew near.

He thrust the drawer closed with a grunt. He would not be captivated. He needed answers. Not silly romantic notions.

He tugged open the next drawer. A small wooden box sat beside a stack of woolen stockings. He slid open the lid. Inside there was a folded piece of paper, some beads, and a dried flower. Gifts from a lover? Guilt stung him. He shouldn't be thinking such thoughts, much less going through her personal belongings. Yet the welfare of the townsfolk trumped a little indelicate snooping.

He unfurled the paper and read the neatly scrawled

missive. *May St. Sophia guide and protect you. Never give up on your dreams, Moira. They are the lamps that light the way. Love always, Mildred Campbell.*

What dreams did she hope for? In his experience, most women wanted a husband, a family, and a place to call home. Miss Devlin seemed to desire more from life. Helping folks and administering to the sick and injured took precedence over her own needs. Just like him. The connection wrapped around him like a comforting blanket.

He returned the note to the box and closed the lid. Where to next? There wasn't much left to search in the sparsely furnished room. He'd already gone through the armoire. It held the same plain cotton garments as the bureau. She would look stunning in a satin ball gown, the material hugging her curves and perfectly showcasing any exposed skin…silky creaminess a man could drown in.

He ground his teeth around a curse. He had to put such lustful thoughts out of his head. Miss Devlin was forbidden fruit. One taste and he'd be lost.

He shoved the drawer shut and stalked to the bed. Perhaps she had secrets hidden under the mattress. One of his classmates from medical school had stashed a bottle of whiskey under his mattress, an expensive Scottish malt shared only with a select few chums. It stayed concealed until the whale Henry Buckley flopped onto the bed. The bottle shattered and spilled precious spirit all over the floor. Some treasures were simply not meant to be hoarded.

Dropping to his knees, he pushed back the bedcovers and thrust his hands between the downy mattress and the webbing. The soft scent of vanilla and lavender nuzzled him. It was a pleasant scent. Her scent. He closed his eyes, unable to stop the image of the two of them on the bed, naked, his fingers twined in that silky mane, his lips tasting hers. She would writhe beneath him, calling his name. It would be heaven on earth.

He doused the image with a grunt. What the devil was wrong with him? He was a man of medicine. A man of refinement and self-restraint. Not a low-bred rogue allowing free rein to his carnal cravings.

He thumped onto his belly and ducked his head under the bed. No more distractions. He had a job to do. Perverse thoughts would only slow his search.

The space under the bed was bare except for a pair of slippers and a dog-eared lady's magazine open to a page displaying stylish bonnets and lavish gowns. Interesting. The single-minded Miss Devlin did have dreams and desires like other women.

The thud of the front door rammed into the room. He jerked, and his head struck the wood bed frame. Pain blasted down his neck. Cripes. Either a patient had arrived, or Miss Devlin was returning. Whichever, his investigation was over. For now.

He backed away from the bed and pushed to his feet. A quick scrub revealed a slightly raised and very tender spot at the back of his skull. The lump would recede after a few days. Until then, it would be a reminder to keep his mind on his mission.

He crept to the door and craned his neck around the jamb. In the bedroom across the hall, Mrs. Lidle dozed in a chair by the window, warming herself like a cat in a slash of sunlight. Perfect. He stole into the hallway and down the stairs. Near the bottom, he slowed and angled to one side. There was a loose tread waiting to herald his presence. He heard it often enough from his office, squealing most annoyingly and breaking his concentration.

He made it safely to the landing. A quick tug set his contortion twisted jacket back to rights. Doctor turned burglar. He never imagined such a thing of himself before Miss Devlin. He also never imagined craving another woman after his failure with Alice.

He let his heels click loudly down the hallway. The need for stealth was over. Instead of Miss Devlin, he found a patient had arrived. Part of him was relieved. He'd never been good at concealing his emotions. Henry had often chided him for his inability to bluff at cards. His recent foray into the criminal would surely be written all over his face.

In the waiting room stood a short, squat man wearing a plain suit of brown tweed, a brown necktie, and a brown shirt. The only coloring breaking the drabness was the man's face. He was greener than a summer frog.

Anson extended his hand. "Good afternoon. I'm Dr. Locke. What can I do for you, sir?"

The man took his hand in a weak grasp. "John Hammock, Doctor. I've been meaning to come by and welcome you to town but…" The man grimaced and rubbed his stomach. "I haven't been feeling well lately. Thought it might just be a passing illness, but it seems to be getting worse."

John Hammock. The owner of Hammock Savings and Loan. He'd caught a glimpse of the man inside the bank as he walked past on his way to the mercantile. So far, he hadn't the need for a bank or a banker, considering his only payment since arriving had been a salted quarter of venison from the Smithers.

Anson motioned to the doorway across the hall. "Please, come into the examination room and have a seat on the table. I'll see if I can figure out what's plaguing you."

He followed the banker into the room. Although a good dose of sunlight poured through the window, he turned up the flame on the lantern. The brighter, the better for examinations.

He moved to the table and gave his patient a quick assessment. Mr. Hammock sat slightly slouched, his eyelids and jowls droopy. His green-tinted skin was dry, and his lips slightly chapped. Something had him out of sorts.

Using his thumb, he lifted an eyelid. The white vitreous of the eyeball was shot with tiny red veins. The iris was pale and cloudy. All symptoms pointed to some sort of malaise.

He released the eyelid. "What ailments have you been experiencing, Mr. Hammock? And for how long?"

"It all started about a week ago. Had a throbbing in my head that wouldn't go away. Then the trots to the outhouse began. I have no pep a'tall."

"Have you been feverish?"

"No. No fever." The man's face buckled, and he cupped his stomach. "But it feels as if my gut is being ripped in two."

Definitely something going on. He collected his stethoscope from the counter and set it on the table. While a little outdated, the instrument had been a gift from Dr. Giles and did the job required.

"I want to palpate your stomach, Mr. Hammock.

Check for any abnormalities. Then I'll use this listening device to see if I can detect anything amiss. Is that all right with you?" An explanation of what was to come often eased anxious minds. As did putting control back into the patient's hands.

The banker nodded. "Do whatever you need, Doc. I just want to feel better."

"Very well. Unfasten your jacket and lie back."

His jacket undone, Mr. Hammock sank onto the table. Anson gently probed the upper quadrants of the man's fleshy abdomen. Plenty of give. No rigidity. He moved his examination to the lower section. Soft and pliable. Nothing to indicate a trauma.

He picked up the stethoscope and placed the bell on the banker's belly. He then leaned over and set his ear to the earpiece. Gurgles and soft rumbling filtered up the tube. No stoppage. That was good.

He straightened and held out a hand. "You can sit up now, Mr. Hammock."

The bank pulled upright. "What did you find, Doc?"

"I didn't feel or hear anything irregular. You could just be experiencing a touch of the stomach ills. Have you eaten anything unusual or tainted recently?"

"Not that I'm aware of. The pretty young lady who took over from Dr. Troutman gave me a tonic for a scratchy throat week before last. It cured my discomfort almost immediately. Then all this nonsense started."

Could Miss Devlin's potion be the cause of the man's illness? It was too coincidental to dismiss. "Has anyone else in your family experienced the same problems?"

Mr. Hammock shook his head. "The missus and

the children are doing just fine."

So, it wasn't something being passed among family members or tainting their drinking water. "What about your neighbors?"

"Claude Gunderson complained he was off his feed a bit. He runs the livery just down the street. Do you think we have the same sickness?"

"I don't know. But I'm going to find out." He replaced the stethoscope on the counter. "For now, I want you to consume only weak broths and gruel. Give your stomach a rest from any heavy foods. Come back if you're not feeling better or if the symptoms worsen."

"What about whiskey? That seems to help with the pain."

Restricting a man's spirits could cause a rebellion. Best to offer a compromise. "Whiskey is fine; just keep your consumption to small doses."

"Thanks, Doc. I'm feeling better already."

He wished he was. Suspicion fumed in his gut. Miss Devlin could very well be the source of a developing pandemic.

Was it by accident or by choice?

Chapter Six

Moira lifted the small crate off the store shelf. Inside, multi-colored bottles rested on a cushioning bed of straw. Luckily, the fragile glass had survived the quake. She would need all the vessels she could find to replace the ones that had been destroyed. Twenty-four bottles wouldn't be nearly enough for the upcoming winter season, but they would have to do until Mr. Cavendish placed an order for more stock.

She tucked the crate under her arm. Meredith had insisted on furnishing the funds to purchase the bottles. There was no one more generous than Meredith Booth. Or wiser. Yesterday's visit to the orphanage had been just what she needed. The dark clouds that had been hovering over her were lighter now. Less disheartening. Nothing would stop her from getting what she wanted in life. She would do as Meredith suggested. If a relationship developed between her and Anson Locke, fine. If not, he would merely be a stepping-stone on her path to becoming a much sought-after healer and herbalist. She didn't need a man for that. All she needed was perseverance and patience. A lot of patience.

"Is that you Moira?" came a familiar voice.

She turned to find Nelda Sawyer standing at the end of the aisle. Younger by eight months, Nel had become a close friend and confidant during their stay at Seaton House. She was the sister Moira never had.

Over the years, they had shared many an adventure, some ending in mud-caked disasters that had the orphanage housekeeper lapsing into colorful Scottish rebukes.

"Nel." She rushed to give her friend a hearty, one-armed hug. "How are you doing? I didn't realize you were back." It had been nearly two weeks since Nel and Mrs. Clement had taken the train to Leavenworth, Kansas. A grand shopping adventure, the housekeeper had called it. Moira couldn't imagine traipsing through such crowds. She liked people, she just preferred them in smaller doses.

"We arrived about an hour ago," Nel said. "While waiting for Mr. Hoggard to collect us, we visited with the dressmaker. Mrs. Stone has so many design ideas. Lace on this. Pearls on that. The long trip combined with her incessant chattering set my head to spinning."

"Are you all right? Do you need to sit?"

"No. I'm fine now." Nel jiggled the items clutched in her hand. "Mrs. Clement sent me to get some fresh air and to purchase some thread and pattern paper. The walk cleared my head."

"Good. The last thing you need is to become ill. So how was your trip to Leavenworth? Did you find the perfect material for a gown? What about shoes? You'll have to tell me every little detail."

Nel was getting married at the end of the month. Her fiancé wanted her to have the wedding of her dreams and had sent her to Leavenworth where there would be a better selection of dress material to choose from. Nel was fortunate to have found such a thoughtful and generous man. Men like Sergeant Reese were few and far between.

"I promise to tell you everything, but not now. I have to get back to the dressmaker's shop. Mrs. Clement is waiting for me. We have a lot to do and not much time left before…" Nel stiffened and looked beyond her. Frown lines dug into her brow.

"What is it?" Moira glanced over her shoulder and saw nothing. "Is there something wrong?"

"No. It's nothing. I'm just tired from the trip and all the tedious planning." Nel reached out and gripped her arm in a gentle squeeze. "Please come by the orphanage when you get a chance. I'll tell you all about my trip. And I want to hear about your adventures as the town healer."

"There's not much to tell."

Nel's scowl deepened. "They're still not warming to you? What's wrong with these knot-headed people?"

Knot-headed. Nel always did have a way with words. She waved a dismissive hand and shoved on her brightest smile. Nel didn't deserve to have cold water tossed on her high spirits. "It's just going to take time to win them over, that's all. Nothing to fret about."

"Well, you let me know if there's anything I can do. I have an inroad to some pretty remarkable persuaders."

While Nel's *persuaders* would make her mission easier, she had to wage this battle on her own. She shifted the box cradled under her arm. "I appreciate your offer. But truly. All is well…or it will be once I get these bottles filled. I lost most of my stock in the earthquake."

"Earthquake? Here in Mineral?"

As they walked to the front counter, she related the details of the earthquake and assured Nel that everyone

80

was safe and sound, including her beloved fiancé.

After paying for their purchases, they went outside. Nel slowed and leaned closer. "I didn't want to stay anything until I was certain, but there's a woman trailing you, Moira."

She looked behind her. The closest person was a man about to enter the nearby feed store. "Where? I don't see a woman."

"She's not of this world."

Of course. Nel had the gift of seeing and talking with the departed. And they had plenty to say about the living. Sometimes nice details, sometimes not.

"Who is she? Is it my mother or Granny Tate?"

"No. She's much younger. I've not spoken with her before."

"What does she want?"

Nel cocked her head and stared into empty space. Anyone seeing her would think she was touched in the head.

Shouts echoed down the street. A group of boys raced by, laughing and shoving at one another. A scuffling sounded beneath the boardwalk. A second later, a mongrel emerged and set off down the street, barking and chasing after the boys. A horse shied at the commotion and his rider wagged a fist at the frolicking youngsters. There was never a dull moment in Mineral. From the living or from the dead.

"I understand," Nel finally said, the clouds veiling her eyes clearing. "She says she means you no harm. She knows you have a good heart and only wants the best for you."

"Well that's a relief."

"She wants her husband to be happy. And she

believes that can happen with you."

"With me? Who is the woman? Is she anyone I know?"

"Her name is Alice. Alice Wentworth Locke."

Her heart tripped. She clutched the crate tighter against her. "As in the departed wife of Dr. Anson Locke?"

"Yes. And she has a warning for you. Danger is coming. You must be vigilant."

"What sort of danger?"

"Miss Devlin. Hold up." Heavy footfalls accompanied the greeting. She turned to find a soldier approaching at a purposeful clip. It was Private Bolton from Fort Dent. He was her most avid caller at the office, more for personal reasons than medical she suspected. His sprained wrist was well on its way to mending, yet the man came almost weekly for a checkup.

He slowed and shucked off his wide-brimmed uniform hat. Moira avoided meeting his gaze. She didn't want to encourage any lingering. She wanted to hear more about the ethereal Alice Locke.

It was not to be. Private Bolton stopped, a pleased grin stretching into the short-cropped beard shadowing his face. He had pale green eyes and a face that many women would call heart-fluttering. Her heart kept a steady beat.

"Good morning, Miss Devlin. Miss Sawyer." He dipped a nod to each of them. "A lovely day is it not?"

Only if he continued on his way. "Lovely, indeed. I wish we had time to chat, but…" She caught Nel's elbow. "We're expected at the dress shop, and we're already late."

Nel dug in her heels. A mischievous gleam stole into her eyes. "We can spare a few minutes for a fine soldier like Private Bolton. Can't we, Moira?"

Moira contained a grunt of annoyance. Now was not the time for Nel to be playing matchmaker. She liked Private Bolton, but only as an acquaintance, and not a close one at that. His friendly behavior hovered just under improper.

She tightened her grip on Nel's arm. "We really should be going. Mrs. Clement is waiting for us. You know how bothered she gets when we dawdle."

"Pshaw. We're not dawdling. We're just being sociable. What brings you outside the fort, Private? Do you need Miss Devlin to have another look at your wrist?"

Moira dug an elbow into Nel's side. Friend or not, Nel was going too far.

Private Bolton waggled his wrist. "It's feeling much better now, thanks to the wonderful care I've been receiving."

His appreciative gaze rolled over her, a mudslide of scrutiny that left her feeling unclean. If Anson Locke looked at her like that, her skin would tingle and burn and ache for more. Dingled men. A pox on both of them.

"I'm glad you're on the mend, Private." She mustered a smile. "Although I didn't do all that much. Just supplied bandaging and some instructions. You did all the hard work."

A shout pulled their attention to the General Store. Another soldier stood in the doorway, wagging a hand. "Bolton, what in blue blazes are you doing? Sergeant Wilson wants us back at the fort by noon. He'll have our hides if we're late."

"Coming, Rafe." Private Bolton tipped his hat. "Pardon me, ladies. Duty calls. I hope to see you again. Soon. *Real* soon."

She could do without the real. Or the soon. She murmured a "good-day" and watched as he strode away. His legs were a bit bowed, and he walked with a hitch in his gait. Probably from sitting astride a horse all day. Odd that she hadn't noticed the imperfection before.

Nel scowled and rubbed at her ribs. "You didn't have to poke so hard, Moira."

"And you didn't have to play matchmaker. I'm not interested in finding a husband."

"You should be. A man could take care of you. Keep you safe."

She'd been taking care of herself for as long as she could remember. She didn't need anyone, least of all a man. "I can look after myself just fine. Always have. Always will. Now, what was the danger Alice Locke warned me of?"

"I don't know. She vanished when Private Bolton arrived."

"Can you summon her back?"

"No. Her mist trail is gone." Nel's tone turned solemn. "Be careful, Moira. The danger she warned about is grave. I could feel the fear in her. It was quite potent."

****

She was in danger. But from whom? And why? The only person who had her in his crosshairs was Anson Locke. While he was a curmudgeon, he wasn't the type to intentionally cause anyone harm. She would just have to be vigilant. Warnings from beyond the grave shouldn't be lightly dismissed.

She pushed through the door and into the medical office. The tinkling bell drew the attention of several men seated in the waiting chamber. They looked up and relief creased their faces. One man nodded and tipped his hat. Another mumbled about finally getting seen.

Across the hall in the examination room, Dr. Locke stood beside a patient lying on the table. The office had become busy during the short time she'd been at the mercantile. Good. Work would take her mind off troubling thoughts.

"I'll get my apron and come help you, Doctor."

"You will go up to your room and wait until I am done."

His voice was stern and cold and cautioned no argument would be tolerated. She ignored the warning. "There are a good number of patients waiting to be seen. We'll get to them sooner if I assist you."

He wheeled around in a squelch of shoe leather and joined her in the hallway. Red tainted his cheeks and ears. The skin over his jaw ticked. A bothered hornet couldn't look more agitated.

He waggled a finger at her. "What I need, Miss Devlin...is for you to obey my orders...without question. Is that understood?"

Lordy. Whatever had him in a snit was quite potent. For the good of the patients waiting to be seen, she would retreat and save the quarreling for when they had more time and privacy.

"As you wish, Doctor." She adjusted her grip on the crate of bottles and tromped down the hallway. Pigheaded man. How could Alice think she would be the answer to Anson Locke's happiness? He didn't trust her. He didn't even like her. Nothing would develop between them. Nothing.

She huffed up the stairs and into her bedroom. The low flame from the oil lamp did little to cut through the gloom of dusk. Perfect. It fit her mood.

She plunked the crate on top of the bureau and stiffened. Something was wrong. The disorder glowed like a torch. Her tortoiseshell hairbrush sat at one end of the bureau, the matching hand mirror at the other. One of the drawers was canked slightly ajar, caught open by a wedge of clothing. What the devil? She would never leave her things so disorganized. Someone had been sneaking about in her room.

She glanced through the doorway at the closed door across the hall. Mrs. Lidle would never stoop to snooping. She was honorable and respectful of others, traits that made her the perfect companion. Besides, she rarely left her bedroom unless needed. Louise Lidle was not the trespasser.

Only one person had the wherewithal and the gall to do such a thing. Anger climbed in her. How could he be so inconsiderate? She had done nothing to warrant such a personal invasion. It was inexcusable.

She turned up the lamp wick, and then slid the brush and hand mirror back to their places. Even the dresser scarf needed straightening. Rotten skunk. He was as meddlesome as he was pigheaded. How could she ever consider a relationship with a man like that?

With a grumble, she yanked open the dresser drawers and began tidying the disarray he'd left behind. Her pulse quickened at the thought of his fingers brushing over her stockings and clawing at her underthings. Had he imagined the intimate garments on her, or even worse, imagined himself peeling them from her heated body? A ribbon of desire curled inside her, a longing for something wonderful, something new, something exciting.

She shoved the last drawer shut. She had never allowed herself to consider having a man in her life...for good reason. In her experience, men were complications best left unsampled. There was too much that could go wrong. Loss of independence. Loss of reverence. And even loss of life. She'd seen it before. Her grandmother had treated a woman who had been beaten to within an inch of her life by her husband, by the man who had professed before God to love and protect. Not something she was willing to chance.

The faint thud of the front door sifted into the room. She crossed to the window and pulled back the curtain. Lamplight burnished a man stepping off the boardwalk and into the street. He tugged his green overcoat closer against the descending chill. It was one of the men she'd seen in the waiting room. Was he the last of the patients? If so, it wouldn't be long before Dr. Locke arrived, and their battle resumed.

She dropped the curtain and squared herself. She would be ready for him. Whatever his agenda.

Footfalls padded in the hallway, and then the open doorway filled with a towering presence. The breath caught in her throat and her pulse hopscotched. What was it about this man that had her acting like a silly schoolgirl?

His glance skittered from her to the bed and back. She stiffened. He was not thinking of her lying there. He was not. A straight-laced man like Dr. Locke would never allow himself to be drawn into the carnal.

She anchored her arms across her chest, clamping down on errant thoughts. "Good. I'm glad you're here. I noticed some of my things have been gone through. Someone was my room. Was it you? Were you looking through my personal effects?"

He didn't deny her charge. Merely squared his jaw and held firmly in the doorway. Why let propriety stop him now? He'd already violated her with his snooping.

"You had no right," she huffed.

"I have every right. I purchased the building earlier in the week. The office is *my* property now." He gave a brisk, sweeping motion with his hand. "Anything and everything within these walls is subject to my inspection."

He owned the building. He could evict her at any time. For any reason. She softened her tone and her stance. "All you had to do was ask. I would have gladly opened my room for your…inspection."

"Indeed. After hiding any evidence."

"Evidence? Of what? I have nothing of value. Nothing illegal." She dropped fisted hands to her sides. "What is it you think I am hiding?"

"Proof that you are poisoning the citizens of Mineral."

"Poisoning them? I would never do such a thing."

His gaze narrowed. "Are you certain of that? Nearly a dozen patients have come in recently, complaining of headaches, stomach cramps, and diarrhea…all unrelated to any illness. Yet every one of them has consumed one of your herbal potions."

She dug fingernails into her palms, using the pain to cut through the ache of his mistrust. "So, the only possible conclusion you can draw is that I am the culprit?"

"It's a reasonable deduction."

"Their symptoms could be from any number of illnesses. Cholera comes to mind."

"I considered that, but the sickness seems to be limited to the menfolk and specifically to those whom *you* provided a remedy of one sort or another."

No. It couldn't be true. There had to be some other explanation. She barreled toward him, heels clicking on the floorboards. "Who are these men? I want to speak with them. Examine them for myself."

"I won't allow it."

She stopped in front of him, hands hooked on her hips. Oh how she wanted to pummel his chest...to give free rein to the anger and hurt that churned inside her. But he might see that as being unhinged and cast her out. She would be the embodiment of control.

"Step aside, Doctor. I wish to leave this room."

He maintained his barricade of the doorway. Ocean blue eyes crashed over her, hard and fast. A flock of seagulls swarmed in her belly. Her heart thumped against her ribs. Surely he could hear the noise. Her ears rang with the din.

She drew in a calming breath and counted to three. Three was always a good number. Three wise men. Jesus rising on the third day. Three leaflets on a shamrock.

Her wits collected, she tilted her head back and stabbed him with a pungent stare. "May I pass, or are you going to stand at my door all night?"

His gaze again flicked from her to the bed and back. Something darted in the blue depths. Regret?

Guilt? Desire? His lips parted, and his gaze drifted to her mouth. Was he thinking about kissing her? The thought clouded her mind like peat smoke in a one-room cabin. She ran a tongue over lips gone dry as a summer pond.

A soft moan rumbled from his throat. He stretched a hand toward her. She froze, waiting, watching. His fingers halted inches from her face. Long, slender fingers that would set fire to her skin. Tingles rippled across her scalp and down her neck in anticipation of his touch.

"Moir…uh, Miss Devlin. I…uh." He swallowed, his throat muscles convulsing with the effort.

He was as mind-muddled as she. "Y-yes?"

His shoulders rose as he sucked in a draw of air and let it go on a long exhale. "You were right. I shouldn't have gone through your things without your permission. For that, I apologize."

She wanted more than an apology. She wanted his trust. And the kiss that his eyes promised.

"Is everything all right, Miss Devlin?" came a curious voice from across the hallway.

Perfect. Now they had disturbed Mrs. Lidle. "Everything is fine, Mrs. Lidle. Dr. Locke and I were just discussing a patient and lost track of time and place. We're sorry to have disturbed you. We'll take our discussion back downstairs." She hefted her chin. "Won't we, Doctor?"

He gave a grunt and stepped back from the doorway. Coldness had returned to his face, the blaze in his eyes all but extinguished.

She hiked up her skirt and sailed forward. As she brushed past, her arm raked his. He recoiled as if her touch might result in his poisoning. Her insides shriveled. She might as well jump for the moon as to hope for his love and trust.

Mrs. Lidle stood in her bedroom doorway, a Bible in one hand, the other clutching her shawl around skeletal shoulders. Thankfully, her face held more curiosity than condemnation.

"My apologies, Mrs. Lidle. The good doctor and I seem to be at odds over a patient's treatment."

Mrs. Lidle nodded. "I understand, my dear. It's plain to see how devoted you are to your patients. The town is lucky to have the two of you working together for their good."

Hmmph. More like butting heads than working together. "Please, return to your scriptures. I'll see you in the morning at breakfast."

As her companion disappeared back into her room, Moira fled down the stairs to the first floor. She made her way into the office, a place where she could keep her thoughts and her body under wraps. In addition, it held the information she needed.

She flipped open the ledger sitting on the desktop. He'd insisted on maintaining a journal of all patients who came into the office...names, illnesses, and treatments. It was one of the wiser practices he'd instituted.

His hand closed over hers on the journal. "I cannot allow you to speak with or examine my patients, Miss Devlin."

"Why can't you? What has changed?" She couldn't keep hurt from staining her voice. "I thought we had reached an understanding. Started to trust one another."

He pulled her hand off the ledger, holding on for a

fraction longer than was necessary before releasing her. "Until I discover the source of these illnesses, no one is above suspicion. Not even you."

His tone was softer, less infected with reproach. Hope surged inside her. She trailed a shaky finger over the desktop. "What if I agree to stop dispensing my potions until we discover the source? Would that be acceptable?"

His expression remained bland. He flipped the ledger closed with a resounding thud.

"Please, Dr. Locke." She hated to beg, but she needed to be involved in the search. For her own peace of mind. "Surely you've come to know me over the past few weeks. I would never intentionally harm anyone. I want to uncover the source of this sickness as much as you."

His gaze locked with hers. "I want to trust you, Miss Devlin. I do. You have been a great asset since my arrival."

"What does your gut say?"

"Pardon?"

"Deep inside. What do you feel? Am I a bad person?"

His shoulders fell a fraction, the hard line to his mouth softening. "You are not a bad person."

"Then, please...give me this chance."

He crossed arms over his chest and studied her like a hawk eyeing his prey. "I will have your word that you will not dispense any potions, tinctures, or any other medicines without my express consent. In addition, I will supervise all examinations and treatments in which you participate, whether conducted here or outside the office. Can you agree to this?"

Some battles had to be forfeited in order to win the war. She set her hand over her heart. "I give you my solemn promise. I will not dispense any potions, medicinal or otherwise. Together, we will discover the source of this mysterious sickness…whatever it proves to be."

Chapter Seven

Moira snipped off the end of the cat gut thread and scrutinized her work. Nice even stitches. No puckering of the skin. No oozing. The wound should heal nicely without any noticeable scarring. The seamstress Elizabeth Keckley couldn't have done any better. She could only hope the apron-wearing hawk perched beside her was as appreciative of her needlework skills as Mary Todd Lincoln had been with her modiste.

She grasped the shoulder of the man lying on the table. "There, all stitched up, Mr. Gunderson. You can sit up now."

With her help, Claude pushed to a sitting position. He canted his head to the side and scowled down at the two-inch gash on his upper arm. "Thank you, Miss Devlin. It doesn't look so bad all cleaned and stitched up. I'm just glad it wasn't any worse. That dizzy spell hit out of nowhere. I must've scraped my arm against something sharp when I fell."

"That's most likely what happened," she said. "You'll want to keep the wound as clean as you can for the next few days. Protected by bandages would be best. Otherwise infection could set in."

"Clean is not always possible around animals, but I will do my best."

"Wash your hands with soap and water as often as you can. And changing the bandage daily will help.

You're welcome to come by the office if you need help doing that. Isn't that right, Dr. Locke?"

Heavy breaths rasped behind her. Her skin pimpled with awareness. The man could make a rock perspire.

"Quite right," he replied. "Come by at any time, Mr. Gunderson."

She pointed to the patient's arm. "If my suturing meets with your approval, Dr. Locke, I will apply the bandaging."

He leaned forward, his shoulder brushing her arm. Tremors rocketed through her, and her knees went weak. She stepped to the side, away from the contact. She didn't want him to notice her reactions to his touch. It would only add tension to a tenuous truce.

He straightened with a nod. "Very nice, Miss Devlin. I couldn't have stitched any better myself. Apply one last swabbing of carbolic acid, and then you can begin the bandaging."

Well, well. A compliment. Would miracles never cease. She saturated a clean cloth with carbolic acid and gently swiped the stitched wound.

Dr. Locke retrieved a roll of bandaging from the sideboard and set it on the table in front of her. He sure was being nice. Was he making up for yesterday's irascible behavior? If so, she wouldn't complain. Any reprieve from his distrust was welcome.

"How long have you been having these dizzy spells, Mr. Gunderson?" Dr. Locke asked.

"They didn't start until a few days ago. Yesterday I could barely walk a straight line. Today it feels like I've been on a four-day drunk."

"Have you eaten anything out of the ordinary? Taken any medicinal elixirs?"

His gaze raked over her, ending the reprieve. She tossed the wiping cloth onto the table and picked up the roll of bandaging. His distrust cut scalpel sharp. She'd kept her word. No one had been given any potions.

Gunderson shook his head. "Nothing that I recall. The missus did use some special seasoning in her cooking the other day. I remember remarking on how delicious the chicken tasted. Sarah said Miss Devlin gave her some herbs to spice the meat."

Dr. Locke's hard expression condemned her. She hefted her chin. "I gave Sarah some dried rosemary last week. But it's not tainted. I used it myself recently, and neither I nor Mrs. Lidle have taken ill."

Her stomach twisted. Yet people *were* getting sick. Was she the reason? Others had taken her potions and hadn't become ill. She needed to find out what had caused Mr. Gunderson's mysterious illness…and she needed Dr. Locke out of the room to do that.

"Perhaps you could examine a sample of Mr. Gunderson's blood with that fancy microscope you brought with you from Philadelphia, Dr. Locke. It might provide a clue as to what is making him sick."

Mr. Gunderson tipped forward, expression eager. "Microscope, you say? What's that?"

Moira smiled and tucked in the tails of the bandage. If she could get Gunderson on her side, he might lead the unwilling doctor to the trough. "It's a device that magnifies very small particles so you can see them better. Our blood has dozens of them, each with their own job to do. If any are out of sorts, you can see them with this microscope."

"Ain't that something." Gunderson fastened a fervent gaze on Dr. Locke. "I'd like you to do that,

Doc. Have a look at my blood with this microscope device. See if everything's working as it's s'posed to."

Dr. Locke's brow crimped. His narrowed eyes walked over her, accusing her of inciting mutiny. She worked at looking innocent.

He gave an indecipherable grunt. "Very well. I need to gather the apparatus from the storage room. I'll be right back. Don't move. Either of you."

As his footfalls faded into the hallway, she stepped out of Gunderson's field of vision. She only had a few minutes before Dr. Locke returned. She had to work fast.

She briefly closed her eyes and rubbed her hands together. Warmth pooled in her palms and spread into her fingers. Energy pulsed inside her, coiling and twisting. A few seconds later, it gathered into a throbbing ball of heat. Her gift was ready.

She picked up Mr. Gunderson's jacket from the table. He'd removed his shirt and jacket earlier to allow access to his wound. "Your shirt is a bit bloodied and torn. You can put the jacket on if you'd like. It's large enough that it ought to fit over the bandaging. I'll help you with it."

He nodded, and she held up the jacket. As he slid his bandaged arm into a sleeve, she pressed a hand to his bare back as if to lend support. Energy flowed from her fingertips and into his body. She probed his core. Nothing abnormal there. She moved her search to his stomach. Pink and gray and throbbing. Irritated, but not fatal.

She slipped into the blood stream. A metallic taste with a hint of garlic flooded her senses. Fear coiled inside her. Back in Tennessee, Granny Tate had perceived a similar taint in a patient. It was arsenic poisoning. A search of the area revealed tailings from a nearby mine had polluted a creek near the man's house. Luckily, they were able to stop the spread of the poison before anyone died.

As she helped Gunderson into the other sleeve, she sent a quick burst of healing into him. It was risky, but she couldn't let him suffer when she had the power to help.

He heaved a sigh. "You have the warmest hands, Miss Devlin. And soft too. My missus has hands like ice and rough as a mule's tongue."

She chuckled. "I learned to warm my hands before touching a patient's bare skin. It keeps from giving them a shock."

"Well, I thank you for that."

Dr. Locke entered the room, his gaze sweeping over her like a magistrate eyeing a felon. "What are you doing, Miss Devlin? Why is Mr. Gunderson thanking you?"

Her pulse skipped. Had he seen her employing her gift? No, it wasn't possible. He had returned after the healing was completed.

She adjusted Claude's crooked collar. "I was merely assisting Mr. Gunderson into his jacket. With nightfall approaching, it's getting a little chilly in here. I thought he might be more comfortable if he dressed."

Dr. Locke mumbled something under his breath and set the microscope on the sideboard. Ornery pigs didn't grumble as much as he did.

"How are you feeling, Mr. Gunderson?" Dr. Locke joined them at the table. "Any lightheadedness since you've been sitting upright?"

"None a'tall. I'm feeling better now. Much better." He gave her a wink. "Must be the exceptional care I'm getting."

"Good." Dr. Locke extended his hand. "Let me have your hand. I'm going to prick your finger with this lancet and collect a drop of blood. Then I can look at it under that microscope."

"Sure thing, Doc."

He gathered Mr. Gunderson's outstretched hand and singled out a finger. "Hold still. This will only sting for a second."

He jabbed the tip of a small pin-like knife into the tip of the finger. Most people flinched at the invasion, but Gunderson didn't even bat an eyelash. He must have some lingering immunity from her healing.

Dr. Locke spread the resulting droplet of blood onto a small rectangular glass plate. He then crossed to the sideboard and set the glass beneath a long tube-like section of the microscope. He leaned over and peered into an eyepiece attached to the other end.

"What do you see, Doc?" Gunderson asked.

Dr. Locke twisted a knob. "Just a minute…"

"Are any of them so-called particles out of sorts?"

Dr. Locke paused a moment and then lifted his head. Frown lines creased his brow. "They all appear to be normal and at a normal count. Both white and red cells. I don't see anything unusual with your blood, Mr. Gunderson."

Not surprising. Arsenic was undetectable to the eyes, nose, and tongue. The Borgias in Italy had used the deadly powder quite successfully to kill their rivals and amass great wealth. It was doubtful anyone in Mineral was intentionally dispensing the poison. So where was it coming from and how? Thus far, only a handful of people had reported becoming mysteriously ill. They had to find the source of the arsenic soon…before more people became ill or worse.

****

Anson pushed aside the strings of dried plants dangling from the edge of the top shelf. Her herbs. For her potions. Odd how he had so doggedly pressed to find Miss Devlin guilty of quackery, yet now that he had substantial proof, it tore holes in his gut.

Over the past few weeks, he'd come to know more about her than he ever imagined or wanted to imagine. She cared for her patients. She felt their pain and did everything within her power to help them. It was difficult to believe she would knowingly cause anyone harm. She was good and kind and thought of others first. She did for them before doing for herself. She was just the type of woman he envisioned working by his side, lying in his bed, sharing his life.

He shoved the microscope onto the shelf. No matter what feelings he might have developed for her, he couldn't turn a blind eye to the truth. He had an oath to uphold. And nothing should sway him from it. Not even his own desires.

A shuffling noise sounded behind him. The aroma of lavender swathed him, bringing with it a sense of calm, of belonging, of home. Without her, the medical office would be dark and stale.

"Dr. Locke, we need to talk."

He'd uttered those same words in the same ominous tone seemingly an eternity ago. Had they wounded her as much as they stung him now? He turned and fell into ebony eyes that would stay branded in his memory until the day he died. Pink lips parted, and hunger pulsed in his veins. He fisted hands against the ache to slake his thirst. Such insanity had to be contained. For both their sakes.

Fingers toyed with the apron tied at her waist. "I know what you're thinking, Doctor."

No. She didn't have a clue what he was thinking. If she did, she would turn and head for safety in the hills. "The evidence speaks for itself, Miss Devlin."

"Indeed. And that evidence leads me to a conclusion about the cause of this baffling sickness."

"Your potions are responsible."

"Perhaps. But not because of negligence or intent. The men are being poisoned by something undetectable. I believe they are suffering from exposure to arsenic."

A slap to the face couldn't have shocked his faculties more. Arsenic. Of course. How could he have missed it? The ailing men's symptoms precisely mirrored those of arsenic poisoning.

"And just how did you come to this diagnosis? Arsenic is one of the most difficult toxins to detect."

She reached up and straightened the strings of leaves he'd knocked askew. Was she buying time to invent a tactful answer, one that would hold her above suspicion?

She dropped her hand to her side, her expression gaunt. "Years ago, back in Tennessee, folks began getting sick in a similar fashion. Headaches and stomach cramps that could not be attributed to any illness. It was eventually determined that tailings from a local mine were leaching mercury and arsenic into the creek water."

The Wentworths owned a large mining operation in the Shoehorn. Were they responsible for the contamination? Before condemning them, he had to be certain of their guilt. He owed Alice that much.

"If the local water sources are tainted," he said. "Why aren't other folks sickening? Very few of the women and none of the children are exhibiting the symptoms of poisoning."

Hands wrung together, fingers twining and untwining. He wanted to reach out and silence her fretting. But he couldn't. It would only encourage feelings that should remain smothered.

She wagged her head. "I don't know why some people are getting ill and others are not. I discarded all the potions unharmed by the quake, and I have not brewed any new ones. However, I can't dismiss the possibility that the folks who are becoming sick may be taking potions I dispensed before the earthquake."

Tears brimmed in her eyes. Her bottom lip quivered. She was truly suffering with the thought that she might have caused anyone harm.

He eased the tautness from his face and his tone with a soft sigh. "Let's go into my office. We can discuss the situation over a cup of tea. Mrs. Lidle brewed a pot before she left on her errands. Nothing like a hot cup of tea to brighten the mind and the spirit, she says."

Her smile whispered over him. "Tea sounds wonderful."

She turned and sailed across the hall, the muslin folds swishing around boots as faded and worn as the material of her skirt. Although she hadn't asked to be paid, she deserved compensation for her hard work. She had put in long hours without complaint. If she was found innocent of the poisoning, and if he decided to let her stay on as his assistant, he would see about paying her a wage. That was a lot of *ifs* to overcome first.

He followed her into the office. The room was only big enough to hold a desk and two ladder-back chairs. A single painting decorated the back wall. It depicted a gleaming blue lake flanked by a forest of greens and browns. Dr. Troutman's, most likely. His predecessor seemed to favor the simple things in life, from the plain wooden desk to the rudimentary kit of surgical tools he'd found in the examination room.

As Miss Devlin settled in the chair facing the desk, he rounded the desk and took the other chair. Wooden legs squawked at his weight. The sound and the hard surface didn't bother him. He had become accustomed to the lack of amenities…had even become stronger for it. He could now sit in a saddle for hours without suffering muscle fatigue.

He picked up the teapot and filled the pair of porcelain teacups on the tray. Mrs. Lidle had left a service for two on the desktop. Was the woman clairvoyant? She was the size of a leprechaun. Why not a psychic, too?

He set the pot down and glanced at Miss Devlin. She sat primly, hands folded in her lap. "Sugar? Cream?"

"Sugar. One cube will do."

Sweet, but not too sweet. Just the way he preferred his tea. And his women. Gripes. He had to get a rein on his thoughts, take a page from her Bible and adopt more puritanical demeanor.

He stirred a cube into each cup and then slid one of

them across the desktop. She picked up the teacup and took a sip. Lips framed pearly white teeth. "Wonderful," she murmured. "Just the right amount of steeping."

Indeed. He sipped his tea, giving her time to enjoy the soothing beverage and relax. After a few minutes, the tautness in her shoulders slackened. Her face lost its worry lines. It was time.

He set his teacup on the saucer. "As to the arsenic...let's start with the obvious. Where do you draw water for your potions?"

Fingers anchored around the porcelain cup handle. "From several places. I have used water from Dancer's Creek as well as from the community well. But hundreds of folks in Mineral do the same. More people would sicken if those were the sources."

"Agreed, but we should test them for arsenic regardless. Rule them out before we look elsewhere."

She leaned forward and set her cup on the desk. Her expression perked up. "How do we do that? I don't know of anything that can detect arsenic."

He kept his gaze rooted on her face and not on those rounded breasts swelling with each draw of breath. "There's a simple test I learned in medical school. It's not always accurate, especially if the concentration of arsenic is very low. But it's worth trying."

"What is required for this test?"

"I'll need a chunk of fresh charcoal and several glass containers for collecting water specimens. Preferably sanitized."

"I just cleaned out the potbelly stove. There should be some useable charcoal in the ash bucket." She rose from the chair, face flushed, arms animated. "I boiled a fresh supply of bottles the other day in preparation for making potions...er, but that was before you ordered me not to."

"Good. Go gather five or six bottles. We can collect a few specimens while there's a lull in patients. The sooner we determine if folks are being poisoned by arsenic, the sooner we can stop the sickness from spreading."

She whirled for the door. "I'll go get them right now."

As she disappeared into the hallway, the dark clouds hovering over him lifted. She wouldn't be leaving. At least not yet. He should be dreading the fact that they would be spending more time together as they searched for the source of the arsenic. But he was looking forward to being with her. She was like the sunshine after a long spell of rain. If he was honest with himself, he needed the brightness.

Chapter Eight

Could her potions, however inadvertently, be the cause of the arsenic poisoning? Her stomach pulled suture tight. She could be making people ill, not helping them as she'd vowed. Mrs. Campbell would be so disappointed. Yet, there was little she could do other than find the source and make sure no more people suffered. She would make this right, no matter what it took.

The sun sat directly overhead, beating down on the valley with thick beams of heat. Only a handful of people had ventured outside. A pair of riders and a mule-drawn wagon laden with burlap bags navigated the deserted roadway. On the other side of the street, old man Turner napped in a chair outside the feed store. Most likely folks were inside, enjoying the shade and their midday meal. It was the perfect time to carry out their investigation.

Dr. Locke walked with quiet determination, eyes forward, back straight, and legs churning. He was like a hound on a scent. She had to extend her stride just to keep up.

His medical bag swung in his hand as he moved, the clink of glass ringing softly from within. When she emerged from the storage room, he had immediately appropriated the sterilized bottles, announcing that he would conduct the collection of the specimens. Was he concerned that she might try to perform a slight of hand to absolve her guilt? As much as his distrust rankled, she couldn't fault him. Were their situations reversed, she would have done the same.

The woodsy aroma of tobacco smoke issued from the open doorway of Cavendish's mercantile. Memories surfaced of Tennessee and Uncle Spivey sitting on his porch, surrounded by a billowing white cloud. The man had few teeth and less hair, but he loved his pipe. He was rarely seen without it. Said there were few pleasures left to him after ninety years, and he was a' going to enjoy all of 'em.

Speaking of pleasures...Mrs. Stone's millenary loomed ahead. On the other side of the large display window, the shop owner bent over, rearranging the hats and bonnets set out to entice customers to venture inside. Moira's heart sank. The green felt decorated with white tulle was missing. Had someone purchased it? She always seemed to be a day late and a dollar short.

"Is something wrong, Miss Devlin? You groaned."

Dingles. She would have to work harder to keep her emotions in hand. She shook her head. "Nothing is wrong."

"You're certain? You appear to be distraught over something in that display window. What is it?"

A hawk with a spyglass wouldn't be as perceptive as he was. She shrugged. "Mrs. Stone had a hat sitting in the window. A green felt with white tulle. A pretty little gee-gaw that caught my eye. It's no longer there. I just wondered if someone bought it."

"If they did, I'm sure the shop owner would craft you another one."

And she could purchase it with coins plucked from her money tree. She waved a dismissive hand. "I have no need for fancy trappings. My straw bonnet is more than adequate."

He grunted. "You are a curiosity, Miss Devlin. In my experience, most women would bankrupt themselves or their husbands to own such gee-gaws."

"In case you haven't noticed, I'm not like other women."

"No, my dear. You most definitely are not."

Was that a compliment? With him, one never knew. They fell into silence as the false-fronted business district gave way to the two-story saloons with their bat-wing doors and piano music emanating from within. Dr. Locke angled closer and rested a hand at the small of her back. His protection was unnecessary; she could take care of herself. But she wasn't going to say anything. She didn't want to upset the comfortable truce that had settled between them. Besides, she rather liked having his hand guiding her. It made her feel worthy of his protection…accepted.

A red-haired woman leaned over the upper balcony of the Starlight Saloon, her barely concealed breasts spilling over the top rail. "Good afternoon, Miss Devlin. What brings you and your gentleman friend out our way on this fine afternoon?"

She recognized the woman from an earlier visit to the office. The lady of the evening had purchased a bag of pennyroyal, a common remedy against unwanted pregnancies.

Moira smiled up at her. "Good afternoon, Miss Birdie. This is Dr. Locke. He has taken over Doc Thompson's medical practice. I'm giving him a tour of the town. We're on our way to visit the sawmill." Not quite the truth, but it would have to suffice. The true reason for their mission might incite a panic.

The woman chortled and pressed a hand to a red-rouged cheek. "The new town doc? La, and handsome, too. I think I might just have to take you up on that offer to come by the office for a thorough medical examination."

Since many diseases could be passed from person to person through intimate contact, she had suggested the ladies get routine examinations. Keeping the prostitutes disease-free ensured they and the menfolk they served stayed healthy.

"Please do. You and your ladies are welcome any time."

Fingers pressed deeper into her back, urging her forward. She cut her companion a glance. The skin covering his jaw twitched and his lips were pulled taut as bowstrings. Definitely not an admirer of prostitutes.

Once they were past the saloon, she shrugged out of his heavy-handedness. "I can see by the set to your face that you disapprove of my association with such women."

"You shouldn't be speaking with them in public...much less inviting them into our office."

Our office. She quite liked the sound of that. "They are people just like anyone else and deserve medical care."

"Yes, they do. But we can't have them mingling with the good folks of Mineral. It's just not done."

He sure held some puritanical notions under that derby hat. "Miss Birdie is doing what she has to in order to survive. Surely you can understand that."

"I understand perfectly. However, others are not so forward thinking and will hold any such associations against us. We can't afford to alienate the townsfolk. In the future, all medical visits for those…er, types of patients will be conducted at their place of business…not ours."

She wouldn't fight him on this. Not now. Maybe later, when she had earned his and the townsfolk's trust. "As you wish, Doctor. I'll arrange a schedule that suits both you and the *women*."

He grunted and fell silent. Buildings soon gave way to an open field. Dancer's Creek loomed ahead with its clear water burbling peacefully over partially submerged rocks. There had been little rain lately, and the water level was lower than normal.

Dr. Locke stopped at the edge of the creek and shrugged out of his jacket. He turned his head from side to side as if looking for a place to set it.

"Let me hold your jacket for you," she offered. "No sense getting it dirty."

He nodded and handed her the jacket. Heat lingered in the folds. Did his scent? It took all her willpower to keep the garment draped over her arm and not shoved against her nose.

Unaware of the foolish thoughts swimming in her head, he extracted a blue bottle from his bag and crouched at the water's edge. He dragged his fingers through the creek bed in a back and forth motion. Muddy silt rose up and clouded the water.

An odd thing to do. She bent beside him. "Why are you stirring up sludge from the bottom?"

He plunged the bottle into the murky water. "Metals like arsenic or mercury are heavier than water and will settle to the bottom. Stirring flushes them up for easier collection."

Quite the knowledgeable man he was. She could learn a lot from him...provided he allowed her to stay.

After filing the bottle, he fastened the stopper and stowed the bottle in his medical bag. He pointed downstream. "We should collect a few more specimens at different spots along the creek just to be thorough. That bend should be a good location. Heavier particles will gather at the top of the curve."

Methodical and precise. He was the perfect investigator. Hope climbed inside her. They would uncover the source of the arsenic in no time.

He pushed to his feet and walked several yards downstream. As he squatted to fill another bottle, she stopped behind him and stared off into the distance at the Shoehorn blanketing the horizon. Purple and gold patches shimmered like gems among the greens and browns.

She sighed. "Just look at that mountain. It's hard to believe anything so beautiful could harbor something so dangerous."

He lifted his head and peered across the creek. "It is quite a sight to behold. The mountains of Pennsylvania are drab cowbirds compared to it. But as you say, danger can lurk in even the prettiest of peacocks."

Her stomach twisted. Was he referring to her as well? She moved her gaze to the mountain crouched in front of her. He filled the cotton shirt nicely. No bulk, no knobby bones. He kept himself fit, that was for certain.

A grasshopper vaulted onto his back, and she

leaned forward to brush it away. Before she could pull back, he pushed to his feet and plowed right into her. Startled legs wobbled. She gasped and threw out her arms for balance. His hands caught her waist. Heat boiled under his touch and spread through her like a wind-fed wildfire. She couldn't contain a moan.

He scoured her face as if searching for the answer to a plaguing question. She couldn't move. Couldn't speak. Hands and eyes held her firmly under a mesmerizing sway.

Flames leapt into the depths of his eyes. With a moan of his own, he dipped his head and firm lips covered hers. His kiss was gentle at first, then more demanding when she didn't resist. How could she? Her bones had turned to mush.

She splayed her fingers over his chest. His heart thudded beneath her fingertips, racing like hers. He nibbled on her bottom lip, teasing, tasting. Her head reeled. A twister couldn't whirl as fast.

He slid his tongue over her lips, basting her with pleasure. He yanked her closer. They molded together like well-fit puzzle pieces. Her body quivered, aching for more. So much pleasure. So much urgency. The blast of her healing power was nothing compared to this explosion.

She'd only been kissed a handful of times. Mostly quick busses that left her feeling disappointed and empty. Not so with this man. He filled her with wonder and excitement. She wanted it to go on forever.

A blackbird's raucous crow exploded like cannon-fire over a quiet field. She started and pulled away. Anson dropped his hands from her waist and stepped back. *Anson.* After sharing a kiss like that, it was the only way she could think of him.

He lifted his derby hat and scrubbed a hand through his hair. "I'm sorry. I shouldn't have done that."

Probably not. She touched a finger to lips that continued to burn. But, lordy what a kiss. It was as if he had branded her.

"It won't happen again, Miss Devlin. I assure you."

Miss Devlin. Not Moira. Not sweetheart. Not my love. Yet, keeping their relationship on formal footing was for the best. Romance would only complicate matters. He knew it. She knew it. Why then did her insides contort as if she'd been poisoned?

****

Anson set his medical bag on the ground next to the community well. A simple rig of hewn saplings flanked an adobe cylinder that looked to be about three-feet tall by three-feet in diameter. A bucket hung from a rope that fed into an overhead pulley which allowed the bucket to be lowered and raised. Based on the length of rope coiled on the ground, the well was deep and would make drawing reliable samples much more difficult.

Something brushed his arm, and he turned. Moira stood beside him, her lavender scent teasing his senses. *Moira.* He couldn't think of her any other way after that mind-robbing kiss. Even now, his lips ached for another taste. But he couldn't let that happen. Their relationship stood on shaky ground to begin with. Adding emotions into it would only make things worse. He would hold himself to a more benign path. Business-like and friendly.

She leaned over the side of the well. "I don't think we'll be able to find anything long enough to stir up the bottom as you did at the creek."

His knees went weak. The urge to grab her ratcheted through him. Not to touch her, although his hands playing over that slender waist would be pleasant. But to keep her from falling in. During a game of hide-and-seek, one of his playmates had attempted to hide in an abandoned well. It was deeper than his friend thought. Johnny didn't survive the fall.

He edged closer. "I don't think we'll need anything. We'll just splash the bucket around and hope that stirs up the water enough."

She pulled back from the well and peered up at him with eyes a man could drown in. "Are you feeling ill, Dr. Locke?"

"I feel fine. Why do you ask?"

Pretty lips pursed. "You look a bit green about the gills. Are you coming down with the same ailment as the other men?"

The only ailment he suffered from was a lust that refused to be contained. Focusing on the task at hand should help. "I'm perfectly fine. Let's get this collection started. You can prepare the bucket for lowering, and I'll get the bottles ready."

"Yes, Dr. Locke."

Dr. Locke. Formal and business-like. As it should be. He unbuttoned his jacket and squatted beside his medical bag. There were two green bottles left to fill. Moira had suggested they use blue for the creek and green for the well. That would make the sources easier to identify when they began the testing. Such a clever lady. Was it any wonder he was drawn to her?

He rose and set the bottles on the well ledge. Moira stood off to the side, holding onto the rope. Her blouse stretched across generous breasts. Perfect for suckling infants. And for hungry men. Heat that had nothing to do with the mid-day sun blasted through him. His groin stirred.

"I'm ready when you are," she said.

Oh, he was ready. But not for the reason she intended. He turned back to the well and nodded. "Lower away."

Rope slid through the pulley mechanism. The bucket dipped and swayed as it dropped into the vertical tunnel. It was soon swallowed up by the darkness.

After a few minutes, a splash drifted up from the depths. Anson held up a hand. "You can stop lowering. The bucket is at the bottom."

He turned back to her. Her breaths were coming in short pants, the effort pushing those breasts up and out for inspection. He forced his focus on her face, flushed now with exertion. "You'll need to give the rope several good hard yanks. Can you do that, or do you need my help?"

He hoped not. That kiss in the meadow had been hard enough to forget. Touching her would only burn the memory into his brain.

She swiped a stray lock from her forehead. "It's no trouble. I can do it."

Lips pursed into a taut line, and she hauled on the rope. Soft grunts punctuated her movements. Would she make those same sounds while in the throes of lovemaking? He gave himself a mental yank. No more of that. Such thinking would only make keeping her at a distance all the harder.

He lifted a hand. "That should be sufficient. Let the

bucket rest a moment so it can fill with water. Then you can raise it."

After a few moments, she adjusted her grip and began backing up, heels digging into the ground. Just as in life, she wasn't going to back down...not for a bucket weighing half her weight, and not for a man who wanted to stomp on her precious ambitions.

The bucket appeared out of the darkness and wobbled toward the edge. He reached for the handle. "That's good. You can stop now."

The rope went slack, and he set the bucket on the ledge. He picked up the ladle and scooped up a generous dose. The well water was clear with only a slight trace of sediment. He took a sniff. No detectable odor either.

Moira joined him. "How does the water look? Do we need to collect another sample?"

"I think this should do. No need to collect more."

"Good. I—" she broke off, shoulders squaring, her expression tightening. Something had set her on edge. Was it something he did?

"There you are, Anson. I've been looking for you everywhere," came a high-pitched voice.

Not him then. Someone much worse. He turned. Mrs. Wentworth walked toward them with a quick, purposeful gait. Her face was set in a determined mask. She didn't appear to be suffering from anything that required a doctor's attention. That meant she had other business with him. Business he most likely wasn't going to like.

He tipped his hat. "Good afternoon, Mrs. Wentworth. What can we do for you?"

"I went by your office." Her gaze slipped to Moira

and narrowed. "Mrs. Lidle said that you were out touring the town."

"I'm sorry we weren't in. Is something wrong? Do you or Mr. Wentworth require help with a medical matter?"

"No. We're both fine. I just stopped by for a visit. We haven't seen hide nor hair of you since you arrived in town." She glanced at the bottles lined up on the well ledge. Her brow bunched, adding more wrinkles to the mix. "What are those for?"

He ladled water into a bottle. "We're collecting samples from the town's water sources."

"Why? Is there a problem with the water?" Her eyes widened. "It's not cholera, is it? Last year, Eagle Ford had an outbreak that was traced back to the well water. It sickened half the town and killed dozens of people."

Good Lord, the last thing he needed was for her to start a panic. "No, no. It's nothing like that. We're just testing the water to be sure it's safe for everyone to drink. The city managers in Philadelphia conducted the same assessment once a year. I figured we could do the same here in Mineral. Prevent any contamination before it starts."

Wrinkles waned. "I knew asking you to take over the medical practice was a good idea. You'll keep everyone safe and healthy."

Perhaps. He stoppered the two bottles and handed them to Moira. "Place these in my bag if you would, Miss Devlin."

Their fingers touched in the exchange. Fire shot up his arm. Their gazes met and locked. A rope-like energy stretched between them, taut and twining to be released. It was magical. And most pleasant.

Moira blinked first and yanked her hand away. She busied herself with stuffing the bottles into his medical bag.

Mrs. Wentworth's disgusted sniff scraped the air. "Why is *she* still in your employ, Anson? I thought we agreed her presence was bad for business."

Moira's gaze fled to him, filled now with accusation and hurt. His stomach sank. The last thing he wanted was to cause her pain.

"Miss Devlin will remain working at the office for the time being. I have need of her assistance."

"Her assistance? She'll cause you nothing but trouble, Anson. She's the devil's spawn."

"You go too far, madam." Anger polluted his tone. "Miss Devlin has been nothing but professional in all her medical dealings…with me and with our patients."

"Harrumph. Alice would be disappointed in your attachment to this…" Her gaze raked hard over Moira. "Creature."

His blood boiled. He bent and snagged his medical bag. If he didn't occupy his hands, his fingers might just find themselves clamped around a wrinkly, over-critical neck. "Alice is dead, Mrs. Wentworth. It would be best if you accepted that and moved on with your life. It's not good for your mental or physical well-being to remain rooted in the past."

He didn't want to be harsh with her, but she had to be given a dose of reality. Truth be told, he needed a good dose as well. It was time to move on with his life. Stop wallowing in the what-ifs and the what-should-haves.

Moira's face glowed with gratitude, and his heart

lifted. Perhaps he should reconsider having a romantic relationship with her. She could very well be the future he was avoiding.

Chapter Nine

The flame on the oil lamp flickered and flashed. Macabre shadows flailed on the exam room walls. A chill snaked up her spine. Was Mrs. Wentworth the danger Alice had warned about? Earlier, at the community well, the hatred stamped on the older woman's face had sent gooseflesh crawling over her skin. Yet, it didn't seem likely. Other than having a tongue that could slice through steel, Edeline Wentworth seemed harmless.

A thump sounded. She whirled and nearly collided with the man coming up behind her. She tamed her racing heart with a hand to her chest. "Oh, pardon me, Dr. Locke. I didn't know you had returned."

Frown lines creased his brow. "Did I startle you? I apologize. I thought you heard me enter the room."

"No, no." She turned back to the counter and busied herself with arranging the teacups she'd assembled for their test. "It was my fault for woolgathering. I shouldn't let my mind wander so."

"Was it Mrs. Wentworth's behavior that has you on edge?" He reached out, hand hovering over her arm as if to offer a soothing touch.

She froze and eyed his fingers, waiting, breath hitched. His hand moved away, and he seized the nearby medical bag. A mixture of disappointment and relief washed over her.

She managed a shrug. "She's harmless. No one I should worry myself over."

"True, but her words were overly harsh. She's having a hard time accepting Alice's death. She needs to stop looking for someone to blame and move on. Let go of her daughter."

And let go of her daughter's husband as well it seemed. She waved a dismissive hand, more to assuage her own concerns, than his. "It's nothing to fret over. I'm used to being maligned."

He fished a bottle from the bag and plunked it on the countertop, sending water sloshing inside. "You shouldn't have to be *used to* such cruelty. It's wrong and completely unacceptable."

Was he starting to believe in her? To trust her? A sense of calm settled over her. "Thank you for defending me."

His gentle smile nearly knocked the feet from under her. "You deserve to be defended. You have done nothing to warrant such treatment. If these tests produce the results I believe they will, you and your potions will be found guiltless."

Was he being hopeful because he wanted her to continue as his assistant, or was there more? Bird wings fluttered in her chest. Oh, how she wanted there to be more. More tenderness. More touching. More...everything.

She dropped charcoal pieces she'd collected from the ash bin into each of the teacups. Her hand thankfully remained steady, unlike her swirling insides. "As much as I appreciate your support, I hope you didn't fracture your relationship with your mother-in-law by championing me."

"Ex-mother-in-law." He fished more bottles from his bag. "Don't let her concern for me fool you. We were never close. She always considered me an outsider who stole her precious daughter. Alice's death merely added another layer of distance between us."

The worry knot in her stomach returned. Mrs. Wentworth's obsession with her former son-in-law wasn't as benevolent as it appeared. It sounded almost fanatical. Perhaps the woman required closer watching.

The thud of bottles being set on the countertop thumped into her thoughts. She would worry about Mrs. Wentworth later. For now, they had a task to attend to…one that would hopefully answer a more immediate and very real threat.

"We should get started." She slid a box of matches closer. "I'm eager to see the results."

He nodded and uncorked a green bottle. "As am I. We'll test the well water first. That appears to be the most commonly used source in town and the one most likely to contain contaminants."

He dribbled a few drops of water onto the charcoal resting in the first cup. He had long fingers. Well-manicured. And very skillful. His touch would make a woman's body sing.

"Miss Devlin?"

She broke off her examination of his hand and looked up. "Yes?"

Blue eyes quizzed her. "Would you hand me a match, please?"

Dingles. She'd best keep her mind on their mission, else she risked his inquisition.

"Certainly, Doctor." She fished a match from the box and handed it to him.

He remained silent about her inattentiveness and proceeded with the testing…a reprieve she wasn't going to squander. A cat crouched beside a mouse hole wouldn't be as attentive.

He struck the match head on the countertop and set the resulting flame to the charcoal. The match burned almost to his fingertips, yet the stubborn coal refused to catch. He snuffed out the match and tried another. And another. On the third try, the dampened charcoal flared with a weak flame. Finally.

Anson extinguished the match with a flick of his hand. "Good. Now, we wait. If there is any arsenic present, a shiny powdery film will form over the charcoal as it burns."

They both leaned closer to watch. Soft, even breaths huffed beside her. She kept her gaze rooted on the burning charcoal, and not on the head hovering in her periphery. If she turned even a fraction, their lips would meet. A fiery collision that would most certainly send her fragile control into a death spiral.

The yellow-blue flame sparked and sputtered and finally died out. Anson straightened and picked up a pair of tongs. He prodded the charcoal. "I see no evidence of arsenic, though I didn't expect there to be any given that only a select few people have exhibited symptoms of poisoning."

"Should we try another sample from the well?"

He shook his head. "I suspect that will result in the same outcome. Let's test the creek water next."

While they waited for the second piece of charcoal to burn, she made sure to keep a proper space between them. The less her mind was tempted to skip off to the land of fairy tales, the better.

The flame sputtered and died out. Once again, the burning did not leave a film, shiny or otherwise, on the charcoal. She nodded. "No arsenic present. I had my doubts about the creek water, considering Dancer's Creek is used just as often as the community well."

"Agreed. That leaves one last item to test."

They had only collected specimens from the well and the creek. What else was there? She looked up at him. "What is that?"

His gazed locked with hers. Something flashed across his face. Guilt? Regret? It disappeared before she could be certain.

"You know I am duty bound to expose any evidence of harmful behavior…wherever it may originate."

"Yes, of course. I wouldn't expect anything less."

"Good…" He fished an amber bottle from his medical bag. "Because earlier this week, I collected one of your potions from Mr. Gunderson."

His distrust squeezed, hard, with little mercy. She managed a nod. "You have to put the interests of the people first. I understand."

"Exactly. I'm glad you understand. I must look at everyone through the same glasses. It's not a personal vendetta."

Not personal? Why then did she feel as if he was standing on her throat?

He poured a few drops of her potion onto a piece of charcoal. Two matches later, the charcoal glowed with a reddish-orange flame. It sputtered and danced and after a few minutes, the flame died out. No film coated the charcoal. The weight on her shoulders lightened.

"Well, that eliminates your potion as the source."

Was that relief staining his voice? The presence of arsenic in her potion would be the perfect excuse to send her packing.

She fingered the teacup. "I have to admit, I was worried my remedies would be the culprit. I'm relieved to know they are not."

"As am I."

Maybe she was wrong. Maybe he did want her to be innocent. "So, what's next?"

"We keep looking. The source must be out there somewhere. We just have to find it."

We. He wanted her included in the search. It wasn't a declaration of acceptance, but she would take it. Every step, however small, brought her closer to her goals.

****

Fiddle music and gaily dressed people swarmed inside the town meeting hall. Freshly-picked wild flowers and colorful streamers decorated the windows and walls. Platters of finger cakes, pies, and candies crowded a linen-draped table. Weddings were festive occasions in Mineral. Everyone came to celebrate and wish the newlyweds a happy and fruitful life.

She wanted to be cheerful for Nel, but it had been three days since the testing of the water samples, and they were no closer to finding the source of the arsenic poisoning than when they started. The owner of the Spade Hotel and Restaurant had come into the office seeking relief from the same symptoms as the other afflicted men. How long before others succumbed? The dance floor would be a lot more barren and subdued if they didn't uncover the source soon.

Her gaze lit on Nel twirling with her new husband

amid the dancers. Lamplight sparkled on the dozens of sequins sewn into the overskirt of the satin wedding gown. The pale blue highlighted her pretty face and set off green eyes, glowing with love and adoration. She'd never seen her friend so happy. Marriage suited her. She could only pray it lasted. Men were fickle creatures. Papa hadn't stayed around long enough to celebrate her first birthday. Granny Tate said Grandpappy had bolted for the gold fields at the first opportunity and never returned. Happy endings just didn't happen to people like them, no matter how much they wanted them.

"Moira? Are you listening to me?"

Fingers snapping under her nose jolted her back to the present. She shook off her ugly thoughts. She shouldn't let her mind wander so. There were too many people with the skill to read her thoughts. Literally. The last thing she needed was someone meddling in her life.

"I'm sorry, Lily. My mind was elsewhere."

"I can see that. Your aura is glowing bright yellow. Something is weighing on you. Is it the medical office? Meredith said a new physician came to take over the practice. Dr. Locke, isn't it? Is he making things difficult for you?"

Difficult? That was an understatement. In more ways than one. "Yes, his name is Dr. Locke, and he is not causing me any trouble. We're getting along just fine. Perfectly, in fact."

Eyebrows arched as if questioning the veracity of her claim. Younger by two years, Lily Kendrick had the gift of seeing the mystical halo that surrounded people. The aura's color indicated what a person was feeling. Apparently, her emotions were as marked as an albino deer in a forest.

"Is there something else about this doctor that has you so disjointed? What does he look like? Is he handsome?" Blue eyes narrowed. "Ho. Ho. That's it. He makes your heart go pitty-pat."

Good grief, the girl was clever. Too clever. Moira flicked her fan, hoping to wave Lily off the scent. "It's nothing like that. My thoughts have been troubled by work. We can't seem to figure out what is making some of the townsfolk sick. It's quite frustrating." Not a lie. Just not the entire truth.

Lily patted her arm. "You will figure out what is making them ill. I have faith in you. We all do."

If she had one tenth of their faith, her worries would lessen. Finding the source of the arsenic was going to take time. Time she didn't have. Her one-month grace period was drawing to an end. She could very easily find herself out on the street without answers…without a life.

On the other side of the dance floor, a slender figure glided into the hall. A stylish top hat crowned his head. A dark evening suit hugged his lean form. He looked the perfect gentleman, right down to his polished brogans. Her pulse began dancing a polka.

"Who is that?" Lily drawled.

"Who is who?"

"That tall, prince of a man who just brightened the hall. I can't take my eyes off him."

Neither could she. "That is Dr. Anson Locke."

"Oh my. I can see why you're taken by him. He has a most unusual aura. A brilliant turquoise. I've only seen that color on people who are ruled by their hearts."

She grunted under her breath. He must have a heart

of stone for all the compassion he'd shown her.

"I might just set my cap for him," Lily added. "If you're not of a mind to, that is."

Moira shot the girl a quelling elbow. "Stop it, Lily. I know what you're trying to do."

Lily feigned a look of puzzlement that was as genuine as paste gemstones. "Whatever do you mean?"

"You know exactly what I mean. There's nothing between me and Dr. Locke. And there never will be. We are business colleagues. Nothing more."

"You might want to rethink that assessment. He's coming this way, and he only has eyes for you."

Moira fanned her face, flushed now with heat. Lily was just being fanciful. Anson Locke did not have "eyes" or anything else for her. He merely tolerated her presence for the well-being of the townsfolk. Nothing quixotic could, or should, be read into his behavior.

"Pink," Lily whispered.

Moira cut her companion a glance. Eyes of periwinkle blue sparkled and gleamed. Not a good sign. Trouble usually trailed close on the heels of that look. "Pink what?"

"The closer Dr. Locke gets, the pinker his aura becomes. He is definitely interested in a relationship with you…and not as a colleague."

Perhaps. But it would be pointless to raise her hopes. He would never accept her for who she was. And she didn't want a relationship filled with lies.

"That's enough, Lily. No more talk about setting caps or any other such nonsense regarding Dr. Locke."

"As you wish."

She dipped a nod as the source of her feverishness arrived. He had deposited his hat and overcoat with an attendant. Lamplight burnished his head in a golden halo. He'd been recently barbered. Brown locks curled above his ears, and his jaw glowed from a fresh shaving. Would his skin feel as soft and smooth as it looked?

She fanned faster. "Good evening, Doctor. May I introduce Lily Kendrick? She's a fellow orphan from Seaton House. Lily, this is my *colleague*, Dr. Locke."

He inclined his head. "A pleasure to meet you, Miss Kendrick."

"My, my. You cut quite the figure in your evening attire, Dr. Locke. You'll have all the ladies clamoring for a dance."

Moira stuffed down a groan. That sugary tone edged with cunning often heralded trouble.

"You do dance, I hope?" Lily continued.

Bewilderment creased his brow. "I am schooled in the art of dance."

"Wonderful. Moira has been worrying herself sick over discovering what is making folks ill. She needs a distraction. Perhaps you could give her a turn on the dance floor? Take her mind off her worries?"

He looked as if he'd rather wrestle with a rattlesnake. Moira shook her head. "I'm sure Dr. Locke has more important things to do. He has yet to meet everyone in Mineral. This would be the perfect opportunity to make their acquaintances."

Lily dodged her lob. "La. There's plenty of time to greet everyone. Besides, a person in need comes first, do they not, Doctor?"

"I suppose they do." He held out his hand. "May I have this dance, Miss Devlin? For the sake of your good health?"

She shouldn't. Being in his arms would only encourage thoughts of a romance that would never happen. Shouldn't happen. They were as fit for one another as oil and water.

Despite her doubts, she found her hand settling into his. When he placed his other hand at her back, heat surged through her veins. His touch was every bit as magical as her healing power. She bit down on her bottom lip, using the pain to keep her mind on dancing…a difficult task considering her bones had gone soft as aged butter.

He whirled her around a slower-moving couple. "You look lovely this evening, Miss Devlin."

She glanced down at the mint green dress overlaid with a delicate lace overskirt. Mrs. Lidle had worked wonders with the hand-me-down, turning it into a gown fit for a princess. She felt almost pretty. Almost.

"Relax. I won't bite."

Maybe he was as empathetic as Lily had said. She forced a chuckle. "Wouldn't that make for a titillating headline in *The Town Herald*. Doctor trades scalpel for fangs."

His lips curled into a smile that rivaled the lamplight. He had perfect teeth. Even and white as the purest snow. He could charm the deadliest of snakes into submission if he had a mind to.

He leaned forward, his warm breath teasing her ear. "Fangs are employed only on very special occasions."

Her head spun like a toy top. She missed a step, and he drew her closer. His heat scorched through the material of her gown. She managed to recover her footing and leaned out of his embrace. Being so close to him was more dangerous than any poisonous snake.

She tilted her head back and tumbled into an ocean of blue. A pleasant stirring coiled in her lower belly. "And just what special occasions require the use of fangs, Dr. Locke?"

His cheery chuckle washed over her. "That, my lovely Miss Devlin, is a well-kept secret."

He'd called her lovely. Twice. He was attracted to her. The flames flickering in his eyes said so. As did the soft set to his mouth. Was he thinking about kissing her again? A shiver danced through her. She wanted his kisses more than air in her lungs.

She closed her eyes. The noise crowding the hall dimmed. The flow of movement around them faded until it was just of the two of them, dancing as one, as if they were soulmates for eternity.

Chapter Ten

The music dwindled to a stop. Heat and desire simmered inside her. Moira wriggled out of the arms trapping her and rushed for the door. She needed to get away. Quickly. Before she made a fool of herself and turned all her progress to ruin.

Once outside, she drew in a deep breath and then another. Stars winked like fireflies in the broad black expanse. The three-quarter moon shimmered and glowed. She leaned against the hitching post and let the air cool her bubbling veins. Her heartbeat slowed. The spinning in her head settled. She sighed. Good. Now she could think.

As much as she enjoyed being held in his arms, Anson Locke was far too charming to be allowed that close. She had little control around him. Her body craved his touch. Her mind went blank. In such a state, her secret could easily slip out. Not only would he send her packing, the trauma of her betrayal might cause him to crawl back into his shell. He'd only just begun to let go, to enjoy himself again after the death of his wife. She couldn't send him back into that darkness. She cared about him. More than she was willing to admit.

She grazed a finger over the wedding placard propped on a nearby easel. Clouds filled her eyes. Nel and Sergeant Reese had so much to look forward to. A home. A family. Someone to love and rely on for the rest of their lives. Things she could only dream of having.

"Moira, are you all right?"

She swiped tears from her eyes and turned to find Gabriel Hunt standing behind her, hat in hand. He'd grown since she'd last seen him at the orphanage. He was a head taller than she and sported a faint dusting of hair on his upper lip and chin. He looked quite dashing in his Sunday best. With those tawny eyes and gold mane, he was going to be a most handsome young man. The local mamas had best keep a close eye on their daughters.

"I'm fine, Gabe. It just got a bit too hot and stuffy inside. I needed a breath of fresh air."

"I thought something was wrong. You ran out of the hall like your dress was on fire."

She smiled. He always had an outlandish way with words. He'd once compared her to a turkey, hard to sneak up on and harder to pluck. "Nothing's wrong. I assure you."

"Good. I'm glad." He jabbed a finger at the doorway. "Are you going back inside? I wanted to ask you to dance with me. Maybe a waltz or a polka. Mrs. Campbell taught me how. I won't step on your toes or whirl you into the wall or anything."

She bit back a chuckle. He looked so earnest and sincere, an altar boy without the Cossack. "I would love to dance with you, Gabe. But later, all right? I'm still a feeling a bit overcome."

"I could get you some punch if you'd like. We can sit out here while you perk up." He ducked his head and dug a toe into the boardwalk. "Talk some and maybe hold hands?"

Oh dear. How to let him down without hurting that tender pride? "Gabe...I care for you, but not in that way. You're like a brother to me. A little brother whom I adore. Do you understand?"

His mouth crumpled. "It's that new Doc, isn't it? I saw the way you looked at him while you were dancing...like he was a big ol' peppermint stick."

Dingles. If Gabe could read her emotions, how long before others saw them too? She'd best get a handle on herself before things got out of hand.

"There's nothing between Dr. Locke and me. We're just colleagues."

"Yeah, right." His skeptical tone said he wasn't buying it.

"It's true. I promise. I don't want a man in my life right now. *Any* man. My work as town healer is all I care about." It was the truth. Mostly. A man would only make her life more complicated than it already was.

She reached for his arm. "Why don't you go back inside and find Lily? I'm sure she'd love to dance with you."

He looked past her and into the hall. His expression hardened. He dodged her outstretched hand. "I have better things to do besides dumb ol' dancing."

He shoved on his hat and took off down the boardwalk, heels thumping his displeasure. She started after him, calling for him to stop. He ignored her and kept going. At the end of the walkway, he turned and disappeared into the darkness. She sighed and halted her chase. It was probably best to let him work out his anger on his own. Her words would only salt his wounds.

"Miss Devlin?"

Anson. Gabe must have seen his perceived rival approaching and fled. Poor fellow. Jealousy could cause as much pain as any physical injury.

She turned and faced the door. Anson stood just outside the doorway, his slender profile outlined by lamplight. He'd cocked his head, and even through the gloom, his expectant gaze tunneled into her. Her pulse quickened. A big ol' peppermint stick indeed.

"Wait there, Doctor. I'll come to you."

As she started forward, the easel propped near him began to wobble and shake. A second later, it toppled over as if pushed by a stiff gust. Except there wasn't any wind. Not even a hint of a breeze. Only one person could move inanimate objects without touching them. She cast a quick glance over her shoulder. Gabe was nowhere to be seen, but that didn't mean he wasn't hiding and watching, waiting for an opportunity to use his gift. She'd have a word with him later. She couldn't allow him to take his frustration out on Anson.

She trotted the last few yards to the doorway. "Are you all right, Dr. Locke? Did you get hit?"

"I'm fine." He collected the easel and set it back on its three legs. "Don't know how the thing fell. I must have brushed against it and knocked it over."

That wasn't why the easel had fallen. But she couldn't let him know the real reason. The truth would make his head reel.

She nodded. "It's easy to miss in the dark."

A shadow fell across the boardwalk, and a young girl filled the doorway. "I saw the easel fall," she said. "Did anyone get hurt?"

It was Sally Hunt, Gabe's sister. While he had the ability to move things with his mind, she used hers to send mental messages across vast distances. All she needed was to hold onto a personal object of the person she wanted to communicate with. A handy gift to have when time was of the essence.

"No one was hurt…" Anson retrieved the wedding placard that had skittered across the boardwalk. He brushed at a brown streak. "Except for this. I'm afraid it took the brunt of my clumsiness."

Sally opened her mouth to respond, but Moira stopped her with a wag of her head. The girl reached for the placard. "It's just a little dirt. Nothing a good dusting won't fix. May I borrow your handkerchief, Doctor?"

"Certainly." He fished a handkerchief from his pocket and handed it to her.

"Perfect. I'll see to cleaning this up. Why don't you and Moira take a walk? It's a nice night. Good for a stroll. There won't be many more like this once winter sets in."

Moira gave Sally a quelling look and formed a few select words in her head. *Mischief-maker. Meddler.*

Sally merely smiled. "Go on, you two. Enjoy. I'll launder your handkerchief and return it to you later…if that's all right with you, Dr. Locke?"

"That's fine by me. Thank you for cleaning up my mess." He held out his arm, crooked at the elbow. "I find I could use a bit of fresh air. How about you, Miss Devlin? Care to join me?"

It appeared she had no choice. It would be rude to refuse such a gentlemanly offer. She rested her hand on his arm. "I suppose a short walk wouldn't hurt." She hoped.

****

Silky skirts swished against his legs. A warm, tingling sensation travelled over his skin and settled in his groin. After Alice died, he didn't think he would feel desire again. An empty numbness had taken hold and refused to let go. Yet this woman with her every touch, with her every breath, had awakened his body. He wanted her with an ache that left him reeling.

Using his free hand, he unbuttoned his jacket. The evening air seeped through his shirt and cooled his overheated skin. Perhaps he just suffered from desiring something that was unattainable. The curiosity. The excitement. The challenge of the chase. It was normal behavior after all. And last time he checked, he was human.

Their footfalls clicked softly on the wooden boardwalk. The street was well lit. But not by lamplight. Out in the back country, with no tall buildings or smog to block its luminescence, the moon shined as brightly as the dawning sun. It was soothing and easy on the eyes.

Speaking of easy on the eyes…he cut a glance at Moira. Moonlight played over her skin and danced on her lips. Her satin gown hugged every dip and curve. She was lovely and most desirable, there was no denying that. Had she felt the stirrings of passion as well? Her ebony eyes flamed when he'd pulled her close during the waltz. Her breaths had become short and uneven. Fright also caused such a reaction. Did she fear him? The thought sent daggers into his chest.

"Why did you leave so abruptly after our dance?" he asked. "Did I upset you? If so, I apologize."

Her grip on his arm loosened and dropped away. Was she afraid of telegraphing her thoughts through her fingertips? He was a fair hand at reading people, but not that astute.

"You didn't upset me. The meeting hall became too hot and stuffy. I simply needed some air."

"Are you feeling better, then?"

Dangling ribbons twined in her hair bobbed. "Yes, much better. Fresh air is just what I needed."

Her coloring looked normal. Her gait was even and steady. The only anomaly was the hoarseness in her voice. But that could be from taking in cool air too quickly after being overheated.

"Good. I wouldn't want my best assistant to take ill."

Her chuckle slid like a waterfall over his skin. "I'm your only assistant, Dr. Locke."

"Indeed. One I am most grateful to have working by my side. Between the two of us, I have no doubt we will uncover the source of the arsenic."

They reached a store window filled with pies and breads and various other baked goods. She slowed and ran a finger along the glass. "What if we don't find the source? What then?"

"We'll just continue to treat those who take ill as we have been doing. Have a little faith, Miss Devlin. We won't give up until we find the source."

She turned her face to him. He wanted to trace a finger over that silky skin. Set his lips to her mouth. Take her in his arms and cover her like a stud stallion.

"You must be a bull."

He coughed around the cotton that had sprouted in his throat. "Pardon me?"

"From the star charts. When were you born?"

"In May. The fourteenth to be exact."

Her pretty smile rivaled the moonlight. "I knew it. Taurus. The sign of the bull. Nel studies the star charts. She can tell a lot about people based on when they were born."

"And what does being a Taurus say about me?"

"Let me see if I can remember..." She scrunched up her face and tapped a finger to her cheek. A few seconds later, her expression lightened. "Oh yes, I recall Nel did a reading for Timmy Rowe. He was a May baby. Children born under the sign of the bull are reliable, patient, and practical. They commit wholly to completing their tasks. That's why you won't give up on finding the source. And it's what makes you such a wonderful doctor."

It's also what made him a horrible husband. His commitment to his profession took precedence over his marriage. And Alice had suffered for it. He wouldn't make that mistake again. Bachelordom was safer and much easier on the heart.

Gunderson's livery stable loomed ahead. Four men had gathered at the main entrance. The faint hum of conversation and tobacco smoke rode the air.

"There appears to be others seeking fresh air as well," he said.

She nodded. "And refreshments. Mr. Gunderson just took a swig from a crock jug. Moonshine whiskey, perhaps? I've heard talk of someone selling home-brewed spirits to the folks in town."

"Mr. Hammock did ask if he could continue having his whiskey. But he didn't mention which brand."

Fingers drummed on his arm. "Perhaps this stroll will provide more than a restoration of our health. All four of those men have come into the office, complaining of stomach ailments. And all four are drinking from that jug. It could be the clue we've been searching for."

It could very well be. But he wasn't going to get his hopes up. Practical and patient. Just like his star chart said.

"Let's have a chat with them, shall we?" He cupped her elbow and guided her across the street. She might not want his assistance, but he wasn't going to risk her safety. Even though the roadway was deserted, one never knew when a drink-addled rider could come barreling down the street. He'd treated many a patient who'd been unlucky enough to meet with such a disaster.

"Good evening, gentlemen," he said when they reached the other side. "Enjoying a bit of fresh air?"

"We sure are." Claude Gunderson glanced skyward. "It's a good night for it. Not too warm, not too cold. In the sweet spot my Sarah would say."

Anson gestured to the jug clutched in the livery owner's hand. "And a good night for a drink as well, I see."

"Just a little something to wet our whistles."

The man looked healthy…as did the others. Normal pallor with just a touch of flushing, but that could be from the whiskey. "I take it you are feeling better after your pumpkin seed treatment?"

Moira had suggested the sickened men eat raw pumpkin seeds. The ruffage would purge their bowels and hopefully purge any lingering arsenic as well.

Gunderson nodded. "It helped some, but I still have stomach cramping. This here moonshine helps dull the ache."

Anson eyed the other men. "Is this the same for the rest of you? Does this drink dull the pain?" At their nods, he held out his hand. "May I have a look?"

Gunderson handed him the jug. He poured a sample into his palm. Clear, with no sediment. He lifted his hand and sniffed. It smelled of slightly sweet corn. No chemicals. A perfect distillate.

"Did someone local brew this?"

"It came from right up there on the Shoehorn. Henry Jukes has a still on his property. Makes the best moonshine whiskey this side of the Mississippi."

His skin prickled. It could be the answer they were looking for. "Can you provide directions to this Henry Jukes' place? I'd like to visit. Have a look around. Ask him about his brewing process."

Gunderson frowned and scratched his chin. "Don't know about that. Henry ain't too keen on visitors. Especially folks he don't know."

Skirts swished closer. "That won't be a problem," Moira said. "I know Mr. Jukes and where he lives."

He turned and gave her a speculative look. He didn't take her for the moonshine type. More apple brandy or a light port.

Her mouth scrunched into a delightful pout. "It's not what you think. I was gathering witch hazel on the mountain last fall when I stumbled upon his place. It's only about an hour's ride from town. We can go together tomorrow."

Go with the woman who aroused his body and clouded his mind? Curiosity, as was often quoted, killed the cat.

Chapter Eleven

Dark clouds hugged the horizon. They'd have to hurry if they wanted to beat the approaching weather. The temperature had dropped enough that they could expect snow or an icy rain. Either would put a damper on their trip, if not halt it altogether. The last thing she needed was to be trapped on the mountain with a man who turned her insides to porridge.

Anson Locke was far too keen-eyed and would surely notice any unseemly behavior. He would question her, just as he'd questioned her flight from the meeting hall after their dance. He thought he had upset her. He was partly right. He had upset her. He'd turned her world upside down. With his touch, with the rich timbre of his voice, with his scalpel-sharp intelligence. She couldn't risk exposing her attraction to him. It would only complicate a tenuous relationship. They needed to focus on finding the source of the arsenic and saving the townsfolk from any further harm. Not on fruitless entanglements.

She reined her mount to a stop at the base of a steep incline. Witch hazel twined throughout a thicket of pines that paraded up the side of the slope. In its midst, a grizzled tree leaned on its neighbor as if returning from a night of drunken revelry. This was the right spot.

She pointed up the slope. "Mr. Jukes' place is just

over that rise. It would be easier if we leave the horses here and travel the rest of the way on foot."

Anson cocked his head back and eyed the incline. "This Jukes fellow sure did pick a most inaccessible place to live. I see now why you suggested we wear more serviceable garments."

She unhooked her leg from the sidesaddle and slid to the ground. The bulky jacket and heavy wool clothing would do more than keep him safe from the underbrush. It would also keep his lithe form hidden. The less distractions she had, the better.

"What do you know about Mr. Jukes?" He dismounted and led his horse closer. "How long has he lived up here?"

"When I spoke with him last year, he said he has lived on the mountain nearly half his lifetime. All alone, except for Miss Ruby."

"Miss Ruby? Is he married?"

"No. That's what he calls his donkey. He's very fond of the animal. She's like family to him."

Anson looped his horse's reins around a low-hanging tree branch. The gelding nosed into the foliage and began foraging. He gave the horse a pat. "That's encouraging. Mr. Jukes must have some compassion in him to care so deeply for an animal. Perhaps it will give us an edge in gaining his trust and cooperation."

"Perhaps. But, we should still be cautious."

"Is he dangerous?"

She secured Dolly's reins to a bush, yanking the knot tight. "Only if you threaten him or his brewing operation."

"Well, I will make all attempts to put his mind at ease. I prefer to avoid digging bullets out of my own hide."

A shiver skipped down her spine. As much as she wished Anson Locke out of her life, she didn't wish him any harm. He was a good man. And a great doctor. The world would miss him. She ignored the voice yelling, *as would she*.

She gave Dolly a pat and turned toward the incline. It was going to be a tough climb, but it would be worth the effort if it provided the answer they were seeking.

"I'll take the lead going up," she said. "That way when we crest the hill, Mr. Jukes will see me first and hopefully remember my visit last year."

"As much as I balk at the idea, your suggestion has merit. Take your time and be careful. If you need any help, I'll be right behind you."

Was he concerned because of his physician's oath, or was there something more? Something deeper. Silly to be speculating on such a thing. There could be nothing between them. He was sophistication and education. She was earthy and plain. The two simply didn't mix.

She gathered her skirts and began slogging up the hill. Heavy footfalls trailed behind her. He was close. Too close. She could almost feel his panting breaths warming her backside. All she had to do was make a misstep and she'd tumble into him. She shook off the notion of being held in his arms. Best to concentrate on climbing and avoid *any* calamities.

The top of the incline loomed ahead. She pushed over the edge and stopped at the edge of a small clearing. A wood-hewn cabin sat nestled in the center. The chimney was quiet. Nothing moved in or around the dwelling. The place was still as a cemetery.

She cupped hands to her mouth and called out, "Mr. Jukes? Are you here? It's Miss Devlin, from town. I've come for a visit."

The only reply was a fervent braying. Corralled in a pen just off from the cabin, Miss Ruby trotted frantically around the enclosure, nose in the air, hollering for all she was worth. Surely such a racket would bring Mr. Jukes running to find out what had his long-eared companion in a tizzy. Yet the cabin and surrounding woods remained still.

She crossed to the pen and leaned over the railing. Miss Ruby raced over and nuzzled her hand. Her tail flicked back and forth like the pendant on an overwound clock. Something was wrong. The few times she'd seen the donkey, it had been quite placid, almost indifferent.

Footfalls thumped behind her. "There's no one here," Anson said. "Mr. Jukes must be away on an errand."

"He's not close. That's for certain. All this noise would have surely brought him running."

"You sound concerned?"

She pointed to the empty water bucket. "If he planned to be gone for any amount of time, he wouldn't have left Miss Ruby without any water. And her feed tub is dry as a bone. It's not like him to mistreat her so."

"Perhaps his errand is taking longer than expected." He reached over the pen and picked up the water bucket. "I'll fill this from the water barrel I saw sitting by the wood shed. Then I'll have a look around. See if there are any clues as to his whereabouts."

She nodded. "Good idea. I'll look inside his cabin."

As she headed for the log hut, a light spattering of rain began to fall. Drat, she'd hoped the weather would hold off until they finished their task. If it wasn't for bad luck, they'd have none at all.

She pulled the leather latch on the door and pushed inside. What little sunlight there was dribbled into the small, single-roomed shack. Two chairs flanked a table that held a half-eaten plate of food and a coffee tin. The fireplace was silent and dark. Not even a hint of a glow shined in the grate.

Worn, but clean, floor planks squeaked under her steps. She stopped in front of the fireplace and stooped, holding her hand over the ashes. Cold. He'd been gone for at least a day, if not more. And hastily, based on the clutter left on the table.

A quilt-covered cot sat near the hearth. A trunk rested at the foot with its lid raised. She didn't want to snoop through his personal affects, but a quick peek wouldn't hurt.

She crossed to the trunk. Inside was a folded stack of clothing, a pair of moccasins, and a heavy fur coat. He clearly planned to return, otherwise he would have taken his things with him.

"Miss Devlin," Anson called out. "Come outside. I believe I have found our brewer."

Good. Her examination of the cabin had only raised more questions. She ducked through the doorway and paused on the stoop. The clearing was empty. Miss Ruby stood in the pen with her nose sunk in the water bucket.

The surrounding woods were silent except for the occasional *birdie-birdie* call of a cardinal.

She turned in a circle. "Dr. Locke? Where are

you?"

A movement near the woodpile caught her eye. Anson stepped from behind the stack, hand upraised. "I'm over here."

She crossed to his side. He was alone. "Where is Mr. Jukes?"

He gestured behind him. "He's over there just beyond the wood line near a creek."

Realization dawned. "He's dead, isn't he."

"I'm afraid so. Based on the stage of *rigor mortis*, he passed sometime yesterday. Come I'll take you to him. You can make sure it is our Mr. Jukes."

Dear Lord. Not what she expected at all. She trailed him into the woods. As they neared a shallow creek, a vile odor waved a greeting. She fished a handkerchief from her pocket and covered her nose. That must be why Miss Ruby was so upset. The animal could probably smell the rot.

A coverall-clad body rested at the edge of the creek. An up-ended bucket sat beside it. Pale eyes stared skyward. A gaping mouth, sliced into a swollen, gray-tinged face. There was nothing she could do at this point. Her healing only worked on the living.

"Do you recognize him?" Anson asked. "Is this Henry Jukes?"

She leaned over and gave the body a closer look. "The bloating has contorted his features a bit, but it appears to be him. I recognize the cottony white hair. I had commented on its striking color when we met. He said it came from his mother's side of the family. Can you tell what he died from?"

Anson squatted and rolled the man onto his side. "There aren't any obvious signs of trauma. No blood, or open wounds. An autopsy would reveal more, but if I had to hazard a guess, I'd say he succumbed to an internal failure of his organs."

"From arsenic?"

"We'll have to test his water source, but if I were a betting man, I'd wager it was arsenic poisoning that did him in."

"Poor man. He probably had no idea he was killing himself."

Thunder cracked overhead, startling gasp from her. A few seconds later, the drizzling shower turned into a hard, icy rain that pelted the earth and cut visibility to a few yards.

Anson pushed upright. "That's it then," he shouted over the din. "You go back to the cabin and get a fire started. I saw a shovel propped against the wood shed. I'll get Mr. Jukes buried as quickly as I can and join you."

****

Anson shoved the cabin door shut with the heel of his boot and set the bucket of water he'd collected from the creek on the floor. Shivers crawled over his arms and down his legs. That was a damn cold rain. And damned inconvenient. He'd hoped to be back in his office, warm and snug…and alone. Now he had to endure sheltering in a small, one-room cabin with a woman who set his body on fire.

She leaned over the hearth, poking at the flaming logs, her backside swaying in invitation. He stuffed down a groan and stripped off his jacket and hat. There was nothing for it. The rain didn't appear to be letting up, and dusk was fast approaching. It would be too dangerous to attempt riding down the mountain in the

148

dark. They would just have to hunker down and wait for morning.

Moira straightened from her task and faced him. "There's a clean towel on the table if you want to dry off. I have coffee brewing. It should be ready soon."

Perfect. He could use something to warm his insides. And it would give him something to focus on besides his cabinmate. Floorboards creaked as he crossed to a table with hewn logs for legs and a slice of tree trunk for the top. In contrast, the two chairs flanking the fireplace were professionally crafted and polished. Henry Jukes had been as eclectic has he had been reclusive.

He gathered the towel and began scrubbing his face and rain-sodden hair. A sneeze drew his attention to the hearth. Moira had pulled a chair up to the fire and sat with a thin wool blanket draped around her shoulders. Steam rose from her skirts, dark now and drooping with rain water. She should get out of those wet clothes before she took ill. But he was reluctant to suggest such a thing. It was bad enough being in such intimate quarters together. To have her undress might be his undoing.

A vision emerged of smooth, silky skin, exposed for his viewing and touching pleasure. Heat that had nothing to do with the fire rose inside him. He fisted the towel and scrubbed harder, attempting to wipe away his randy thoughts.

"There are a pair of trousers and a shirt in the trunk if you want to change into something while your clothes dry by the fire," she suggested through a sniffle. "They're not much, but they are clean."

She appeared to be comfortable being alone with

him…even suggesting he undress. If she could maintain her composure, so could he. With a little adjustment.

He arranged the towel over a chair back. "That won't be necessary. You have a good fire going, and there's plenty of kindling. My clothes should dry soon enough."

He gathered his jacket and hat and crossed to the hearth. After hanging the wet things on a peg, he settled on the chair next to her. A pair of boots and thick wool stockings rested on the hearth. Propped at the edge of the stones, pink toes peeked from beneath a muddied hem. The slender digits were perfectly formed and smooth. Would she moan if he took them into his mouth? Another wave of heat surged through him and settled in his groin. He ground his teeth around a curse. What the hell was wrong with him? He was torturing himself with such thoughts.

Heaving a grunt of annoyance, he leaned over and worked on removing his rain-soaked boots and socks. Once done, he stretched his bare feet out to the fire. Heat bathed his throbbing toes, and he sighed in contentment. There. That's the only pleasure he should be thinking about.

"Did you…um…get the horses settled?"

Her question croaked out on a raspy breath. Was she taking ill? He straightened in the chair and gave her a quick check. Only a slight flushing pinked her cheeks, but that could be from the heat blasting from the fireplace.

"The horses are under the lean-to with Miss Ruby. They should weather the storm just fine."

"Good. I was worried about them."

She was considerate of all of God's creatures. Was

it any wonder he was drawn to her? He picked up the iron poker and jabbed at the logs, sending flames licking at the coffee pot hanging over the fire.

"Where did you draw water for the coffee?" he asked.

"Not to worry. I cleaned the pot and then set it outside the door to collect rainwater. The coffee should be just fine. I found a jug of whiskey under the bed, though I don't think we should drink any of that."

Even if the whiskey wasn't tainted with arsenic, they shouldn't consume anything that would loosen inhibitions. He barely had a rein on his lust as it was.

"Agreed. We don't want to take any chances and make ourselves sick." He pointed to the bucket by the door. "Don't use that water for anything either. I collected it from the creek near Juke's still. It may be contaminated."

"I wonder why Miss Ruby didn't get sick? You would think she drank the same water as Mr. Jukes."

"It's hard to say. Perhaps he watered her from the rain barrel. Any contaminates would have settled to the bottom. Or, wherever he drew water from the creek for her wasn't contaminated. Testing will answer many of our questions."

"Why don't we do that while we wait for the coffee to brew? There's a crate of glass jars over by the bed. They appear to be unused and should be sterile enough for testing."

"I suppose there's no sense in waiting. The sooner we know for sure if there's arsenic contamination up here, the better. Let's start with the whiskey. That's what most of the menfolk in town have been drinking."

She pushed upright, her pretty toes disappearing

under her skirt. "I'll get the jug. Since you have the poker, you can fish out a piece of charcoal."

He nodded and thrust the poker into the embers. The logs cracked and popped, complaining of the intrusion. Orange embers danced upward and disappeared into the flue. It was a mindless task and served to ease the tension coiled inside him.

Skirts brushed his legs, and the sleeping serpent roused once again. He groaned and fisted the poker handle. He had to stop reacting to her every touch or it was going to be a long and most uncomfortable night.

The jug thumped onto the hearth. "Is everything all right, Dr. Locke?"

Hells bells, had she heard his moan? He wagged his head. "Everything's fine. Just having a little difficulty finding…" He jabbed deeper into the embers and unearthed a walnut-sized chunk of charcoal. "There. Got one."

"Good." She set two glass jars onto the hearth next to the whiskey jug. "Now we can get started."

Using the poker head, he broke the charcoal in half and scooped a piece into each of the jars. He then uncorked the jug and poured a small amount of whiskey onto the shard in one jar.

Moira leaned closer and held out a match. He pinched the stick just above her fingertips, making sure not to touch her. He finally had his desires tamed enough that he could work without making a fool of himself. Even the slightest graze could undo that.

He struck the match head against the hearth stones and set flame to the whiskey-soaked charcoal. The blaze glowed a cool blue.

He shook the match dead. "At least it's a good

quality distillate."

Her head cocked in that curious way he was coming to adore. "How do you know it's good quality?"

"I used to accompany my grandfather on his monthly trips to Virginia to restock his supply of moonshine. He said the clear, cool water of the Blue Ridge made the best whiskey. He would pour a sample into a spoon and set fire to it. If the flame burned blue, it was good quality. A yellow flame meant the whiskey was tainted. Grandfather was meticulous if he was anything."

"You are close with your grandfather then?"

"Was. He died six years ago this month." Even now, sadness clamped around his chest, making breathing an effort. He scrubbed a hand over his mouth and worked to bring himself under control. Weakness was not tolerated. It only led to mental deterioration.

"I can see how much his passing affected you. I'm sorry for your loss."

Her soft voice spread over him like a soothing balm. He rose and fished in his drying jacket for the photograph tucked in an inside pocket. The keepsake was a little worn, but thankfully dry. He smiled down at the familiar face washed in sepia.

"He took me in when my mother passed…and my father couldn't cope with her death. Not a day goes by that I don't think about him."

She shifted closer, her shoulder brushing his. "He has a kindness in his eyes. Like you."

The ache slicing his heart eased. "He was the kindest man I ever knew. Never judgmental. Always encouraging. I wouldn't be the man I am today if it wasn't for him."

"He must have been a very special gentleman then. You are a wonderful person and a most caring doctor."

"Not so wonderful to everyone." He looked up from the photograph and into soft ebony eyes. His chest tightened. "I'm sorry I have been so harsh with you, Moira. I let my emotions take over my good sense. You don't deserve to be treated like a criminal. Grandfather would be disappointed in my behavior."

She rested a hand on his arm. "Please don't worry yourself over it. I understand how grief can take hold of a person. I also lost someone near and dear to my heart."

Her tone turned wistful, her expression sad. He wanted to take her in his arms. Comfort her as she had comforted him. But that would lead him down a path he wasn't yet ready to travel.

"I don't deserve your understanding…but I'll take it." He returned the picture to his jacket pocket. Best get back to the task at hand before things got *out* of hand. "Let's return to our testing, shall we?"

Chapter Twelve

The blue flame sputtered and died out. Unlike the other two tests, this time a thin grayish powder coated the charcoal. Goose pimples crawled over her skin. "That's it, isn't it? That's the film we're looking for."

The scowl that had puckered Anson's brow ever since he joined her in the cabin lifted. "Yes, that's it. The whiskey *is* contaminated with arsenic. Though we don't know if the contamination came from his water source or from his distilling equipment."

"Let's try the creek water you collected and see what that shows." She'd already moved the bucket of water next to the hearth in anticipation of testing it.

"Very well." He dipped a piece of charcoal into the water and dropped it into a glass jar. "Match, please."

She scooped a match from a box on the hearth and held it out. His fingers brushed hers as he took it. Quivers skittered across her hand and skipped up her arm. She jerked away and worked at fluffing her drying skirts. After an initial awkwardness, they had settled into a comfortable companionship. She didn't want to disturb that with her silly yearnings.

Thankfully, he didn't appear to notice her unseemly behavior. Lighting the wet charcoal consumed his attention. After several attempts, the charcoal caught fire. It burned for several minutes and then went out, leaving behind the same powdery film.

A weight lifted from her shoulders. "We did it." She couldn't keep a girlish giddiness from coloring her voice. "We found the source."

"We sure did."

Sparkling eyes poured over her. She averted her gaze and picked up the rag she'd set on the hearth. "How about some coffee now that we're done? I hope black is all right. I couldn't find any sugar."

"Black is fine."

Using the rag, she lifted the pot off its hanger and poured steaming coffee into two tins she'd washed earlier with rainwater. He gathered one of the tins and settled back in his chair, stretching his long legs out in front of him.

He had slender feet and toes. The skin bared below his trouser legs was smooth with no cracking or scaling. He took care of himself. Without a doubt, the rest of him would be just as well maintained. Lean and muscular. Her fingers would find touching him most pleasurable.

She snatched up her coffee tin and sank onto the chair. What was wrong with her? Only tarts imagined such things.

"I would love to hear more about your grandfather," she said "What did he do for a living? Where did the two of you live?" Mundane conversation would surely tame her wayward thoughts.

He cupped his hands around the tin. His expression turned wistful. "We lived in Pennsylvania in a small town just over the border from Maryland. Grandfather was the station master for the B&O Railroad. I spent many an afternoon in that stationhouse, helping with the passengers and studying my lessons during the lulls."

"You said he took you in when your mother died. How old were you when she passed?"

"I was ten." Sadness crept into his eyes. "She died of a lingering illness of the lungs. No one could seem to help her. Her death is the reason I decided to go into medicine. I couldn't help her back then, so I vowed to never again be so powerless."

She understood completely. Wanting to help someone and being powerless to do so could be quite maddening. She'd lost count of the number of times she'd been unable to help a patient who was too far gone for her healing to work. Each death took a piece of her heart.

He sipped his coffee and peered at her over the rim. "What happened to your family that caused you to end up at the Seaton House orphanage?"

Hen's feathers. How had the conversation turned to her? She lifted the tin to her lips and blew across the top, gaining some time to formulate a benign answer.

"My father left for the California gold fields just after I was born. He never returned. My mother and I moved in with her mother, Granny Tate. We lived in the mountains of Tennessee for nearly ten years."

"Is that where you learned your trade? I've heard you mention your Granny Tate's teachings several times." At her nod, he added, "What made you leave Tennessee?"

That explanation required time and something a lot more potent than coffee. She supplied him with the condensed version. "It was hard making a living in the remote mountains. Most folks were too poor to afford our wares. The rough terrain made it difficult to travel.

We decided to move to a more accessible and populated area. Unfortunately, my mother passed during the journey. Granny and I settled outside a small town in Texas. She died five years later. That's when I came to live at Seaton House." He didn't need to know the tragic circumstances surrounding her mother and granny's deaths. That was her cross to bear.

"And now you're on your own. I'm surprised there's no man in your life. You're a remarkable lady. I would expect men to be lining up at the door for a chance to court you."

Would he join that line? She scrubbed her thumb over a wrinkle on her skirt. "My dedication to healing is not a suitable trait. Most husbands wouldn't cotton to having their wife called out at all hours of the day and night."

"I know what you mean. Alice was always complaining about my long hours. That I was never home. That I never had time for her."

"Those who knew your wife said she was extremely beautiful."

"She was. She had the most extraordinary hair. White gold like an angel's halo. She had a voice like an angel too. Everyone loved listening to her sing."

"You must miss her."

He stared into the fire, his hands clamped around his coffee tin, his expression grim. She hadn't intended to cause him distress. Yet there it was, plain as humps on a toad. Pain. Gut-eating pain.

She stirred on her seat, seeking a more comfortable spot for her bottom and her guilt. "If it's too difficult to talk about her, I understand."

He took a swig of coffee and winced. Too hot? Or

not the mind-numbing spirit he really wished he was drinking?

"No. It's all right. I just wish things had turned out differently for her. Wish I had done more or paid attention to what she was going through."

What could she say to that? She'd shouldered the same regret many times over the years. It was a connection she felt clear down to her soul.

He set his tin on the hearth and leaned forward, the spindly-legged chair squawking in protest. He snagged the poker and began prodding at the burning logs. Embers popped and sizzled.

"Alice's pregnancy was difficult," he said between prods. "She stayed sickly much of the time and emptied her stomach more often than not. She was bedridden from the first trimester."

She wanted to reach out and comfort him. But wasn't sure how such a gesture would be received. She sipped her coffee instead. "That's not unusual. I have known many women who experienced extreme sickness during their confinement."

"As have I." He poked harder at the logs. Sparks shot upward, spitting and darting like angry bees. "Yet everything I tried failed. Nothing seemed to help. She slipped deeper and deeper into despair."

She had seen that before as well. Women so weakened by the battle, they simply gave up. One even went so far as to rid herself of the babe. Both mother and child had perished. Had that happened to Anson's wife?

He rested the poker against the hearth, but remained leaning forward, elbows braced on his knees. "My practice was starting to build, and I was busy with patients. As much as I wanted to stay by her side, I couldn't. So, I hired a woman to sit with her. Unbeknownst to me, Alice had this woman purchase elixirs from a snake-oil salesman who claimed the tonic would cure any illness, even confinement sickness."

"I'm guessing the tonic didn't help."

"It made things worse…much worse."

So that was the reason for his distrust of her potions. He associated them with his wife's demise.

His heavy sigh clawed the air. "I had no idea she was poisoning herself. She began slipping away, turning into nothing but skin and bones. I tried everything I knew to help her. Nothing worked. Perhaps if I had known about the tonic, I could have saved her…could have saved our child."

A soft ache filled her chest. She had regrets as well. Many of them. "I'm so sorry for your loss. But you must know her death was not your fault. There was nothing you could do if she kept things from you."

"I should have done more…should have put my practice on hold and cared for her myself. I failed her and my child."

"You did not fail anyone. In the short time we have worked together, I feel I have come to know you. You would sacrifice your own wellbeing to help a person in need. I imagine that would be doubly true for someone you loved."

"Love? I'm not so sure I'd call what I felt for her as love. I wanted to provide for Alice, give her and our child a good life. But she wasn't in my every thought. I wasn't struck with an overpowering obsession for her. She was just a part of my life, like a lamp or a chair. Perhaps that's why I failed her." His chin fell to his chest. "I just don't know."

She wanted to comfort him with a sympathetic embrace, but that would only invite trouble. She resorted to words. "There are all kinds of love in this world. I'm sure Alice knew you cared for her; just as I'm sure she cared for you."

Thoughts of another woman sharing his love pinched. She reached for the pot. "More coffee?"

He shook his head. "No, thank you. I've had enough."

Enough coffee, but not enough talk of his wife. He needed to purge himself of the poison that clearly still had him in its grip. She set her empty tin on the hearth. "Tell me how the two of you met."

He rose from the chair and braced an arm across the mantle. His face buckled into frown lines. "It was at Mrs. Dalrymple's evening gala. I didn't want to attend...socials are not my cup of tea. I prefer the company of a good book and a fire raging in the fireplace."

So did she. They really were peas of the same pod.

"I watched this lovely butterfly flitting around the ballroom, putting smiles on people's faces and laughter in their hearts. I thought she would make a wonderful complement to my practice."

"She sounds enchanting."

"She was." He wagged his head, a wry smile splitting through the wrinkles. "Did you put a potion in my coffee, Miss Devlin?"

Her heart stuttered. "Wh-what?"

"I've never opened up to anyone about my feelings for Alice. I must be under a spell."

Was that a good thing or bad? He didn't look upset.

He looked…relieved. The hardness had left his face. Even his eyes had softened.

She smiled up at him. "I'm glad you feel comfortable talking with me. It always helps to get things off your chest. Unburden yourself from your demons."

He reached out and cupped her arms, pulling her to her feet. "I feel more than comfortable. I care for you, Moira. Deeply."

"Anson, I…"

"Say it again."

"S-say what?"

"My name. I've never heard it cross your lips before. I quite like the sound."

He didn't give her a chance to reply. His lips fell to hers. A perfect mixture of firm and supple. His tongue teased her lips apart and dipped inside, hungrily searching for sustenance. She melted against him, ready to provide whatever nourishment he needed.

He moaned deep in his throat and lifted a hand to cup her breast. Warmth flowered inside her, and she gave a moan of her own. If this was heaven, she never wanted to leave.

He shifted and thrust against her. A very noticeable bulge pressed into her lower belly. Cold reality flooded her. She wanted to help him heal. But this was not the way it should be done.

She shrugged out of his arms and backed away, putting distance between her and temptation. "We can't do this, Dr. Locke. It's wrong."

He heaved a sigh and dropped his hands to his side. "You're right. We can't. I apologize for putting you in such a compromising situation."

"There's nothing to apologize for. You were caught up in an emotional moment. I understand." So had she. Almost to the point of no return.

"It was wrong of me to push my attentions on you. I should have considered the ramifications."

Ramifications. Like being forced to marry her? Or the possibility he might enjoy being with her and how that could compromise his heart?

****

Birds chirped. Squirrels chattered. Leaves rustled in the wind. Peaceful sounds. Yet a strained silence screeched between them. Anson rode ahead, leading Miss Ruby. His back was rigid as a tree trunk, his shoulders bunched. When the rain refused to let up, they had spent an awkward night in the cabin. She had slept on the cot, while he made a pallet by the fire. Morning had brought sunshine, but not a letup in the tension. He had retreated into his self-imposed dungeon and clearly intended on staying there. He would keep their relationship platonic, even if it killed him.

How could she view him as a mere friend and colleague after that kiss? Nothing she had ever experienced came close to the feelings he evoked. Heat and passion. Fire and yearning. She ached to have more, to be more to him. She couldn't just sweep the incident under the rug as if it had never happened. It was permanently branded into her soul.

The woods thinned and opened onto Dancer's Creek. The water level had risen with the overnight rains and flowed briskly over the submerged rocks. Anson found a shallow spot, and the horses crossed without mishap.

As they rode into town, the toll of church bells

filled the air. It was Sunday. A day of worship. She hadn't seen the inside of a church in years. Not because she didn't believe in God...she did. But in her experience, most who attended church regularly and claimed to be Christians were far from it. If they believed half the words they spouted, the world would be a much better place.

Anson twisted in his saddle, looking at her for the first time in hours. "Let's drop the horses off at Gunderson's livery. Then we can join the others at church. It will be the perfect place to reveal our discovery."

Her belly attempted a dismount. "Is that a good idea? What if they don't believe us?"

"Why wouldn't they believe us?"

Oh, maybe because people rarely believed her. She had to earn their trust before they put their lives in her hands. And she hadn't quite reached that point. Perhaps they would react differently to a certified doctor, to a man.

She shrugged. "The people in this town are a skeptical lot. They don't trust easily. When faced with danger, they shoot first and ask questions later. We will have to tread carefully."

"Everything will be just fine. You'll see."

She could only hope it would. They left the horses and Miss Ruby with Gunderson's stable boy and walked the short distance to Trinity Presbyterian Church. While not the only church in Mineral, it was the most attended. Once they disclosed their findings, word would spread quickly throughout the town.

White-washed clapboard walls gleamed in the sunlight. The large double doors had been thrown open in invitation. Her skin prickled, and she rubbed at the scar at back of her neck. She knew first-hand how very *unwelcoming* church-goers could be.

She tugged in a fortifying slug of air and climbed the stairs. Footfalls trailed behind her and urged her forward. She stepped into the church. Conversation droned in the nave, low and threatening, like the buzz in a busy hive. She kept her head bowed, eyes averted. An empty pew appeared, and she slid onto the polished wood bench, quick and quiet as a mouse.

Anson settled beside her, his thigh pressing against hers, strong and comforting. Her agitation eased. Some, but not entirely. Just enough that she wouldn't squirm like a worm on a hot rock.

The congregation rose and began singing *Rock of Ages*. Granny Tate's favorite hymn. She stood and sang along, the familiar words further easing her tension. Everything would turn out just fine. All she had to do was believe.

As the last notes of the hymn faded, Reverend Turnage moved onto the raised dais at the front of the church. He looked out over the congregation, his sallow face pleated with a smile as genuine as iron pyrite. Moira hid behind the bulky shoulders of the man seated in front of her. If the good reverend caught sight of her, it might doom their cause.

"Welcome, everyone. Welcome. We gather today on this glorious Sabbath; the body of Christ assembling like Ezekiel's dry bones coming together in the resurrecting power of God's Holy Spirit." He lifted his hands. "I ask you to greet one another in love, as family. For even if we haven't met, in Christ we are brothers and sisters, children of God."

Moira choked down a grunt. If only he practiced what he preached. A low hum boiled around her as the congregation turned to one another to shake hands and offer greetings. The woman seated next to her held out her hand. Moira pasted on a smile. When in Rome…

She shook the woman's hand, repeating the salutation of "peace be with you."

The hum subsided, and Reverent Turnage motioned to the gathering. "Are there any announcements? Family news?"

Anson set his hat on the pew and pushed to his feet. "There is, Reverend. I have something of grave importance I wish to announce."

"Please. Dr. Locke, is it?" At Anson's nod the reverend waved him forward. "Come up to the dais, so everyone can hear you."

Anson eased into the aisle and strode to the front of the church. He stepped onto the platform and turned. Sunlight dove through the stained-glass windows and painted his hair and face with colorful slashes. He looked like an angel. A loving, trustful seraph. And was just as unattainable as one.

"As you may have heard," he said. "Some among you have been struck with an unusual and quiet persistent stomach ailment."

Someone coughed. Others nodded, including Claude Gunderson who sat a few pews in front of her. Most looked on with curious expressions.

"The healer Miss Devlin and I have been working tirelessly to uncover the cause of this ailment. After much research and collecting of samples, we have discovered the source. It's coming from a creek located near the summit of the Shoehorn."

Indrawn breaths and disturbed mumblings carved the air. Expressions blanched. Reverend Turnage's bushy brow knitted together in one formidable line. His piercing gaze flew over the crowd. Moira slouched more, hoping the giant in front of her shielded her from his view. Why did Anson have to mention her? He was more than welcome to claim the glory for himself.

"Is it cholera?" someone called out.

"No. No. Please, do not panic," Anson said, his tone calm and steady, the Rock of Gibraltar. "I assure you, it's not cholera. Our investigation revealed that the patients complaining of these stomach ailments had consumed Henry Jukes' mountain brewed whiskey."

Sniggers and tsks-tsks greeted this announcement. Moira risked a peep around her barricade. Reverend Turnage had thankfully given up his search. His beady gaze riveted on Anson. Was he calling on God to rain fire and brimstone on the good doctor for associating with a witch?

Anson lowered hands he'd apparently raised to garner calmness. "Miss Devlin and I took a trip up to Henry's place to further explore this connection. We found Mr. Jukes, but unfortunately, he had perished days before our arrival. Tests of his moonshine and of the water from a nearby creek exposed a deadly secret. Both were contaminated with arsenic."

"Arsenic, you say?" Claude Gunderson asked.

"Yes, we believe a vein recently opened up tainted the creek he used to brew his moonshine."

The lady beside her gasped and clasped a hand to her chest. "What about the town? Has it tainted our drinking water as well?"

Claude twisted around to face the anxious woman.

"Not to worry, Mrs. Smithe. The creek that runs by Henry's place empties into Dancer's Creek a few miles below town. Our drinking water should be just fine."

The banker, Mr. Hamilton rose to his feet. "Do you have any idea what could have opened up that vein, Dr. Locke?"

"Anything that moves the earth," Anson supplied. "Mudslides, earthquakes…mining blasts."

"Was it that earthquake? It shook everything rather fiercely."

Claude wagged his head. "Couldn't have been. I bought my whiskey from Henry weeks before that quake hit. And there haven't been any mudslides in months. It must be the Wentworth's mine."

Shuffling and grunts filled the air. A second later, Mrs. Wentworth shot into the aisle, hands waving as if shooing away a swarm of bees. "That is not true. Our mine is on the other side of the mountain. It could not be the cause of the tainting."

"Then what else could it be?" Gunderson fired back.

Mrs. Wentworth stalked to the pew where Moira sat and stopped. Pale eyes flamed with Satan's bonfire. A bony finger took aim. "You should be looking at that one for the cause. Miss Devlin has the most to gain from polluting the water."

Dozens of gazes shifted in her direction. All warmth left her body. She'd been discovered.

Anson vaulted from the dais and rushed down the aisle. "Why would you make such an accusation, Edeline? Moira would never do such a thing."

"Of course, she would. By discovering the source of the poisoning, she makes herself look good in the

168

eyes of the townsfolk." Mrs. Wentworth turned her pointed gaze on Anson. "And in your eyes. I've seen the way she looks at you. All cow-eyed. She wants you for herself."

Heated blood rushed to her head. Moira bolted upright. "You have no right to say such things."

"Do you deny your attraction to him? A prominent doctor would be quite the catch for a jezebel like you."

"That's enough," Anson bellowed. "Moira is not responsible for the tainting."

Mrs. Wentworth puffed up like a bothered hen. "And just how do you know this?"

"Because I know Moira. She is good and kind and only has the best interests of this town at heart."

"Bah. You're just bewitched by her."

"If being in awe of her dedication and selflessness is being bewitched, then I am. And so will the folks of this town once they get to know her. Miss Devlin will continue to serve this community as herbalist and my assistant. On a permanent basis." He stood there, a mountain, daring anyone to naysay him.

Mrs. Wentworth's face turned a mottled shade of red. If she were a train engine, she'd be spouting steam. "You'll regret your choice, Anson Locke. Mark my words."

Chapter Thirteen

Anson accepted her. He wanted her to remain and work beside him at the medical practice...permanently. A drunk with the keys to the saloon couldn't be happier. Yet there was more to her than just being able to mix herbal potions. A lot more. Learning about her abnormal ability could cause him to rethink his decision. To renounce her. It would mean an end to their partnership. And if she was honest with herself, it would ruin any hope of discovering if anything special could develop between them.

He was at the very least intrigued by her. That kiss at Henry Jukes' cabin had been full of passion and want. But he still mourned the death of his wife. She didn't want to push a relationship on him. Besides, she still had plenty of misgivings about getting involved with a man. There was too much danger in such closeness. For now, she would continue as his colleague, making her potions and only using her special gift when necessary, covertly, just as Mrs. Campbell had instructed. It was the best course of action...for everyone.

Wagons and carts congested the roadway. People scurried along the boardwalk. Like her, they'd risen early to conduct their errands. Mondays were always busy after a day of respecting the Lord. Shop owners had thrown their doors open to welcome the throng and the moderate weather. The temperature had climbed since the rainstorm and didn't appear to be abating.

Standing outside his mercantile and holding a long-handled broom, Mr. Cavendish tipped his hat. "Good morning, Miss Devlin. A wonderful day to be out and about."

She stopped and nodded. "And a good morning to you, Mr. Cavendish. It's hard to believe winter is right around the corner."

"For certain. We should enjoy this mild weather while we can. My Mary says she saw a wooly caterpillar near the woodpile. It's going to be an early winter, I'm afraid."

"Let's hope not too early. Most folks, myself included, are just starting to stock their pantries."

"Indeed, they are. I wanted to thank you for convincing me to try that hay fever remedy. It worked wonders. I shall certainly come to see you when I need more."

"I'm glad it worked for you. Come by any time."

A woman approached, basket in hand. Mr. Cavendish backed into the doorway. "Please excuse me, Miss Devlin. I must cut short our conversation. Mrs. Brown has arrived to collect her order. You have a nice day."

"I understand, Mr. Cavendish. A good day to you, too. I'm glad you're feeling better."

Well, he didn't seem to have been affected by Mrs. Wentworth's rantings at church. Perhaps her remedy and Anson's backing had nipped any fears that might have sprouted.

She continued to the end of the walkway. There, she traded the boardwalk for a narrow lane leading to the railroad stationhouse. It was much quieter and less congested. Unfortunately, it was also dry as a desert. In a matter of seconds, a powdery red film coated her boots. She sighed. She wouldn't be enjoying much of the temperate weather. Not with her to-do list growing by the minute.

Just ahead, a small shack sat atop a raised platform. A thin, black wire stretched from the roof in either direction to poles placed at intervals along the train tracks. The telegraph was a marvelous invention, that is, when weather and malicious vandals left the wiring intact.

She climbed the stairs and went inside. A well-dressed gentleman approached, toting a paper-wrapped package bound with twine. He tipped his hat and murmured a polite "good morning." Another genial greeting. Such a welcome change from the wary gazes that had hailed her in the past.

On the far side of the room, a woman stood at the counter with her back to the door. She wore a fashionable suit with rear bustle and matching cape. The ostrich feather adorning her hat bounced a lively jig.

"Just as I dictated, Mr. Brown. Not a single word more."

The clerk nodded, his bald pate barely visible over the countertop. "Yes, ma'am. I'll only send what you require."

As the clickety-clack of the telegraph machine filled the room, Moira moved a safe distance from the counter. The woman's haughty voice was quite unmistakable. *Edeline Wentworth.* The self-appointed town matriarch. There wouldn't be any genial welcome from that corner. Might as well avoid any unpleasantness.

She gazed up at the wall shelf lined with jars of preserves. Apple, elderberry, pear...any flavor that could be imagined. She picked up two jars. Might as well start stocking her pantry, although two jars would most likely not carry her through the winter. There was nothing better than Mrs. Brown's blackberry preserve spread over hot bread. She could eat the sweet treat at every meal. Probably would, much to the dismay of her expanding girth.

The clacking stopped, and chair legs rasped over the floorboards. "Your telegram has been delivered, Mrs. Wentworth. It will have to be transferred from the relay station to its destination. I expect you will receive a reply from the recipient within a few days."

"Let me know as soon as you receive the reply. Not a minute later." Mrs. Wentworth turned and stopped short, her brow crumpling like old paper. Pale lips thinned. Blue eyes turned to smoke. A storm cloud couldn't look more menacing.

Moira hefted her chin. She had never cowered before. She wouldn't start now. She forced a pleasant tone. "Good morning, Mrs. Wentworth."

The ostrich feather swayed like a vulture feeding on a fresh carcass. "There's nothing good about a morning when you are in it."

Moira fisted the jars, resisting the urge to toss them at the woman. "It's a pleasure to see you, too."

Mrs. Wentworth gave a grunt and stuck her nose in the air. She sailed for the door, heels clacking like a runaway railcar. She yanked open the door and pounced through the opening.

As the door slammed shut, Moira rolled down her shoulders. What a shrew. She put on as cheery a smile as she could muster and crossed to the counter. She wouldn't let Mrs. Wentworth ruin a perfectly good day.

"Good morning, Miss Devlin," the clerk said with a nod. "What can I do for you?"

Smudges of ink slashed his shirt. His necktie sat at a crooked angle. Tufts of hair poked like hedgehog spikes above his ears. It appeared to be quite the hectic morning for the telegraph clerk.

"And a good morning to you, Mr. Brown. How is your wife? Hard at work keeping your shop stocked with preserves, I see."

"Oh, yes. A day doesn't go by that my Emily isn't brewing some sort of sweet concoction."

"She makes the best."

He pointed to the jars she'd set on the countertop. "Is this all for you today?"

"These, and I came to collect Dr. Locke's mail. You sent word that a package had arrived for him. He asked me to get it."

"Absolutely. It's in the back room. I'll go and—" The click of the telegraph machine broke in. He frowned and moved to small table where a metal flange bounced up and down, belting out a staccato tune. "Give me one moment…"

He sat in the chair and picked up a pencil. The stub rasped over a piece of paper. It was amazing that anyone could turn those bursts of noise into words.

After a few minutes, the clicking stopped. Mr. Brown scooped up his deciphering and returned to the counter. "Sorry about that, Miss Devlin. It has been quite a busy morning."

"I'm in no hurry. Please, take your time."

He set the papers on the counter and disappeared through a doorway behind him. Moira hefted her reticule and searched for coins to pay for the preserves. As she fished, the paperwork on the counter caught her eye. Mr. Brown had such elegant handwriting. The lines were straight and precisely formed. It looked like artwork. Two words jumped out. *Willoughby, Texas.* Her heart started its own clickity-clacking. She knew that town. Knew it well.

She shouldn't snoop, but curiosity and a good helping of dread overtook her. She leaned over and cocked her head to better read the telegram.

To Jack Thacker. Willoughby Texas. The healer you seek is living in Mineral, in the Indian Territories. Contact Edeline Wentworth.

A glacier formed in her stomach. Willoughby was the town where Granny Tate had been burned to death. Where she had narrowly escaped with her life. Where Jack Thacker had accused her of murder.

****

A spinning sensation seized her head. Dark swirls flecked with gold clouded her vision. Moira set down the tin of gypsum plaster and gripped the counter. It wasn't her first episode of dizziness, and it probably wouldn't be the last. Over the past two days, her mind and her body had been all out of sorts. Not from illness, but from worry.

Edeline Wentworth despised her...there was no denying that. The town matriarch made no effort to hide her feelings. But to send word to Jack Thacker that the healer he sought was in Mineral? That went well and above hatred. And how had the woman known to contact the man? Someone at the orphanage must have carried the story of her rescue into town. The betrayal pinched, but fear of Thacker overrode her pain.

There was only one person in Mineral Jack Thacker would want to locate. Her. As she fled from her burning home in Willoughby, he had screeched a warning of finding her…of finishing what he started. That had been five years ago. A lifetime to her. Maybe not so long for him. Would he answer the telegram? Would he come to Mineral? Her roiling gut said he would. Few people in her experience ignored a chance at retribution…especially fanatics like Jack Thacker.

Thankfully, Mrs. Lidle had packed her things the day before to stay indefinitely with her ailing sister who had taken a fall and was now bedridden. While unfortunate, the accident held a silver lining. She wouldn't have to worry about keeping her companion safe from Thacker. Louise would be out of harm's way.

A knot gathered in her stomach. But what about Anson? He spent most of his waking hours at the office. Should she tell him about Thacker? Prepare him for what was to come? There was so much about her past she couldn't reveal. He wasn't ready to hear the truth; worse, she wasn't ready to disclose it. Her insides were raw enough without adding his scorn to the mix.

She would just have to be extra vigilant. If…no, when…Thacker showed up, she would do everything in her power to keep him from causing anyone harm. Mrs. Wentworth may have started the rock rolling with her telegram, but she wouldn't have the last word. Thacker would not get the best of her. Not this time.

Her head finally settled to a mild buzz, and she let go of the counter. No more dawdling. It was time to get back to work. People were waiting on her.

She gathered the tin of plaster and tugged on the lid. It refused to budge. *Dingles.* She dug her fingers under the rim and tried again. Nothing. What the devil? Why did everything in her life have to be so difficult?

She leaned over, ground her teeth together, and pulled. The lid popped off, sending white plaster dust exploding from the can. She coughed and fanned at the billowing haze. Good grief. She didn't need this. An uncooperative mule had mashed Mr. Gunderson's oldest son against the stall door and fractured the boy's lower arm bone. She needed to get the plaster mixed and back to Anson as quickly as possible.

"What's taking so long with that...oh, I see."

She swiped plaster dust from her face and blinked at the tall silhouette filling the doorway. "I'm sorry, Anson. The lid was particularly uncooperative. It stuck and well...this happened."

"Opening gypsum tins can be tricky. I've taken many a bath in the powder myself. You should have called for help."

The only help she needed was to be granted more time. More time to figure out how to handle Thacker. More time to gather the courage to tell Anson about him and her gift.

She swept spilled powder into a pile with her hand. "I knew you were busy setting Jonah's arm. I didn't want to pull you away to help with what should have been a simple task."

"The bone is set, and Jonah is resting peacefully now that the laudanum has taken affect. We're just waiting on the plaster."

At least the child wasn't suffering while she

fumbled around. She picked up a ladle and spooned gypsum powder into a large bowl. "I'll get this mixed and bring it to you right away."

"I can help if you'd like."

"No, thank you. Now that the lid is off, it won't take long to prepare." She grasped the handle of the water pitcher, but powder slickened fingers refused to grip. Her hand slipped. The pitcher listed, and water sloshed over the rim. An unladylike curse bubbled to the surface. Thacker wasn't even in town, yet he was already impacting her life…and not in a good way.

Footfalls scraped closer, and steadying fingers closed around hers. "Easy, there. I have you."

His warm breath played over her neck. Her skin tingled and burned. Her muscles shuddered. The spinning in her head returned with more force, with more color. Yellow, this time. And bright. She groaned and slumped back against the sturdy chest behind her, the strength gone out of her.

His arms went around her. "What's wrong, Moira? You're weak as a sapling in a nor'easter."

Moira. Would he say her name with such affection once he learned about Thacker? About her? About what she could do?

She forced steel into her spine and wriggled out of his embrace. "Nothing's wrong. I'm just upset with myself for spilling that plaster. I shouldn't let my mind wander while working. It only leads to trouble."

Concerned eyes poured over her. "I think I know what the problem is."

"Y-you do?" Had he felt the seesaw of emotions tugging at her insides? The hunger warring with the knowledge that it was too dangerous to eat?

"You're worried about how we will move forward together...as associates, as partners, especially after our rather shaky start."

Shaky was putting it mildly. She was still shaking, but in a different, much more pleasing way. She busied herself with scrubbing her hands on the apron tied at her waist. Best to cleanse her hands and her mind before more than just water got spilled.

"I have been wondering how this partnership of ours would work. You didn't exactly welcome me with open arms when you arrived."

A wry smile tugged at his lips. "I'm sorry for that. I should have been more open minded...more hospitable. I was in a bad place, and I took it out on you. To make amends, I have a proposal for you."

A proposal? Of marriage? Excitement trotted inside her. She reined it in with a fisted hand. How ridiculous to think such a thing. She was not the woman for him. She was complicated and messy. He was straightforward and tidy. Besides, he had his own baggage to carry. He didn't need to add hers to the load.

"What is this proposal?"

"Something that will get us started on good footing, a foundation to build on, so to speak."

All the buildings from her past had crumbled, solid foundation or not. No reason to think this would be any different. The wise thing to do would be for her to pack her things and leave. But she was tired of running. Bone tired. And the thought of leaving Anson made her insides curdle.

"What do you have in mind?"

His face split into a smile that reached into dimpled crevices. "A picnic. I'll have Mrs. Gilliam pack a basket for us. We can eat and enjoy the temperate weather on the banks of Dancer's Creek. It will be a simple outing where we can relax and talk about our partnership. Make plans for the future of the practice."

Simple. Nothing in her life had ever been simple.

Chapter Fourteen

Anson set the wicker basket on the blanket he'd spread under a tree overlooking Dancer's Creek. Mrs. Gilliam's raised eyebrows as he made his request for a picnic supper had spoken volumes. But he refused to offer the landlady any explanations. She and the rest of the townsfolk could speculate all they wanted. This outing was for the express purpose of discussing his future partnership with Miss Devlin, as business associates. Nothing more.

The sun sat like a fireball a hand's breadth above the peak of the Shoehorn. They would have just under an hour of daylight before darkness set in. That should give them plenty of time to eat and talk. He wanted to hear her opinions. Wanted to hear what she most desired from life. He would do his best to see that she got everything she wanted. She deserved it after the way he had treated her.

Anger and frustration had clouded his judgment. All his life, he had sought the good in people, had given them the benefit of the doubt. Not so with Moira. He had branded her as evil from the moment they met. It was wrong and completely unfair. He would make certain it never happened again.

The leafy canopy stretching overhead dipped and swayed in the gentle breeze. A soft gurgling bubbled up from the creek winding around the foot of the hillock. It was the perfect place to unwind and enjoy the scenery. Yet his supper companion was anything but relaxed.

She stood with her hands clasped in front of her, knuckles white with strain. Was she afraid of being alone with him? That he might take advantage? The thought that she didn't trust him poked lancet sharp.

He held out a hand. "Here, let me help you onto the blanket."

She hesitated, her eyes widening ever so slightly. Her chest rose and fell with quick breaths. Something had her spooked that was for certain.

"It's all right. I won't bite. I promise. I left my fangs at the office."

A tentative smile dimpled her cheeks. She unfurled her fingers and grasped his hand. Warmth snaked up his arm and coiled in his belly. He imagined having her right there on the blanket, that ebony hair fanned out around her, silhouetting her creaminess. He stuffed down a grunt of annoyance. A perfect outing if he could keep his mind out of the gutter.

She floated to the blanket like an angel alighting on a cloud. He reluctantly released her hand and settled beside her.

"It's quite lovely this evening," she said, her words coming out on a breathy exhale.

"Indeed, it is." He pointed to the flock of blackbirds performing acrobatics in the sky. "Even the birds are enjoying the weather."

She tilted her head back, allowing sunlight to pour under her bonnet brim. Tension left her face. Taut lips eased. She sighed and rolled down her shoulders. She was loosening up. Good. She deserved some joy in her life.

"Let's see what Mrs. Gilliam has packed for us." He lifted the linen draped over the top of the basket. "Ah, I see bread, fried chicken pieces, and sliced apples. And a jug of what I hope is lemonade. She has fresh lemons freighted in from California. They make the most delicious lemonade. Just the right amount of sweetness and sass." Just like Moira Devlin.

He uncorked the jug and poured the bright yellow drink into two tins. He handed her one. "Try it. Your taste buds will dance a jig."

She took a sip and treated him to a sunny smile that never failed to warm him. "It's delicious...and most refreshing."

Lips moistened with lemonade called to him. He busied himself with unpacking their supper. "Speaking of refreshing...what would you like to see for our office, Moira? What do you see for our future?"

A gleam sparked her eyes. "I'd like to expand my herbal business. Turn it into a service that offers herbs not only for medicines, but for use in cooking as well. To encourage good, healthy eating. That should make seeing the doctor more appealing than just when people are sick."

"A sound proposition."

"What about you? What do you see for the future of the practice?"

He really hadn't considered his future. All he had done since Alice died was put one foot in front of the other. It was time he started running.

He fished a plate from the basket. "I like the notion of promoting good health and well-being. We could expand on that initiative. Invite people to come in for routine wellness exams. Head off major problems before they start."

"I like that, too. We could offer courses on wholesome foods and good hygiene."

She really was an intelligent and caring person. He had misjudged her. Greatly.

He filled a plate with chicken, bread, and apple slices and handed it to her. "If this initiative catches on and business grows, we may have to move into a larger building. And perhaps one day, build a hospital for folks who need around-the-clock medical care."

His pulse quickened, and he couldn't stop from grinning. Where had that come from? He hadn't been this excited about something in…well, in forever. And he owed it all to one person.

Laughter danced in dark eyes. "A hospital? My, my. Aren't we getting a bit ahead of ourselves?"

He shoveled food onto his plate. His appetite had returned. For many things. "Not at all. You've seen how rapidly the town is growing. New buildings are going up every day. There's talk of a railroad spur coming in from the south. That will draw more people into the community. A hospital will become a necessity."

"I suppose you are right. Mineral is expanding. It won't be long before they start building settlements further along the creek."

"There you go. A hospital it is then."

He sunk his teeth into a chicken leg and groaned. Savory juices poured through the crispy outer crust. Excellent fare. And excellent company. He couldn't ask for a more perfect outing.

They lapsed into a comfortable silence. He could easily see them years from now, enjoying each other's company without the need for conversation. The perfect partnership. Fortunately, she did not bear him any ill will for the way he had treated her at the start. For that, she deserved to be rewarded.

He set down his empty plate and rose. He crossed to the buggy and extracted a ribbon-wrapped box from the boot. This ought to put a smile on her face. His heart was already grinning.

He returned to the blanket and set the box in front of her.

She dabbed her lips with a napkin. "What's this?"

"It's a gift. A token of my appreciation for your unflagging patience with me and my foul disposition."

"You don't have to give me anything."

"I know I don't. I want to. Please, open it."

She undid the ribbon and slid off the lid. Eyes widened to the size of saucers. "It's the hat I admired at Mrs. Stone's shop. I thought it had been sold."

"It had. But I cajoled Mrs. Stone into making another." At quite an extravagant cost. But the look on Moira's face was worth every penny.

She lifted the hat from the box and held it out in front of her. Frown lines creased her brow as she fingered the gold broach pinned to a lace bow. "What's this? I don't recall seeing a broach on the original version."

"No, it wasn't. I had Mrs. Stone add it."

"It's such a lovely piece. I've never seen such a brilliant gemstone before. It's almost…magical."

She twisted the hat to and fro, her face beaming like a child on Christmas morning. Sunlight caught on the amethyst gem and shot lilac rays across her creamy skin. Magical, indeed.

"It was my mother's," he said. "And my grandmother's before that."

Clouds darkened her sunshine. She guided the hat back into the box. "I can't accept this, Anson. The hat, and especially not the broach. It's a family heirloom. You should be giving it to your…"

She broke off, teeth clamping down on her bottom lip. He wanted to kiss away her unease.

"You deserve it, Moira. Consider the hat and broach my way of apologizing and welcoming you into my family so to speak. A symbol of our newfound friendship."

He could offer more than friendship. His body was ready. His head was ready. But his cracked heart balked.

"It's too much. I couldn't possibly accept your gift, no matter what the reason."

"You deserve this, and much more for putting up with me. As your employer, I order you to accept my gift." He lightened his tone. "Please don't make me take the hat back to Mrs. Stone. It wasn't easy convincing her to make a replica of the original one. She said her creations were one of a kind. Works of art."

Moira's chuckle washed over him. "She can be a bit over-dramatic."

"A bit?"

"Very well, I accept your gift. Thank you, Anson. I shall think of you every time I wear it."

And he would think of how happy she made him every time he saw it adorning her lovely head.

Laughter spilled up the hillock, drawing their attention. Two bare-footed boys waded in the creek below. They splashed in the water, kicking at currents, and tossed rocks across the surface.

He pointed at the acrobats. "It appears our peaceful interlude has been invaded."

She smiled. "I quite like the sound of children playing. So innocent and pure. It's music to my ears."

He let his gaze slide over her. She would make a wonderful mother. She was kind and protective and gave her entire heart to those she loved. He envied the man who took her to wife.

Sadly, it wouldn't be him.

****

Moira skimmed a finger over the broach pinned to her new hat. Such a lovely gem. Such a lovely gesture. She'd never received such an extravagant gift before. Yet, Anson wanted her to have it. To be part of his family. A symbol of their friendship. She wanted more than just friendship. But was he capable of giving more? Was she capable of accepting it?

He kneeled on the blanket, packing the picnic items into the basket while whistling a cheery tune. He seemed more relaxed...as if a great weight had been lifted from his shoulders. A smile tugged at his lips. One foot waggled in time to the whistling. She smiled. They should have more outings like this if it made him so happy.

A scream pierced the air, making the hairs on her arm stand on end. She yanked her head around and followed the sound to the creek below where Charlie Gunderson and Patrick Cavendish had been playing in the water. Little Charlie sat on the creek bank, crying and holding onto his ankle.

Anson leapt to his feet and rushed down the hill.

Heart pounding, she unfurled her legs and bolted off the blanket, racing after him. He reached the creek first and squatted beside the wailing child. She pulled up behind him.

"Hush now," Anson urged. "Tell me what happened."

Pain and fear streaked the boy's face. Charlie sucked down a sob and swiped at his tears. "R-R…" was all he managed to get out.

Patrick edged closer. "It was a rattlesnake. We didn't see it until it was too late. The dang bugger bit Charlie on the leg."

Ice filled her veins. Rattlesnake venom was quite deadly, even for adults. A six-year-old didn't stand a chance against the toxin.

She glanced around but didn't see any coiled serpents or tell-tale slither marks. "Where did the snake go?"

Patrick pointed to a cottonwood standing sentinel over the creek about twenty feet away. "The bugger slunk over there. Probably hiding under that snarl of roots."

Good. They didn't need any more snake-bit patients. One was enough. She pointed to the hillock. "Patrick, I want you to run back to town. Tell Charlie's parents what happened, and that Dr. Locke and I are looking after him. Have them go to the doctor's office and wait for us. We'll bring him there once we've seen to his bite."

Patrick nodded and charged up the hill. The Gunderson's would be beside themselves with worry. Hopefully, she and Anson could get the boy back to them alive and kicking.

Anson scooped Charlie into his arms and toted him up the hill. She joined him as he placed the boy on the blanket. Charlie reclined back, writhing and moaning. The youngster had saddled Dolly for her on many an occasion. He was a jolly little fellow who always had a smile on his face. Except for now. His pain gouged into her. Treating injured children was always the hardest. All she wanted to do was take away their suffering.

"We have remove as much venom from the bite as quickly as we can," Anson said. "Try to calm him while I get my medical bag. Agitation will only make the toxin spread faster through his body."

As Anson rushed to the buggy, Moira knelt on the blanket and rested a comforting hand on the boy's shoulder. His muscles quivered beneath her fingertips. He was pale as his white cotton shirt, and sweat coated his forehead. She ached to send healing power into him, but Anson was much too close for that. She would just have to help him in the normal fashion.

"Lie still, Charlie. Everything is going to be all right. I promise."

The writhing slowed. A watery gaze latched onto her. "A-Am I going to…d-die, Miss Devlin?"

She gave him a reassuring squeeze. "Of course not. Dr. Locke and I won't let that happen."

"I 'member S-Sally Younger," he said through hiccupping sobs. "She was six. She got bit l-last year. Sh-she died."

"You're a strong young man, Charlie Gunderson. I've seen how you handle your father's livestock. No rattlesnake is going to get the best of you."

The boy hauled in a deep breath, seeming to take strength in her words. Good. He would need to be courageous for what was to come.

Anson returned and dropped to his knees at the boy's feet. He fished inside his medical bag and extracted a knife and a vial of clear liquid.

Charlie's eyes grew round as wagon wheels. "Wh-what're you gonna do with that knife, Doc?"

Anson uncorked the vial and poured liquid over the tip. "I'm going to save your life, young man. This may hurt a bit, but it will give me access to those bite punctures. Lie still as you can now. Hold onto Miss Devlin's hand if you need to."

He set the vial down and glanced at her, eyebrows arched in question. She nodded and gathered the boy's hand in hers. Clammy fingers shackled hers. She ignored the pinch. If Charlie needed a lifeline, she was there to provide it, no matter how painful.

"Charlie is ready. Go on, Doctor."

Anson grasped the boy's ankle and dipped the knife tip into a fang mark, making a slight incision. Charlie gasped and went rigid as a board. But he didn't thrash or wail. Such a brave boy.

Moira squeezed harder. "You're doing great, Charlie. Hold tight."

Anson set the knife aside and leaned over, pressing his mouth to the bite mark. His cheeks puckered as he drew blood from the wound. After a few seconds of sucking, he turned his head and spat out a red stream. He did this three times and then wiped his mouth on his sleeve.

The boy's grip on her fingers slackened. "A-Are you done, Doc? D-Did you get all the venom out?"

"Most of it." Anson picked up the vial. "I'm going to apply a little ammonia to the wound. It will sting, but only for a few seconds. Hold still a while longer, and then we will be all done."

The boy eyed the vial. "Ammonia. My pa puts that on his animals when they get cut."

Anson nodded. "That's right. It's an antiseptic. It kills germs. Ready now?" At Charlie's nod, he poured a good dose of ammonia over the incision mark.

Charlie didn't move. Didn't even bat an eyelash.

"That's it, Charlie," she crooned. "All done. My, you are such a brave young man. Your father would be so proud of you."

Charlie merely gave her a wan smile. His coloring had turned pale as the wispy clouds racing overhead. His eyelids drooped. He was fading…fast.

Anson shoved the knife and ammonia back into his bag. "We've done as much as we can here. Let's get him to the office where we can watch over him."

Charlie wasn't out of the woods yet. The boy had a long battle ahead of him. Hopefully one he would win.

Anson gathered Charlie in his arms and stood. "Go and get into the buggy, Moira. The boy's too weak to sit on his own. You'll have to hold him on your lap. He's small enough you should be able to manage for the short ride to town."

She would do whatever was needed to keep the boy safe. She hurried to the buggy and climbed in. Once she settled on the seat, Anson handed up the boy. Charlie sagged against her, his arms limp and lifeless.

Anson stowed the picnic basket and her hat box in the boot and then joined her on the seat. He draped the blanket over the boy. His concerned gaze met hers. He knew Charlie was in dire straits.

He gathered the reins and urged the horse into a

fast clip. As the buggy bolted forward, Charlie's head thumped against her chest. His eyes were closed; his breaths were coming in shallow draws. The life was going out of him. She couldn't let that happen. She wouldn't. She had to help him…risk of discovery be damned. Perhaps the blanket would hide most of her efforts. She shifted for a better position on the buggy seat.

Anson tossed her a worried look. "Are all right, Moira? Is he too heavy?"

She wagged her head. "I'm fine. The boy fainted, and I needed to get a better grip. I'm good now."

He frowned and scoured Charlie's face. "I hope we don't lose him."

She would do her best to see that they didn't. As Anson returned his focus to handling the galloping horse, she hunched over and rubbed her hands together under the blanket. Energy gathered in her core, spinning and churning. Pulsing heat coursed down her arms and pooled in her palms. She slid her hands under Charlie's shirt. His skin was cold and clammy. She closed her eyes and concentrated on probing. His blood was black and icy. Anson hadn't extracted all the venom.

She sent healing waves into the blackness. The ice thawed. The blackness lightened.

Charlie moaned and lifted his head. "W-Where am I? W-what happened?"

"Shh," she whispered. "Everything's all right. You were bitten by a rattlesnake while playing at the creek. We're taking you to the doctor's office where your parents are going to meet us."

"Your hands…so warm. Tingly. Made me… better."

Anson's puzzled gaze moved from her to the boy and back. Her heart thudded against her ribs. There were going to be questions for which she couldn't give any answers.

Chapter Fifteen

Moira tossed her apron onto the bureau. Worrisome thoughts and the need for sleep had her head spinning. She and Anson had taken turns watching over Charlie during the night. To her delight, the boy greeted the sunrise with a weak smile. While she cheered his recovery, the repercussions of using her gift nagged like a festering hangnail. Not because of Charlie. She would do it all over again if the situation arose. It was a man with the eyesight of an eagle and the wit of a fox who had her on edge.

During Charlie's final examination before leaving with his parents, Anson had tossed numerous puzzled looks in her direction. He'd opened his mouth twice but held his tongue. Probably out of consideration for Charlie and his parents. It was a reprieve. Slight, but she would take it. Her head was already buzzing. The longer she staved off a confrontation, the better.

As the door closed behind the Gunderson's, she'd made a beeline to her bedroom with the excuse of requiring a nap. Which she did need. But she also needed time alone to think.

Anson would give her a few hours to rest. He was that considerate. But after that, he would demand answers. Answers she couldn't give. He liked her, might even care for her. But he wasn't ready to hear about her gift. He barely accepted her potion-making ability. How could he accept her magical talent? He would toss her and her potions out into the street.

As bad as that would be for her, she knew deep down he would be more tormented. He'd come to trust her, had allowed her into his life, into his beloved medical practice. He would be devastated by her betrayal. Leaving would be the best course of action. Now. Before either of them fell any deeper into the morass.

With a heavy heart, she tugged her trunk from under the bed. She didn't want to leave. She'd come to adore Mineral and all the people who lived in the mining town. Claude Gunderson who always had a humorous anecdote on hand. Generous Ben Cavendish. The ever-optimistic and caring Mary Lidle. Most of all she would miss Anson. She'd fallen in love with him. Didn't know when or where it had happened, but it had.

She yanked open a bureau drawer. There was nothing for it. She had to leave. There could be no future for her and Anson. He was better off without her. If she loved him, she had to let him go.

She scooped up a handful of clothes and dropped them in the trunk. Like a puppet marching on strings, she went back and forth from the bureau to the bed, gathering and packing her things. Each step was a dagger to her heart. But she had to do it.

Her hands paused over the green felt hat nestled in its box. A soft ache filled her. It was the most wonderful present she had ever received. A gift from the heart. But she couldn't keep it. It was far too personal and far too painful to hold onto. It would be a constant reminder of what she couldn't have.

He wanted her to be part of his family. To work by

his side. She traced a finger over the broach pinned to the hat. Sunlight sparkled on the multi-faceted gem resting in a gold filigree setting. A stone of many colors. Like him. She couldn't bear to be the cause of dulling that luster.

Footfalls shuffled in the hallway outside the door. He was here. Her reprieve was over.

An insistent rapping tapped into the room. "Moira, I know you're awake. I heard you moving about. We need to talk."

His deep voice rumbled through her just as it had from the day they met. She briefly closed her eyes and gathered her courage. She needed to be strong. Anson wouldn't let her go without a fight. He was a very determined man. It was what she loved most about him. Nothing swayed his convictions.

"Moira, open the door. Please."

She heaved a sigh and crossed to the door. Her hand hovered over the knob. She didn't want to hurt him, but remaining at the practice was not an option. He would only suffer more if she stayed.

She grasped the knob and tugged open the door. He filled the doorway, an impressive mountain of tweed and bay rum cologne. She would treasure that sight and smell during the long, empty days ahead.

"Yes, Dr. Locke?" She couldn't call him Anson. It would imply intimacy. An intimacy they couldn't share.

Blue eyes pried into her. "I would like to discuss what happened with Charlie Gunderson."

"There's nothing to discuss. Your heroic efforts saved the boy."

"That's poppycock, and we both know it. Children that young rarely survive a rattlesnake bite, no matter what *heroic* efforts are performed."

"Then we'll just say his recovery was a miracle from God and leave it at that." She pushed on the door, but his foot stopped its progress.

"This discussion is far from over." He leaned in, his face smudged with determination. "I've seen my fair share of miracles, but Charlie's rapid recovery goes well beyond that. He began improving before we even reached the office. What did you do to that boy?"

The answer danced on her tongue. Oh, how she wanted to free the words. Let him know exactly who she was and what she could do. She didn't want any secrets between them. But she had to keep the truth caged. For both their sakes.

"What do you think I did? You were sitting right there beside me in the buggy."

"I don't know. I'm just so baffled by it all. I don't know what to think. You were the one holding onto him. Is there more to you than just being an herbalist?"

Too close. Much too close. She stepped away from the doorway. He could pry the truth out of her with one look, one simple touch. Best to put some distance between them.

He surged into the room like a locomotive with a full belly of steam. He waggled a finger at her traveling trunk. "What is that?"

"It's my trunk."

"I know it's your trunk. Why are there clothes packed inside? Are you leaving, Moira?"

The anguish in his tone sliced into her. She hauled in a bandaging breath. At least his focus had shifted to something other than Charlie's miraculous recovery. "I intended to tell you once the Gunderson's left. This business arrangement between us…it's just not going to work."

"Why not?"

"Because I'm all wrong for the practice." *For you.*

"How can you say that? I thought we discussed this? You want to expand your herbal services. Provide healthier options for folks."

She crossed to the bureau and slipped the lid back onto the hat box. Out of sight, out of mind.

"I do want that. But I can't do it here in Mineral. These people don't trust me. They may never trust me. I'm a burden. My presence will only stifle the practice and you."

"You are not a burden. Far from it. Whether they realize it or not, the people in this town need you. They will come to trust you."

Like he trusted her? The hollow assertion only strengthened her resolve. "What the people need is you. A trained medical profession. Someone they can rely on and trust. You have goals for this practice. I don't want to be the reason you fail to achieve those dreams."

He stepped closer and clasped her upper arms. "Those dreams include you as well, Moira. I've come to care for you. A great deal. I want us to succeed together."

Her heart stuttered. He cared for her. Wanted her to succeed with him. She wanted that too. But he needed normalcy and honesty. Things she couldn't give him.

"I care about you too, Anson. It's for that reason I must go. You will do much better without me holding you back. I'm poison to your future."

Fingers pressed into her skin. "For someone so in tune with others, you have failed miserably to see what's right in front of you."

A commotion blasted through the open window. There was a shout and then another. Something boiled in the street below.

"Moira Devlin, bride of Satan," came a heated greeting. "Come out and meet your judgment."

Her insides turned to ice. She knew that voice. It had haunted her every waking and sleeping moment for years after fleeing Willoughby.

She shrugged out of Anson's grip and rushed to the window. In the street below, dozens of people congregated behind a tall, slender man clutching a Bible to his chest.

He shook a fist in the air. "Come out, witch. Tell these good people what you did. Bare your evil to one and all."

****

A stiff breeze plowed through the bedroom window, lifting the curtains. The sheer fabric curled around the woman standing still as a statue, her fingers clamped on the sash. Her breaths were coming in shallow draws. Her skin was as pale as a corpse's. Whoever was shouting from the street below had her terrified.

"Moira, who is that man? How does he know you?"

She stared out the window, shoulders quivering. She scrubbed hands over her arms as if warding off a chill. "His name…is Jack Thacker."

"Why is he here? What does he want with you?"

"He's here because Edeline Wentworth sent for him."

"Why would she do that?"

"In order to tarnish me in the eyes of the townsfolk…" She turned, her tortured gaze spilling over him. "And in yours."

"There's nothing he can say that would turn me against you. I've seen your goodness. You care deeply about people no matter what their circumstances. There's not an evil bone in your body."

"I'm not evil. But I'm not ordinary either. There's more to me than you know. I've done things…"

Her voice trailed away on a quiver. He held out a hand. "Tell me. What hold does this man have over you?"

She ignored his offer of an anchor and paced to the bureau and back. Pearly teeth clamped down on her bottom lip. A fist gripped his heart. What could she have done that had her so afraid? Steal? Murder? Neither seemed likely. She was too kind to have committed such sins.

She stopped in front of the window, glanced out, and then faced him, her expression defeated. Tears swam in her eyes. He wanted to take her in his arms and comfort her. But he couldn't. She clearly needed to purge herself of whatever poison held sway inside her.

"Do you recall me telling you that I left Tennessee with my mother and grandmother years ago?"

"Your mother didn't survive the journey."

"You have a mind like steel trap, Anson Locke. Yes, my mother died before we arrived at our destination. My grandmother and I managed to make it to Texas where we settled on the outskirts of a small town. We set up shop in our home and sold potions and administered to the sick. That was where I met Mr. Thacker. I was fourteen at the time. He came to us, begging for our help. His son was gravely ill. Granny Tate had become too frail to travel, so I went alone." Her arms dropped to her sides. "I tried to help, but the boy was too far gone."

Not an unusual occurrence. He'd seen many a patient who didn't respond to treatment, no matter how vigorously applied.

Another raspy exhale scraped the air. "Mr. Thacker refused to accept the inevitable. He pled with me to save his son. In hindsight, I should have refused, but I wanted to help. So, I provided a remedy that would only ease the boy's suffering, not cure him. Little Jimmy Thacker died a week later."

And the father blamed her. Nothing new there. People handled grief in different ways. Some retreated from the world. Others condemned it. Most recovered and went on with their lives. Clearly Mr. Thacker had not.

A shout spilled through the window, calling for the witch to come down. Ebony eyes widened. Trembling shoulders crouched inward. She shoved a hand to her mouth. He wouldn't get anything more out of her until the source of her torment was removed.

"This verbal lynching has gone on long enough. That man needs to be sent on his way."

As he turned, a shuffling noise sounded behind him, and then her hand closed around his elbow. "No, Anson. This is my fight. I should be the one confronting Jack Thacker."

He turned back to her. "You don't have to do this, Moira. I can send that mob on their way."

"No. I have to do this. I'm tired of running from my past. It's time I faced Thacker, no matter how unpleasant."

"Then I'll come with you. We'll face him together."

A grateful smile tugged at her lips. "Thank you, Anson. Your support means more than you know."

He motioned to the doorway. "Then let's get rid of that rabble, shall we?"

The soft scent of lavendar wrapped around him as she walked by. He stuffed down the urge to pull her into his arms and let his lips soothe her pain. Rabble first, kisses later.

He trailed her down the stairs and out the front door. She stopped on the boardwalk, shoulders thrown back, chin thrust up. She had more strength in her than many men he knew.

A tall, slender man totting a Bible stepped forward. A wide-brimmed hat shadowed his face. "There you are, witch. Tell these good people what you did to my little Jimmy."

"You know very well I tried to help your son, Mr. Thacker. There was nothing more I could do." Her tone was calm and non-provoking, her stance relaxed. The prophet Job couldn't have displayed more patience.

"Bah, you gave him useless potions and laid your hands upon him. You wanted me to believe you were helping him. Wanted me to have hope. But you knew in your black heart you couldn't save him."

Anson fisted his hands at his sides. Weeks ago, he had spouted the same vitriol, hurling accusations when he didn't know the truth, didn't know the woman behind the potions.

He moved beside Moira, unable to remain silent. "Miss Devlin told me she did her best for your son. His illness was too far gone."

"And yet she continued to take my money."

"She was just a young girl. All she wanted was to ease your son's suffering. You should be thanking her, not casting stones."

A hand settled on his arm. "Please. This is my battle, Anson."

He looked down and met ebony eyes filled with sureness. She could do this. He nodded and took a step back.

"My only mistake, Mr. Thacker," she said, "was my failure to help you accept the inevitable. For that I am deeply sorry."

"All you wanted was to make yourself appear the do-gooder, so you could continue lining your pockets."

"My grandmother and I lived in a dilapidated shack and survived only on what we could grow and hunt. Most of our payments came in the form of bartering, a scrawny chicken or a sack of grain. Some couldn't pay at all. We did what we could for the people of Willoughby, out of the kindness of our hearts."

"Hogwash. You pretended to help so folks would come to you with open purses. You're doing the same here with the good people of Mineral."

The crowd parted, and Mrs. Wentworth surged forward. "It's true. Everyone knows how desperately you wanted to be accepted after Doc Thompson passed on. You traipsed about town, handing out your wares in hopes of luring clients into your lair. It's not a stretch to believe you would poison the creek and then make yourself look the savior by *finding* the source."

"I did no such thing."

Mrs. Wentworth turned to the crowd, a gnarled

finger upraised. "Remember Major Allen's mysterious stomach ailment? His wife had been poisoning him so he would go back East for treatment. She hated living out here. Miss Devlin is doing the same thing. Poisoning us so she can steer us into doing what she wants."

"I am nothing like Harriet Allen." Her voice cracked with the barest hint of desperation. "Any of you who know me know this."

"She gave me a potion, but it didn't work," a man called out.

She shaded her eyes with a hand. "Is that you, Mr. Donaldson? I told you to come back if the ointment didn't cure your rash. Treatments work for some people and not for others. We could have tried something else."

"Like a witch's brew?" Thacker hefted his Bible in the air. "Let's tie her to a pyre and see if she burns."

"Hang her," another called out.

Ice filled his veins. He needed to put a stop to this witch hunt before it got any further out of hand. He stepped to the edge of the porch. "Miss Devlin has done nothing to warrant such condemnation. Medicine is sometimes a trial and error practice. I'm sorry for your loss, Mr. Thacker. But even trained medical doctors know that there are some people you just can't help."

Edeline Wentworth waddled closer. "Are you still taking her side, Anson? You should send her packing before her taint rubs off on you."

The only stain would be to allow this farce to continue. It was wrong to accuse someone of something they didn't do. The guilt of the past two years bolted out of him. Not everyone could be saved. Moira couldn't save Jimmy Thacker; he couldn't save Alice. No one was at fault. That was life.

"Yes, I am taking her side, and I will continue to do so as long as my support is needed. Miss Devlin is not to be harmed or forced out of Mineral against her will. Anyone who attempts this will answer to me. Is that understood?" He gave Edeline a pointed look. "Now, go home. All of you. Look into your hearts. You will see what is right and good."

Chapter Sixteen

Her muscles had hardened to rock, her bones to butter. She couldn't move. Couldn't breathe. Thoughts buffeted in her head like vultures riding the air currents. Thacker had come to Mineral. For her. He wouldn't leave because Anson told him to. The grieving man wanted retribution. And he would do everything in his power to get it, even if that meant bloodying the few supporters who dared to stand at her side.

Images surfaced of Willoughby, of angry faces and raised fists…of torch-bearing townsfolk whom Thacker had incited. They surrounded the shack where she and Granny Tate lived in the woods on the outskirts of town, demanding her surrender. Her heart thudded now, just as it had back then, a thundering that clawed up her throat and stilled any sound. Panic. Full and unshakeable panic.

When she failed to come out, the rabble had thrown torches onto the roof. The thatch caught quickly and sent flaming tinders raining down. She tried to rouse Granny, but the ailing woman was too frail to flee. Death seemed certain for both of them.

Then, two saviors had appeared. Armed with a shotgun, Preston Booth had chased off the mob while Meredith helped her escape from the burning shack. She rubbed the scar at back of her neck. She had survived relatively unscathed. Granny Tate had not.

They'd buried her in an unmarked grave next to a creek near the shack. Granny always did love the sound of running water. Said it soothed her soul. Hopefully she rested in peace.

The lock being thrown on the door clacked into her thoughts. She shook off her melancholy. It was time to put the past behind her. Far behind her.

She moved deeper into the foyer. Somehow, she'd made it from the boardwalk back into the building. Good. Thacker didn't need to know just how weak he made her. It would only encourage more fanaticism.

Gentle fingers pressed into her back. "Let's go into my office. We can sit and talk. Finish our discussion from earlier. I've locked the door. We should have plenty of privacy."

Talking was the last thing she wanted to do. Anson wouldn't let her go without a fight. She just didn't have the energy for battling. All she wanted was to lay her head on her pillow and sleep for a thousand years.

The pressure on her back deepened. She shuffled forward. Might as well get this over with. He wouldn't relent until the well went dry.

Their footfalls clicked death knells on the floorboards. Even the wall clock joined in the macabre cacophony. Tick. Tock. Out of time. Out of rope. It's over.

At the office doorway, she stopped. It was cold and dark inside, a coffin for her dreams. Would the grim reaper come calling again? Was it her turn to meet Peter at the Gate? She glanced over her shoulder. Or would she lose yet another person she loved?

Anson brushed past her and surged into the office. A second later, golden lamplight flooded the room. The shadows retreated. The coldness warmed. She forced her feet forward. She had to be strong. For Anson. For herself.

He angled a chair toward her. "Have a seat, Moira."

A seat? She needed a train ticket and many miles of track between her and Mineral and that madman Thacker.

"Sit down, Moira. Before you collapse. You're white as a bedsheet."

His harsh tone slashed into her. She collected herself with a deep breath. Dealing with a shrewd man like Anson required all her focus, else he would see straight through any lies.

She sank onto the chair and worked at settling her skirts. She was dithering. But she just wasn't ready for the inevitable clash. Not with him. Not with her last few hours of being near him. She wanted to remember the happy times, the smiles, the laughter. The way his touch lit up her skin. The way his voice rumbled into her soul.

Anson was having none of it. He paced in front of her, his brow ploughed with thick lines. "Thacker is the reason you were packing to leave."

A statement more than a question. "He is part of it. While at the telegraph office the other day, I inadvertently saw a telegram Mrs. Wentworth had sent to Willoughby, Texas. She told Thacker where he could find me. I knew he would come."

He stopped in front of her, arms crossed over his chest. "Why didn't you confide in me? You had to know I would keep you safe."

"I didn't know any such thing. From the first moment we met, you have questioned everything about me. I wasn't sure how you would react."

His fierce expression softened. He dropped his hands to his sides. "I'm sorry for that. I let anger cloud my good judgment. But I see differently now. I see you. The real you."

No. He didn't see her at all. Because she wouldn't allow him. "I can't stay where I'm not trusted. It's not fair to me, or you, or to any of the patients I may treat."

"But I do trust you. And this town will come to trust you."

"How can you say that?" She bolted to her feet and wagged a finger at the doorway. "You saw how quickly folks rallied to Thacker's side. They wanted to believe his rantings, wanted to believe the worst in me. Not an hour ago, you grilled me about my treatment of Charlie Gunderson. I can't live with such doubts."

His hand shackled her arm. "I was wrong to doubt you. Little Charlie survived because of us, because of our devotion and expert medical care. Nothing more."

The rip in her heart widened. He was partly right. But the part he got wrong was as scalable as a mountain of ice. And neither of them was equipped for the climb.

"As for the others," he continued. "We both know Edeline Wentworth has her own agenda when it comes to you."

"Because of you."

"Exactly. She knows how much I care for you, and it scares her. The other folks just got caught up in the frenzy. They will see how ridiculous their behavior has been once Thacker leaves."

He cared for her. Honeyed words that carried a vicious stinger. Anyone who loved her would be fair game to a fanatic like Jack Thacker. Causing them harm would hurt her. Just like with Granny Tate.

She shrugged out of his grasp "That's just it. He won't leave. Not until he's had his retribution. I won't put you or anyone else I love in danger. I have to be the one who goes."

She fled for the door, hands outstretched. Tears blurred her vision. She could barely make out the doorway. Fingers found the jam, and she hauled herself out and into the hallway. The stair newel post was five steps from there. Twelve stairs up, one screeching tread in the middle. Six steps down the second-floor hallway. Turn left. She pounced into her bedroom and anchored herself against the bed post. Her eyes burned. Her breaths were coming in short, ragged gasps. She was about to lose everything. Again.

Footfalls thudded behind her, then a soothing warmth cuddled her back. Arms went around her. She closed her eyes, saving the memory for later when only darkness cloaked her.

"I won't let you go, Moira."

She dug fingernails into the carved wood. She couldn't give in. If anything happened to him…her heart would crumple under the weight of it.

"I have to go, Anson. My fight with Thacker will at the very least interfere with all your good work. At the very worst…well, I can't take that chance."

Tender lips pressed her head just above her ear. Not a kiss. More as if he breathed her in. Consumed her essence.

"I'm doing all this *good* work because of you, Moira Devlin. You helped me see the light, to come out of my shell. You healed my wounds. You saved me."

"Nothing pleases me more than to know I helped

you. But I can't stay. I won't. It's too dangerous."

His hands slipped to her arms, and he spun her around. A parade of pearl buttons was all she could focus on. If she met his gaze, surrender would be inevitable.

"Look at me." When she didn't obey, he repeated the demand, softer this time. "Look at me, Moira. Please."

His pleading shoveled into her resolve. She looked up and into eyes filled with tenderness and faint flecks of hurt. A pang stabbed her heart. No amount of lye would scrub away the stain her leaving would cause. But she had no choice. His life was at stake.

He thumbed her cheek, swiping at the wetness. "You said you love me. Is this true?"

Had she said that aloud? If so, she hadn't meant to. The words must have tumbled out in her rush to flee. There was no taking them back now. They'd been freed like a bird, never to be caged again.

She leaned into his hand, savoring the softness cradling her cheek. He was everything she wanted. Nothing she could have. "I love you more than you will ever know. You are a wonderful, caring man. Any woman would be thrilled to have you in her life. But it's not fair of me to ask you to risk everything for me and my baggage."

"What isn't fair is for me to lose my first chance at happiness since Alice died. You consume my head, my heart, my soul. I want to be with you day and night. I love you, Moira. Every part and parcel of you."

He loved her. It was all she had ever hoped for. But she couldn't let her joy ruin his.

"I can't make you happy, Anson. I'm tainted...like

Jukes' creek water." She unfastened the top three buttons of her blouse and rolled down the collar. She put her back to him, exposing her neck and the scars of her past. "You see that? Thacker and his radical followers marked me with their hatred. They set fire to our shack back in Willoughby. They killed my granny. All because of what we can do."

Tender fingers traced the back of her neck. Her skin tingled. Her heart ached. If only she could let him in. Let him cure the pain that clouded her days and nights.

His breath whispered over her skin. "It cuts my heart to know someone caused you harm."

She wheeled around, shrugging out his tenderness. "I don't want your pity, Anson. I want you to understand why this can't be. Why we can't be together. I am poison to anyone who cares about me."

"Oh no, my sweet Moira. You are more than wounds and scars. Much more."

His tender words washed over her. She anchored her hands at her sides. "You deserve a woman who will give you light and joy. Not darkness and sorrow."

"You provide all the joy and light I need. You are a special woman, and I would be the luckiest man alive to have you at my side."

He reached out and pulled her to him, arms wrapping her, holding her, tethering her. He was wrong. She wasn't the light. He was. Bright and insistent and warming the coldness inside her.

"I want you, Moira. Now and forever."

Resistance melted in his heat. She collapsed against him, nuzzling his chest like a cat. Smooth cotton rasped her cheek. His scent seeped through the material. Bay Rum. Heady stuff. Her skin prickled with a dozen shocks of want.

Anson scrubbed her back, fingers trailing fire in their wake. Rackety, madcap sensations grew and twisted inside her. She arched her hips against him, seeking more.

He was aroused, the size of him bucking against her belly. He would not skulk or hide it. He was a man of science, of nature. Arousal was as natural to him as breathing.

She tilted her head back and fell into blue eyes flaming with desire. No more fighting. Their last few hours together should be filled with joy and pleasure…a treasure to hold onto when they were separated by distance and principles.

There was only one way to do that.

****

His face held a most stupefied expression. Eyelids fretted. Brow crimped. His mouth opened and closed like a fish tossed on the river bank. For a man of many words, he appeared to have none.

Moira undid the last three buttons on her blouse. "Did you hear me, Anson?"

His gaze darted to her fingers and back. He licked his lips. "You want to take this…to the bed. To consummate our feelings for one another."

She pushed the blouse off her shoulders. Cool air swirled over her bared skin. Her insides quivered. "I want you, Anson Locke. More than anything I have ever wanted in my life. Will you have me?"

"I want nothing more than to have you…"

His words trailed away on a throaty groan. She cocked her head to the side, studying him. Hesitancy buckled his face.

"But…?" she said.

"But once we cross that bridge, there won't be any turning back."

She stepped closer. Her nipples strained through the thin material of her shift, seeking his touch. "I have no desire to turn back."

"You're certain? I don't want you to wake tomorrow morning filled with regret."

"There will be no regrets. Only exquisite joy. Now kiss me, Anson."

He groaned again and dropped his head. His lips devoured hers. Hungrily. Impatiently. He tasted of coffee and honeyed want. A sweeter flavor she couldn't imagine.

He left her mouth and slid slow, blistering kisses over her chin and down the column of her neck, stitching them together in a suture of heat. Her skin had never been so alert, so alive. She arched her neck, giving him better access.

There was a tug on the ribbons of her shift, and then his fingers were under the folds, kneading her breasts and nicking her nipples. Delightful tingles rattled through her. She shuddered and pushed into his hands. If this was Eden, she never wanted to leave.

"You're so lovely."

His voice was another brand of caressing, like silk over her body. Rippling down her breastbone. Tunneling deep in her belly. A fever ignited inside her. She wanted to bare all of her to his touch. She grasped the band on her skirt, but his hands stilled her.

"Let me," he whispered.

Skilled fingers made quick work of buttons and

laces and undergarments. In a matter of seconds, she stood before him, naked and shivering. Not from the cold. From the anticipation of what was to come.

"You're even lovelier than I imagined." Blue eyes burned dark with desire. "I've dreamt of this moment ever since I laid eyes on you. You are perfection. Pure perfection."

She reached out and slipped a button free on his shirt. "Is that your clinical assessment?"

One eyebrow arched. "There are no scientific words worthy of describing you, my dear. You are sprite and queen and temptress, all rolled into one delectable form."

She chuckled and undid more buttons. "Flattery will get you everywhere, Dr. Locke."

His hands closed over hers. "Stop for a moment."

Earnestness had replaced the playfulness in his eyes and tone. Her heart missed a beat. "What is it, Anson?"

"Make no mistake; I want you. In my life...and in my bed." He gave her fingers a squeeze. "But only if that is what you truly want as well. There will be consequences to what we do. There always are. Our joining should not be entered into lightly."

He was right. There would be consequences. Her innocence would be lost. She could become pregnant. Her reputation could be ruined. But just for today, just for a few exquisite hours, she wanted to be with him, to experience the joy of love, without any barriers. "I'm prepared to accept the consequences."

"You may think you are. Such intimacy adds new dimensions to a relationship. Some survive it. Some don't."

She traced his clenched jaw with a finger. "I'm not Alice. I won't break, Anson. We won't break."

Eyelids briefly shuttered. "The last thing I want is to cause you pain and suffering."

"You won't do that. Loving you is good and right. I feel it in my heart. I want you, Anson. More than anything in this world. But if you're having second thoughts, we can stop."

"No. I want this too. We can work through the consequences. Together. Whatever they may be." He cupped her hips and pulled her against him. His rod bucked against her belly. "Are you ready, my love? Because I certainly am."

"I've been ready. Make love to me. Now."

His mouth claimed hers. More demanding this time. Committed. He slid his tongue over her lips and delved inside. Her whole body came alive—a thousand butterflies bursting from their cocoons.

His hands slid up her arms, over her shoulders, and across her neck. Eager fingers dove into her hair, pushing out pins and loosening coiled locks. Freed hair cascaded down her back. He snagged a handful and hauled her closer, his mouth thieving from her like a robber of trains.

She couldn't think. Couldn't breathe. A moan rumbled up from deep within her. She had never wanted anything so intensely. She wanted to feel his bare skin pressed against every inch of her.

She undid the last button and shoveled his shirt off his shoulders. Her fingers played over his bared chest. Smooth and firm with just a light dusting of hair. Beneath her fingertips, his chest rose and fell, his breaths coming in short, ragged draws. He was as eager as she was.

She slid her hands downward, over ribs and a taut, quivering stomach to the band on his trousers. The buttons sewn there weren't as cooperative. Her fingers slipped, and she pressed against his bulging manhood.

He gasped and caught her hands. "Wait. Let me do that. Else this will be over before it even gets started."

Shoes and socks joined the shirt puddled on the floor. Then came trousers and belt. He stood before her, rod hoisted, thick and red and ready. A breath hitched in her throat. He was magnificent. A stud stallion worthy of covering the finest mares.

He grasped her hips and propelled her backward until her thighs met the bed. He gently pushed her onto the mattress. Bedcovers cooled her backside while his body warmed her front. His hands poured over her skin, fingers kneading her hills and skimming her valleys.

He shifted and lowered his head, mouth latching onto her breast. Teeth nipped, and lips suckled. He marked her as his own. Heat coursed through her and pooled between her legs. Fire. She was on fire. Except these flames wouldn't leave any scars.

"Anson..."

He stilled his suckling and cocked his head, peering up at her with eyes the color of a storm-tossed ocean. "What is it, my darling. Am I taking this to fast? Do you want me to slow down?"

Slow down? Not even close. A shudder ratcheted through her. "I want...I need...I don't know. Something...more."

That magical mouth tipped into a smile. "I think I know what."

His hand ploughed a path down her belly and

between her thighs. Fingers thrust inside. A bonfire erupted around the raid. She gasped and arched against him.

"You're ready," he whispered.

She was more than ready. She was at the mountain's peak. "Yes. Please. Now. Join with me."

Fingers withdrew, taking their pleasure with them. His breaths were hot gusts streaming over her breasts. "This is your last chance to say no. I won't be able to stop if we go any farther."

"There will be no stopping." She grasped his hips. "Take me. Now."

He shifted and hovered over her, hands braced on either side of her shoulders. His gentle gaze poured over her. "This first time is going to hurt. Just lie still. The pain will soon recede and then, I promise, there will be nothing but pleasure."

She smiled up at him. The pain would be worth the pleasure. "Come into me."

He took himself in hand and guided his staff between her legs. She pushed her hips upward in greeting, eager for the pleasure to begin. "Now, Anson."

He plunged inside. White hot pain flowered around his invasion. She gasped and wriggled against the ache.

"Easy," he crooned. "Don't fight it. Let the pain ebb."

She forced the tension out of her body and concentrated on the exquisite sensation of his fullness throbbing inside her. It was a strange combination of unnatural and familiar.

He moved his mouth to her breast, licking and flicking the nub with his tongue. A ribbon of heat spiraled inside her. Pain retreated, and pleasure advanced. She wanted all of him. Every inch he had to give. She wrapped her legs around his buttocks and pushed herself tighter against him.

He stilled and exhaled a throaty groan. His muscles quivered. Heat poured from him. He flexed his hips and began moving his staff out and back in. Slowly. Gently, as if savoring every thrust.

Waves built inside her, a tidal wave preparing to crash onto her shores. Her breaths were coming in quick, shallow huffs. She could barely breathe, much less move.

His movements quickened. She clung to him, taking him inside her over and over. Molten heat surged with each thrust. Fire with no pain. Nothing could hurt her when she was with him.

He threw back his head and gave one last plunge. Ragged breaths whistled through his teeth. Liquid warmth basted her insides. His seed. His markings.

Her own wave crested, and pleasure rushed in. Jolts of it splashed over her, sprinkled with her groans. She rode the surge, amazed that even with her mind awash, he could take her higher. It was limitless pleasure that glowed and blazed inside her. She closed around him, again and again.

As the last throb faded, she unfastened her legs and melted into the mattress. Time streamed once more. For a minute they lay there, him poised over her, their heated bodies mingled with sweat. If he never moved, she wouldn't complain. He had taken her on an incredible journey. She would hold onto him, onto the memory of his lovemaking. It might the be last pleasure she felt for a long time…if ever.

He gathered her in his arms and rolled them onto their sides. Tender fingers stroked her hair. "I didn't hurt you too badly, did I? It's been a long time since…well, I wasn't as slow or gentle as I should have been."

Always thinking of the welfare of others. Was it any wonder she loved him? She snuggled against him, her head resting on his chest. His heart thudded like a horse on a racetrack, even and strong. "It was perfect. You were perfect."

"No. I'm not. Not even close. But I know how I can get there." He thumbed her ear, caressing the lobe. "Will you marry me, Moira? Be the half that makes me whole, the half that makes me perfect?"

She toyed with the smattering of hair peppering his chest. Becoming the wife of a kind and devoted man was all she had ever dreamed of. All she had ever wanted. But there were mountains to climb before she could have such happiness. Tall mountains with steep cliffs.

His hand captured hers. "I see my proposal has taken you by surprise."

"Anson, I love you with all my heart, but…"

"But it's too sudden. I know. You are not one to jump recklessly into decisions. You weigh the consequences before acting. It's one of the traits I love most about you." He planted a kiss on each knuckle. "I want you to be happy, Moira. Take all the time you need. You are worth the wait."

Chapter Seventeen

Sleep released her from its grasp. Her mind and body floated to awareness. She opened her eyes and blinked at the brilliant sunlight streaming through the window. It only did that at mid-day. Lordy, had she slept the morning away? She usually rose as the sun poked its head over the horizon. Not today. Not after last night.

She shifted beneath the bedcovers. A dull twinge throbbed between her legs. Odd that the tearing of her virginal membrane hadn't yet healed. Her gift usually cured such minimal injuries within minutes. Perhaps it was because love had been involved. Love and a lot of passion. Warmth radiated through her at the memory of Anson's skillful lovemaking. Oh, the things he had done to her body. He was the one with the magical powers.

She turned her head to the side. A freshly-plucked wildflower and a folded slip of paper sat on the pillow. She went up on one elbow and traced a finger over the indent where his head had rested. Even though he hadn't shown it, she knew her hesitancy in answering his marriage proposal had hurt. It nearly killed her to know she had caused him pain, but she was only thinking of his welfare. Her lies would be far more painful if discovered after they wed, after he had fully committed his heart and soul.

She unfolded the note. *My sweet Moira…* She smiled at that. His Moira. He had definitely branded her. In more ways than one.

I was called out to see a patient. You were sleeping so peacefully I didn't want to wake you. I shouldn't be away for long. We can have a picnic lunch and spend some time together. Yours forever, Anson.

Forever. Oh, how she wanted that. To wake every morning in his arms. To spend every day by his side, performing the work they both loved. The only black cloud on the horizon – her gift. They should start their lives together without any secrets. She needed to tell him about her healing power. If he couldn't accept her for who she was, for what she could do, then there would be no forever.

The clatter of wagon wheels drifted through the open window and rattled into her thoughts. She should rise and get dressed. There were chores to do and possibly patients to see. With Mrs. Lidle away helping her convalescing sister, this was no time to be a slug-a-bed.

She tossed aside the bedcovers and rolled off the mattress. After a quick cleanse with a wet cloth, she dressed and went downstairs. A pot on the stove spewed the heady scent of coffee from its spout. Such a thoughtful man. Was it any wonder he had captured her heart?

A soft noise buzzed in her ears, then came a voice, *"Moira, we need you. Come to Seaton House. Quick as you can."*

It was Sally Hunt. The girl had the gift of sending mental messages over long distances. For Sally to contact her in this way meant something was wrong at the orphanage. Very wrong.

She penned a note to Anson of her whereabouts and left for the stables. Claude Gunderson had Dolly saddled and ready within minutes. She mounted and once outside of town, urged the mare into a steady lope. Nothing too strenuous. Just enough to get her to Seaton House as swiftly as possible without endangering the horse's health.

Dolly's hooves pounded the dirt-packed roadway in a soothing rhythm. Moira relaxed in the saddle and let go of the tension coiled inside her. The stress wouldn't do her or whoever needed her help any good. Mrs. Campbell would expect her to have a clear head and steady hands. Nothing less was acceptable.

The road undulated over hilly terrain where short expanses of thick copses were sandwiched between broad patches of cleared farm land. Years ago, Mrs. Campbell had established Seaton House some twelve miles outside of Mineral. She wanted the orphanage to be as far from prying eyes as possible, but still have the outside world accessible. Unfortunately, with the coming of the railway, the small mining town had expanded into the outlying countryside. Folks were taking advantage of the Homestead Act and securing property in the unassigned lands in the center of the Indian Territories. It wouldn't be long before the orphanage had farmers instead of forests for neighbors.

The road plunged into a dense thicket, dousing the sunlight. Scrub oaks and underbrush lined either side of the roadway. The birds and squirrels were oddly silent and still. A shudder rattled through her. Was this a sign of bad tidings ahead? She prayed not.

Sunlight basted them as Dolly loped out of the

thicket and into the open. The orphanage loomed ahead. As if aware of her impending arrival, Mr. Hoggard stood in the driveway, watching her approach.

She reined up in front of him. Worry shaded his normally sunny expression and clouded his bright eyes. He assisted her off the horse and motioned to the house. "Inside, Miss Moira. Quickly."

"What is it, Joseph?"

"It's Mrs. Clement. She collapsed this morning, and we have been unable to revive her."

No. Not the jovial housekeeper who was more family than staff. Heart thudding, Moira rushed inside. Meredith called out to her from the top of the stairs. "Up here, Moira. Quickly."

She bounded up the stairs and trailed Meredith into a bedroom. Mrs. Clement lay on the bed, eyes closed, her face white as the bedsheets.

"What happened?"

"We don't know. Mr. Hoggard found her collapsed on the kitchen floor. Maddie tried a reviving potion, but it didn't help. We can't rouse her no matter what we do."

Maddie was just as competent with potion making as she was. If the younger girl's remedy didn't work, then the housekeeper was indeed in critical condition.

Moira shucked off her cloak and riding gloves. "I will probe her and see what is going on inside."

She crossed to the bed and pulled back the covers. The housekeeper's chest rose and fell in shallow draws. Her nightgown was damp with sweat. Her body was fighting off something malevolent.

Moira rubbed her hands together. Nothing happened. She rubbed harder. Her hands remained cool and slightly clammy.

"What's wrong, Moira?" asked Meredith

"I don't know. My healing power won't come."

"Try harder. Concentrate."

She focused on drawing the healing power from her core. Nothing happened. Not even a twitch. Panic fisted her chest. "I can't bring it forth. What is going on with me?"

"Have you injured yourself recently? You know healing yourself can drain your powers."

Years ago in Willoughby, after healing the burns caused by the collapsing shack roof, she'd slept for two days. Nothing that severe had happened to her since.

"I haven't done anything recently that would require the use of my…" An image blasted into her head of tangled, blood-smeared sheets. Embarrassing heat flamed in her face. "Oh dear. I think I know what may have caused this."

"What."

"Not what. Who."

Meredith cocked her head to the side and gave her a pointed look. "You and Dr. Locke? When?"

"Last night." She fretted with the bedsheet. "Will my power return?"

"Only time will tell."

Time Mrs. Clement might not have. "I'll send for Anson. He may know what to do."

****

Guardian Angels came in many different forms. Lucky for him, his had a soft body and pliant lips that made his blood sing Hallelujah. Even now, he was having trouble focusing on his patient. Moira's curves called to him like a siren to a drowning sailor.

Last night had been perfect. She had been perfect. His body still hummed with contentment. The only gloom shading his sun…her reluctance to immediately accept his proposal. She needed time to decide if marrying him would impact her calling as a healer. He would never take that away from her. All he wanted was her happiness. But she had to come to that realization on her own. He would give her whatever time she needed to work through her reservations. She was well worth the wait.

She stood across the bed from him, adjusting the bedsheet covering the patient. A frown stitched her brow. He wanted to pull her into his arms and assure her everything would be all right. That her friend would recover. That he could make her happy. But he couldn't do that. Not with a room full of spectators. Later, perhaps, in the privacy of her bedroom.

He pressed the stethoscope bell onto the housekeeper's chest and leaned over to listen through the earpiece at the other end. Her heartbeat was slowing, becoming steadier and stronger. Her breaths were deepening, and her color was pinking up. Mrs. Clement would recover. His assessment of her condition had been correct.

He had just arrived at the livery in Mineral when one of the orphans from Seaton House had ridden up. Moira needed him at the orphanage. The housekeeper had collapsed and couldn't be revived. No one knew what was wrong with her. Even Moira was baffled.

A swift ride across the countryside had brought him to a massive two-story farmhouse sitting like a castle in the middle of the woods. He'd been rushed up the stairs and into a bedroom. After a brief assessment of the housekeeper's condition, he'd queried the small gathering of onlookers.

Mrs. Clement had been off her feed for several days and had exerted herself quite strenuously that morning chasing a recalcitrant chicken. He knew almost immediately what ailed her. She'd succumbed to *Diabetes Mellitus*. He'd treated several patients with the ailment in Philadelphia. The only question...did her blood have high or low glucose from the malady. One was easily managed, the other required a more extensive treatment that more often than not failed.

He had Moira make a simple syrup of sugar dissolved in boiling water. Once the concoction cooled, the two of them managed to get the housekeeper to drink the sugary liquid. That had been ten minutes ago. Thankfully, her rapid improvement pointed to low blood glucose as the culprit. Mrs. Clement would be waking soon and with a restrictive diet, should fully recover from her ordeal.

Translucent eyelids fluttered open. Milky eyes settled on him. "Who...? What...? Why am I abed? 'Tis midday by the light in that window."

Moira patted the woman's shoulder. "This is Dr. Locke, Mrs. Clement. You collapsed this morning in the kitchen and couldn't be revived. We had to send for someone with more medical expertise."

Anson nodded. "Not eating properly caused the sugar levels in your blood to drop. That combined with strenuous activity sent you into an unconscious state."

Lines shoveled into plump cheeks. A confused gaze latched onto Moira. "Why didna you cure me, lass?"

Moira's mouth sagged open. Her eyes went wide as

cheese wheels. She seemed more afraid of the answer than regretful. Odd. When talking of her life at Seaton House, she had spoken highly the housekeeper, that the woman was like family. Why the fear?

A hand closed around his upper arm. He turned to find Mrs. Booth standing beside him.

"Why don't you come downstairs, Dr. Locke. There's a fresh pot of coffee on the stove and a plate of scones left over from breakfast. I'm sure you could use some sustenance after being out of the office all morning. Moira can look after Mrs. Clement."

A smile reached into violet tinted eyes. If she had any ulterior motives, like getting him out of the bedroom and away from Moira, it didn't show in her face. Besides, he was famished.

"Scones and a cup of coffee sound wonderful." He stowed his stethoscope into the medical bag and peered across the bed. "Call out if you need me, Miss Devlin. Though I don't think you will. Mrs. Clement appears to be recovering quite nicely."

The panic on her face was gone, replaced by a tender smile and glowing eyes. "Thank you, Dr. Locke. We are grateful for your quick thinking and expert advice. You saved our Ida. She's special to us and now, so are you."

He smiled at the underlying inference. He was special to her. Perhaps he wouldn't have a long wait for her answer after all.

He followed Mrs. Booth out the door and down the stairs. Less rushed than when he arrived, he took his time and appraised the place where Moira had found happiness and acceptance. The floorboards and furniture gleamed from a fresh polishing. Flowery wallpaper decorated the walls. The glass window panes sparkled and shined. The orphanage was as clean and well-kempt as any surgical office.

A door swung open and a flood of children poured into the foyer, all talking at once. Short ones, tall ones. Ones wearing dresses. Others in short pants. Worry stained their little faces and peppered their voices.

Mrs. Booth stopped, hands cupping two small heads. "Quiet now, children."

The din subsided, and Mrs. Booth smiled down at the menagerie. "There's no need to fret. Mrs. Clement is going to be just fine. She's awake and talking and with a little rest, should be up and about in a day or so."

"What happened to her?" asked a little girl with pink ribbons twined in her red hair. "She didn't look so good when Mr. Booth and Mr. Hoggard carried her up the stairs."

Mrs. Booth patted a slender shoulder. "She merely overworked herself is all. She's not as spry and young as she used to be. We'll all have to pitch in and help, so it doesn't happen again."

"I can have a talk with that ornery hen," a boy with cottony white hair suggested. "Make sure she stays in the yard and doesn't try to run off again."

Anson stuffed down a chuckle. Children invented the oddest tales. He wanted at least a handful of the little creatures. Maybe more. There was no question that Moira would make a wonderful mother. There was no one more loving.

A tug on his coattail drew his attention. He glanced down and met eyes the color of summer violets. Golden ringlets framed the girl's pretty face. No doubt this was the daughter of Mrs. Booth.

"I saw you with Miss Moira. Are you her friend?"

More than a friend, he hoped. He squatted to her level. "Miss Moira and I have been working together in town, helping folks who need medical care. I am Dr. Locke. Who might you be, young lady?"

"My name is Sophia. I'm four." A pudgy finger pointed at Mrs. Booth. "That's my momma. She looks after the orphanage. My daddy works at the reservation. He's the agent for the Indians. He used to be a trooper in the army, but he wanted to be with my momma. So, he re-assigned himself."

"Is that so?"

"Uh-huh. And then they had me."

Mrs. Booth sidled closer, her expression exasperated but tender. "That's enough, Sophia. Dr. Locke doesn't need to hear your life's story. Go on back to the schoolroom with the others."

"Yes, Mama." Tiny fingers waggled. "Bye, Dr. Locke. It was nice meeting you."

As the darling Sophia and the other children filed back through the doorway, Mrs. Booth wagged her head. "I'm sorry. Sophia would talk the ear off an elephant if given a chance. She's quite the social lioness."

"No need to apologize. She's enchanting."

"You sound like my husband. Sophia has him wrapped around her finger."

"Not a bad place to be, I'd say."

She smiled and motioned at a short hallway just ahead. "The dining room is this way. At the end of the hall."

As he trailed behind her, she glanced over her shoulder. "I take it you enjoy children then."

A statement, not a question. "I adore them. I want a whole flock one day. Sons to teach to ride and fish, and daughters to pamper."

"Moira loves children, too. She has a way with them. Always has."

"Moira is very special." Very special indeed.

Mrs. Booth pushed open a door that led into a room with a large dining table in the middle. "We wouldn't take it kindly if she was mistreated in any way."

Was that a veiled warning? If so, it wasn't necessary. He wouldn't harm a hair on Moira's head. "You have nothing to worry about, Mrs. Booth. I only have Moira's best interests at heart."

"She tells me the two of you have become…close. Do you love her?"

Direct and to the point. Mr. Booth must have his hands full dealing with such strong women. "I love her with all my heart. And before you ask, yes, I intend to marry her. I proposed last night as a matter of fact. Moira has requested time to consider her answer, which I am gladly giving her."

"I'm happy to hear it. Moira has had a difficult life, filled with suffering and loss. Trusting others doesn't come easy to her."

"I believe that can be said for many people."

"Indeed. But Moira has secrets hidden deep inside her…secrets that will be hard to expose and harder to accept All I ask is that you keep an open mind. Listen to what she has to say and think well before you answer. If you love her as much as you claim, you will accept her for who she is, not who you want her to be."

Chapter Eighteen

Sunshine poured through the window, basting the small kitchen in a golden glow. The pot belly stove radiated with warmth and the soothing aroma of freshly brewed coffee. Moira sank onto the chair and lifted a steaming mug to her lips. It was good to be back. While she loved Seaton House, the medical office had become her new home. It was where she had ventured back into the world. Where she had regained her confidence. Where she had met and fallen in love with Anson Locke.

She couldn't deny it. She loved him with every fiber of her being. She wanted a life with him. Wanted to be his wife. She just had to find the courage to go after what she desired and not let anything stand in her way…not even her own misgivings.

While at the orphanage, she had sought counsel from Meredith and Mrs. Campbell. Both had found love and acceptance from the men they loved. If they could find a way to live such a life, there was no reason she couldn't. The problem was in the *how*.

The two women offered sage advice about a future with Anson. If she truly loved him and wanted a life with him, then she should be open and honest. Secrets were death to relationships. She needed to trust him with the knowledge of her gift. If he couldn't accept her for who she was and what she could do, then he wasn't the right man.

She anchored her grip on the cup handle. No more dilly-dallying. Anson was a good man. He deserved to know the truth. Tonight, she would tell him about her past, about her gift. She would bare all and let the cards fall where they may. No amount of worrying or wishful thinking would influence the outcome. He would either accept her, or he wouldn't. It was that black and white.

She took a sip of coffee and winced. Too strong. More grounds went into the pot than necessary. She'd best stop her woolgathering else she risked more than blistered taste buds.

The ding of the doorbell announced the arrival of a visitor. She set down her mug and rose. It was time to stow her gloomy thoughts and get on with the day. She could worry about Anson later.

In the hallway, she met a man holding a dusty, weather-beaten hat in front of him. His faded trousers and shirt were gray with dust. Even beneath the grime, he wasn't anyone she recognized.

"What can I do for you, sir?"

His leathery face cratered, and he craned his neck to peer around her. "Is the doctor in?"

Anson had left earlier to call on Zeke Brown, a cattle farmer who lived thirty miles outside of town. The farmer had suffered a kick to his leg while tending a sick cow. It would be several hours before Anson returned.

"Dr. Locke is out at the moment. Is there anything I can do to help?"

The man fidgeted with his hat brim. "I was sent to collect the doctor. There's been a cave-in up at the Shoehorn mine. Some of the miners are trapped. Others escaped but need medical attention."

That meant patients who couldn't wait hours for a doctor. "I am trained in providing basic medical care. I can go with you if you'd like. I'll do what I can for the injured men until Dr. Locke can get there."

"That would be perfect. Any help you can give my mates would be much appreciated."

Well, that had been easy. No hemming or hawing. Maybe folks were finally accepting her.

She whirled for the exam room doorway. "Give me a moment to grab my bag and leave a note for Doctor Locke. Then, I'll be right with you."

"Very good, Ma'am. I'll be right outside with the horses."

She scribbled a quick note on a piece of paper and set it on the examination table. Anson should see the message when he returned and come up to the mine. She would do what she could until he got there.

She gathered her medical bag and cloak and joined the man outside at the hitching rail. Two saddle horses waited patiently beside him.

He pointed to a bay gelding with gentle-looking eyes. "I brought an extra mount, thinking the doctor would be riding back with me. Are you able to ride astride? Or should we get a side-saddle from the livery?"

She moved to the horse and fastened her medical bag to the saddle straps. "There's no need to waste time on a side-saddle. I can ride astride."

His face creased with relief. "I was hoping you would say that."

She gathered her skirts. "Help me mount, if you would please."

He assisted her up and onto the saddle. She settled in and adjusted the stirrups to her shorter length. Her skirts bunched, showing more of her calves than was appropriate. She grunted. The devil with propriety. Injured men needed her help. Society could choke on its indignation.

She gathered the reins and nodded to the man, mounted now and waiting for her. "Let's go."

He nudged his horse into a steady lope. She clucked and reined the gelding to follow. Being early morning, there was little traffic on the main road. Just a farmer's cart laden with vegetables and a man crossing from one side of the street to the other.

They quickly reached the outskirts of town and splashed across Dancer's Creek. On the other side, the man guided his mount onto a well-worn trail weaving north along the foot of the Shoehorn.

"Where are we going?" she shouted.

He slowed his horse and waited for her to catch up.

She reined in beside him. "Why are we going north? I thought the Shoehorn Mine was south of town."

He nodded. "The main operation is. We're going to an older mine that hasn't been used much. Mr. Wentworth had instructed the foreman to send a small crew to inspect the site for possible re-opening."

"Did you not take the proper precautions before entering?"

"We did, but the support posts weren't as sturdy as we thought. The weakened wood gave way, and the tunnel collapsed. Me and two other men made it out safely; three pickers got trapped inside. We could hear them hollering, so we knew they were still alive."

So possibly head injuries and broken bones. She could handle those. Or at least stabilize the injuries until Anson arrived or the men were transported back to town.

"Are you all right? Were you injured?" Other than being coated with dust, he looked healthy.

"I'm fine. I was lucky enough to be standing at the entrance when the cave-in started. I escaped without any trouble. My mate Joe wasn't so lucky. A rock clobbered him on the head just as he ducked out of the mine."

"Did it knock him unconscious?"

"Nah, he's a tough ol' coot. He made it to a nearby tree, but he has a bleeder than may need stitching."

Easy enough to treat. "What about the other man? You said three of you made it out."

"Ben stumbled out a few seconds after we did. I think he took in too much dust. He was having a hard time breathing."

A more difficult injury. It all depended on how much dust the miner had inhaled. Too much, and he could drown in his own mucous.

A fork in the path loomed ahead. The man guided his mount onto the trail leading upward at a sharp incline. "We're going up the mountain now. This is a trickier route, but it will be quicker. Stay behind me and keep your horse in the middle of the path. And whatever you do, don't let him stop."

Heights didn't bother her overmuch. But riding an unfamiliar horse on a steep and treacherous trail set her nerves on edge. She grasped the saddle horn and shot a silent prayer skyward.

The path wound up the mountainside, zigging and

zagging over the sheer rock face. At one point, the edge dropped off to a deep chasm. While her mount plodded on with no hesitation, she stared straight ahead and chanted, "don't slip, don't slip," to the thud of his hooves.

Near the top, the trail flattened and led them into a sparse copse of trees. She patted the gelding's neck and whispered a grateful, "thank you."

After a short trek through the woods, the path opened onto a clearing that stretched to a large hole carved in the mountainside. Nothing moved in or around the mine entrance. Everything was silent and still. Odd. She would have expected to ride up on chaos.

"Where is everyone?" she called out.

The man reined his horse to a stop and dismounted. "I'm not sure. Maybe they're inside digging out the others."

Perhaps so. He crossed to her side and helped her to the ground. She reached to unfasten her medical bag, but something hard pressing into her side stopped her.

"You won't be needing that bag," the man said, his tone harsh and threatening.

Her pulse hiccupped. "What? I don't understand. Why won't I need—"

"You'll find out soon enough." He waggled the pistol at her. "Now, start walking toward that mine, and don't try anything stupid."

Her head whirled. What was going on? Why had this man escorted her to a cave-in, only to stop her from bringing her medical bag? And why hold her at gunpoint?

As they drew closer to the gaping maw, footfalls

echoed from within the black depths. A few seconds later, two figures emerged. One toted a Bible. The other, an older woman with a vulture feather bouncing from her cap, held a length of rope. Jack Thacker and Mrs. Wentworth. Her veins turned to ice. This was no cave-in.

The only one needing help was her.

****

The wall clock welcomed him with joyful dongs, not the death march it had tolled when he'd first arrived. For the first time in years, he looked forward to the future. All because of one woman. Moira had brought sunshine and happiness back into his life. Had helped him conquer his guilt over Alice's death. She showed him that he couldn't control how other people lived their lives. He could only offer help and friendly counsel. It was up to them to heed that advice or not.

A wise woman, his Moira. She was everything he needed. Everything he wanted. He would do whatever necessary to have her in his life, even swallow that monumental pride his grandfather had said would one day be his downfall.

He sailed into the foyer. A quick glance at the examination and waiting rooms confirmed they were both empty. He whistled his way down the hall and stopped at the bottom of the stairs.

"Moira, I'm back," he called out. An image rose up of her reclined on the bed, naked, with those raven locks spread out beneath her. His blood quickened. A toss beneath the bedsheets would be a most invigorating welcome.

The tick of the wall clock was his only greeting. "Moira?" he tried again, louder. "Are you up there?"

Silence. Where the devil was she? He'd only been gone for two hours and most of that had been spent on horseback. Zeke Brown had luckily sustained a minor bruise to the knee. A compress of chilled cloths was all the treatment the farmer required.

He pushed away from the newel post. Perhaps she had been called out to help someone in need. If so, she would have left a note. She was mindful of things like that.

A quick check of the storage room and kitchen turned up nothing. He returned to the examination room. A folded note rested on the table. Thoughts of sweet lips had kept him from seeing the obvious.

He picked up the note. She'd been called to a cave-in at the Shoehorn Silver Mine and urged him to join her as soon as possible. Miners had been trapped and some were injured. The missive fluttered back to the table. A cave-in. There could dozens of patients needing treatment. Moira was a competent healer, but she might be overwhelmed. He had to hurry.

Medical bag in hand, he rushed out of the office and down the boardwalk to the livery stable. Claude Gunderson was just starting to remove the saddle from the horse he'd ridden to Zeke's place.

"Wait, Claude," he shouted. "Don't untack that horse. I have need of him again."

Gunderson stilled his unsaddling and turned. "What's going on, Doc?"

"There's been a cave-in at the Shoehorn Silver Mine. Some miners were injured."

Claude frowned and scratched his chin. "That's strange. Joe Tillman just rode in from up there. He didn't say anything about a cave-in."

"I can only go by what Miss Devlin's note said. She implored me to join her post haste. She has no reason to fabricate something that dire."

"No. She wouldn't do anything like that." Gunderson tightened the girth strap he'd loosened and stepped back. "Alrighty, Doc. Here you go. I hope you find the cave-in was a simple misunderstanding."

Him, too. He reached for the reins. "Thank you, Claude. What's the quickest way to get to the main mine?"

"Only one way to get there. Cross over Dancer's Creek and take the south trail along the base of the mountain. After 'bout a half mile, you'll come to a wide gap. Follow that through to the other side. There, you'll see a path leading up the mountainside. The main mine entrance and outbuildings will be at the top."

Easy enough. He fastened his medical bag to the saddle and then footed the stirrup. Once settled in the saddle, he gathered the reins and urged the gelding into a quick lope through town. A few minutes later, the animal splashed through Dancer's Creek, and once on the other side, he reined the horse to the south.

As the sure-footed gelding loped along the path, worry leeched into his gut. Was Moira all right? Was she rattled by having to treat a large number of patients all at one time? Was she faced with critical injuries and wondering what to do? He grunted. No. Knowing her, she was doing just fine. She was smart and kept her composure. He trusted her to provide the care the injured miners needed.

It had been foolish of him to question her potions or her treatment of Charlie Gunderson. She had done nothing wrong. She was as devoted to helping others as he was. She deserved better from him. As soon as they got through this cave-in fiasco, whatever that turned out to be, he would make it up to her.

A quick ride through the gap and up the steep mountainside brought him to the Shoehorn Mining compound. Several small shacks sat outside a large hole hacked into rock face. Only a handful of men loitered in the clearing, and they didn't look the least bit distressed or impaired. His nugget of fear ballooned into a boulder.

One of the men left the group and advanced toward him. He wore work trousers and a clean cotton shirt. His expression was more curious than concerned. Anson dismounted and turned to meet the man.

"I'm John O'Malley, the foreman of the mine. Can I help you, sir?"

He nodded. "I hope so. I'm Dr. Locke, the new town doctor. I was told there was a cave-in and that some minors had been injured."

"No cave-in here, thank the Lord. It's been quiet all morning long."

Damn. Damn. Damn. Where was Moira? More importantly, was she safe? "Are there any other mines in operation on the Shoehorn?"

The man wagged his head. "None that I know of. The Wentworths own all the mining rights on this range. And right now, this is the only one that's operational."

"Are there any others that aren't operational?"

"There are two. One is to the south about half a day's ride. The other is closer, fifteen miles north of here. Both have been shut down and boarded up for years. Shouldn't be any mining activity in those."

"Is it possible someone trespassed without your knowledge and suffered a cave-in?"

"I reckon it's possible. Not likely, but still possible."

Possible would have to do. He had no other clues as to where to look for her. A mudslide sloughed through him. He couldn't lose her. Not now. Not after he'd just found her.

He dragged in a deep, calming breath. He wouldn't let fear take control. He would be methodical and precise, just as Moira expected him to be. He would search the other two mines, and if she wasn't at either of those, he'd keep looking. No stone would be left unturned.

"You all right, Doc?"

He gave himself a mental shake. A clouded head wouldn't help him find Moira. "How do I get to those other mines?"

The man provided directions which he committed to memory. He thanked the foreman and re-mounted. He sat there staring at the path. Which should he go to first? North? Or South? If he chose wrong, he risked wasting time...time that Moira might not have.

"Go to the north mine," a voice echoed in his head.

He twisted around in his saddle and scanned the clearing. The foreman and his men had disappeared. No one else was about. "Who said that?"

There was no answer. Not even a peep. Whatever the source, he wasn't going to ignore the advice.

As he nudged his mount forward, the voice rushed back into his head. *Hurry, Dr. Locke. Moira is in danger. She needs you.*

Chapter Nineteen

An old, musty smell clogged the air...as if an ancient tomb had been opened for the first time in eons. Cold seeped up from the smooth rock floor and chilled her legs through skirts and petticoats. A blanket and a warm cup of coffee sounded wonderful...but asking for such comforts from captors bent on retribution would be futile.

They stood across from her, talking with the man who had fabricated the tale of a cave-in. He had certainly sounded convincing. Her internal nose for sniffing out untruths and ill-intentions never jangled. Not even a twitch. She had become too complacent, too trusting. And now she would pay the price.

"Go and watch the entrance," Thacker ordered. "No one in or out until this is over."

The man nodded and wheeled around. He strode past her without any acknowledgement and was quickly swallowed up by the darkness. They were deep in the mine. Farther than sunlight would reach. Farther than any cries for help could be heard.

The note she'd left for Anson would send him miles in the other direction. Not finding her or a cave-in, he would have no idea where to look for her. Survival would be hers alone to achieve.

Harsh lantern light spilled over the jagged rock walls and illuminated water trails oozing like blood.

The overhead cross timbers sagged with age and rot. Gooseflesh crawled over her arms. If Thacker didn't kill her, the decaying mine very well could.

Thacker had bound her hands behind her back. She wrestled with the ropes, ignoring the burn of rubbed skin. A little discomfort would be worth the effort if it helped her escape. She wanted a life with Anson. Wanted a home. A family. She couldn't have those things if she died.

"There's no sense fighting the inevitable, Devil woman. You're going to get what's coming to you." Thacker shrugged out of his jacket and slid a thick-bladed knife from a sheath strapped to his waist. "You'll pay for what you did to my boy. Painfully."

She looked up and into eyes that held no sign of life. Just a dark, bottomless pit of hatred. Her stomach knotted. Her mouth went dry. She shoveled strength into her backbone. She had to stay strong. Had to buy herself enough time to get free of her trusses.

"Think about your son, Mr. Thacker. Little Jimmy wouldn't want you to do this. He was good and kind." She wriggled her wrists and worked at getting her thumb under a loop. "Remember when he placed bread crumbs on the sill outside his window? He was so weak; he could hardly sit up. But he found the strength to feed the birds struggling with the harsh winter."

Even now, her heart ached at the thought of the brave little boy who had refused to let death steal his goodness. Why God took the good people early and left the bad ones was beyond her.

Red outlined the harsh lines etched in Thacker's face. His upper lip curled into a snarl. "Shut your mouth. You have no right to say his name, much less talk about him."

Pandering clearly wasn't going to work. The man's anger had him totally unhinged. Any further mention of his son might push him over the edge. She needed more time before he attacked. Best to shift her attention to someone less volatile.

Mrs. Wentworth stood a few feet away, staring at a framed portrait sitting on a rocky shelf jutting from the wall. A nearby lantern poured orange streaks over her sagging face. Tears streamed over pale cheeks and dripped like raindrops from her jowls. Moira sighed. She knew that pain. A desolate, unbreakable ache that never truly went away. It just dulled over time until it merely became manageable.

"Is that a picture of your daughter, Mrs. Wentworth?" Her skin burned beneath the friction of her struggle with the rope. She kept at it. "Surely Alice wouldn't want you to turn your grief into something ugly. From what I have heard of her, she was a beautiful person, inside and out."

Mrs. Wentworth traced a finger over the portrait. "She was beautiful. Like an angel. She was the only one who could make Stanley smile."

Thacker fished a cap from his pocket and set it next to Alice's picture. "You miss your daughter as much as I miss my Jimmy. They were taken from us far too soon."

The familiar cap made her pulse stutter. Tweed with a blue bird embroidered on the brim. Every time she visited, Jimmy had insisted on wearing it. Said he wanted to look presentable for their guest, no matter how badly he felt. It killed her knowing she couldn't save such a gentle soul.

Mrs. Wentworth sniffed into a handkerchief. "Alice pleaded with us to let her live with her grandparents in Philadelphia. I was against it; she was so young. But Stanley convinced me to let her go. I wish I had heeded my motherly instincts. If she had stayed in Mineral where she belonged, she might still be with us."

Soft sobs echoed in the mine. Moira stilled her efforts. She wanted to offer comforting words. Wanted to wrap her arms around the grieving woman. But she knew from experience that grief often twisted people into strangers. Some turned that agony onto themselves. Others projected their pain outward. Mrs. Wentworth seemed to be straddling both. The wrong push could send her slipping onto the dark side with Thacker.

A boot stamped the floor, startling a gasp from her. Thacker's menacing gaze plowed across the short distance. If hatred had a face, it would be his.

"My Jimmy never had a chance to visit a fancy city like Philadelphia," he spit out. "His last days were of pain and suffering…all because of her and her poisons."

Moira swallowed her last bit of moisture and went up on her knees, ignoring the bite of sharp-edged rocks. Time was slipping away. She had to work faster, else she'd be joining little Jimmy in heaven.

"You are wrong, Mr. Thacker." She sawed at the bindings trapping her. Poke hot pain rasped her wrists, but she refused to stop. Giving up would be her death sentence. "My potions allowed your son to pass easily into God's hands. Without pain. Without suffering. You saw that. He died peacefully."

Thacker stalked toward her, eyes bulging, knife

waggling. "What do you know of God, heathen witch? He should strike you down for such blasphemy."

Witch. Lord, how she hated that word. It ground against her soul like broken glass. Her mother had been branded by it, as had her grandmother. Both had died because of it. If she never heard that word again, it would be too soon.

She shoved up her chin, refusing to be marked. "I am as much a Christian as any other God-loving disciple. I follow the teachings of the Bible and attend church when I am able."

He hovered over her, hate buckling his face. "Then you know that the Lord said an '*eye for an eye; a tooth for a tooth.*' Edeline and I shall have our vengeance."

She slowed her tussle with the rope. Thacker mustn't get wind of what she planned, else he might undo all the progress she'd made. He wouldn't win. Not this time. He wouldn't take another innocent from this earth.

She craned her neck and peered around him. Mrs. Wentworth stood at Alice's shrine, head bowed, shoulders quivering. A grieving mother, still feeling the pain of her loss. Perhaps she could reach the woman, prod her compassion to the surface.

"I know what Mr. Thacker claims I have done." She poured gentleness into her tone. "What is it that requires *your* vengeance against me, Mrs. Wentworth?"

The older woman whirled around, her expression switching from forlorn to venomous in the blink of an eye. "Bah. You know very well why I want vengeance. You have cast a spell over Anson. He believes he is in love with you. I won't have Alice's memory besmirched by his replacing her with a witch."

There was that word again. Sympathy for the woman began slipping. She had to grab onto what little tenderness she had left. "Anson has the right to find happiness again. Alice would want that for him. You know in your heart she would."

It was the truth. Alice's ghostly form had said as much. A cool mist brushed over her wrists, soothing her raw skin like a gentle caress. The hairs on her arms stood on end. She'd felt a similar sensation once when Nel had called forth a spirit from the dead. Was Alice at the mine? Was she trying to help? Or was she siding with her mother?

"Don't tell me what my Alice would want." Mrs. Wentworth sliced the air with an agitated hand. "You know nothing of her."

A stiff breeze plowed through the tunnel. The lantern flame flickered. Alice's portrait bounced and rattled on the ledge. A second later, it toppled over and fell to the floor in a shatter of glass. Mrs. Wentworth gasped and jumped back.

Thacker's eyes went wide as wagon wheels. He leaned away from her and made the sign of the cross over his chest. "She has called forth the Devil. We must kill her now before he pulls both our souls into Hell with him."

Mrs. Wentworth retrieved the crippled picture and clutched it against her chest. Her eyes held a fanatical glow. Her mouth twisted into a hateful grimace. She had slipped to the other side.

"Gag her so she can't call for his help," the woman snarled. "Then we will send her to join her master."

Moira's heart thudded against her ribs. Things were spiraling out of control. The ropes weren't loose enough to slip free and fend off an attack. She needed more time.

"Please don't do this." If groveling slowed their plans, she'd clean every speck of dust from their shoes. "I will leave town. Today. You won't ever see me again. I swear on my grandmother's grave."

Thacker grunted and yanked a handkerchief from his pocket. "We're going to make certain of that. To truly kill a witch, a heated blade must be run straight through her black heart. You and your evil will never rise again."

He thrust the cloth into her mouth. Old sweat and stale tobacco basted her tongue. Her stomach roiled. Bile burned in her throat. The strength went out of her spine. This was it. She had lost. Anson would be robbed of yet another woman he loved. Deprived of a life he could have cherished. He would be devastated. He would retreat into his shell. May never come out again. May never love again. All because of her failure.

****

Breaks in the foliage offered a clear view of the gapping maw twenty yards ahead. There was no evidence of a cave-in. No debris littering the ground. No people scurrying about. The only signs of life were several horses tied to a nearby tree and a man standing at the opening.

He was tall and slender and armed with a pistol. He kept turning his head from side to side, watchful and alert. There was only one reason to post a guard…either to keep someone in or to keep someone out.

Was Moira inside? His gut said yes. His head swam with more questions. Was she still alive? Or had he arrived too late? Fear rose in his throat and threatened to strangle him. Would he ever feel her gentle touch again? Hear her lovely voice? Had he lost the chance at having something wonderful?

No. He shook off the maudlin thoughts. She was alive. He wouldn't allow himself to think otherwise. Positive thoughts led to positive outcomes.

He studied the area around the mine entrance. As much as he wanted to rush in, he had to go slowly, plan his attack. Intricate surgeries required patience and a clear head, else the procedure could turn fatal. He didn't want any recklessness to cause her harm or worse.

He'd left his horse tied to a tree back where the slope ended and the trail leveled out. Horses were social creatures, neighing when they sensed others of their kind. Not to mention plodding along noisily, unmindful of the placement of their feet. The whispers in his head had warned of danger. His approach required stealth and silence.

He crept through the thicket, watching where he walked. The snap of a branch or crunch of debris could alert the guard to his presence. He wanted to get a clean jump on the man.

The grove thinned just before the mine entrance where several large boulders standing elbow to elbow offered the perfect concealment. He crouched behind the tallest one and peeked around the side. The guard hadn't moved and appeared to be unaware of his approach. Good. Maybe all those years of playing Hide-and-Seek with his boyhood playmates were paying off.

He grazed a hand over the ground and found a palm-sized rock and another just a bit larger. Now he could direct the guard's attention to where *he* wanted it to go.

He tossed the smaller rock into the brush on the other side of the trail. The guard alerted on the sound and bolted forward, pistol aimed and ready.

Anson prepared himself, hauling in a breath and tightening his muscles. As the man surged past, he sprang from his hiding spot and smashed the rock against the man's head. Not hard enough to kill, but enough to render the man unconscious. The guard crumpled to the ground like a ragdoll.

A woman's scream echoed from within the mine, making the hairs at the back of his neck stand on edge. *Moira.* She was alive. But clearly not unharmed.

He snatched up the guard's pistol and ducked into the mine. Darkness quickly enveloped him. He paused to let his vision adjust to the lack of light. He had never been afraid of the dark, but this dank hollowness had his pulse thrumming.

A faint glow glimmered in the distance. Moira was down there. With whom, he had no idea. But they would pay dearly if they hurt one hair on her head.

He moved slowly down the shallow slope, taking short, cautious steps while running his hand along the rock wall for guidance. Rushing wouldn't do him or Moira much good if he ran into the business end of a weapon.

The light grew brighter. Faint murmurings echoed from deep within the shaft. Not clear enough to identify, but enough to let him know someone was there and he needed to employ caution.

He molded against the rock wall and inched closer. A hundred heartbeats later, a macabre sight came into view. He stopped and pressed into the shadows, his veins filling with ice.

His former mother-in-law stood holding a lantern as she watched the man called Thacker pressing Moira against the tunnel wall. A meaty forearm trapped her throat. A thick-bladed knife hovered over her heart. Thacker was going to carve the sunshine out of the world.

Anger smashed through his fear. Not today he wasn't.

He stepped into the light, pistol aimed at the thug's back…a hand's breadth below the left shoulder. A fatal point should the need arise. "Drop that knife, Thacker, or I'll shoot."

Thacker yanked his head around. Beady eyes narrowed. Pale lips thinned. But the hand on the knife didn't waver.

Moira's gaze washed over him, fearful, pleading. A cloth plugged her mouth. Her hands were bound behind her back. She was helpless as a newborn kitten. One thrust of that knife, and she'd be lost to him forever.

Anson waggled the gun. "Drop the knife, Thacker. Now. Or I'll put a bullet in you."

The man's lips twisted upward as if he held all the aces. He didn't. "Don't think I won't shoot just because I'm a doctor. I'm a man first. A man who won't let you hurt the woman he loves."

Mrs. Wentworth took a step toward him. Her expression was animated, almost fanatical. The lantern swung in her grip, casting dancing shadows on the walls. "Come, Anson. You're bewitched. Let us rid you of this sorceress before you fall further under her spell."

He shifted the barrel a fraction to cover her as well. "Don't come any closer, Edeline."

She pulled up, eyes going wide. "You would shoot me, Anson?"

"If I have to, yes."

Her gaze fled to a rocky ledge holding a boy's tweed cap and a framed portrait of a young lady wearing a familiar blue dress. "What would Alice think of you doing something so heinous to her mother."

"Alice is dead. There's nothing you or I can do to change that. We must go on with our lives. I want to do that...with Moira."

"You don't know what you're saying."

"I know exactly what I'm saying. Now move over by that shrine and stay there." It was sad. She was a lost soul who couldn't get beyond her grief. He almost felt sorry for her. Almost.

"I disown you, Anson Locke," she hissed. "You are no longer a part of our family."

He hadn't been part of a family for years. His parents were gone. Grandfather was gone. Alice was gone. But he now had Moira. She was going to be his family, his future.

"You no longer have any hold over me, Edeline. I don't owe you or Alice anything. I am free of the guilt. Moira helped me see that. So, do as I say and move over to that ledge. Now."

Pale eyes deadened. Shoulders slumped. With the lantern nearly dragging the ground, she trudged to the opposite wall and plucked the framed portrait from the ledge. She stroked a finger over the shattered glass.

"I'm sorry, Alice. I tried. But our Anson is too far gone."

Anson closed his heart to her sorrow. She was the one who had let grief carry her too far. She was the reason Thacker had come to Mineral. The reason a hate-filled man was poised to kill the only thing that could make his life whole again.

He pointed the pistol at Thacker's black heart. "Drop that knife and release Moira. I won't say it again."

The man hesitated. The dirt-coated skin covering his jaw twitched. Was he chewing over his options? It would be a most unsatisfying meal.

Mrs. Wentworth's demented cackle echoed in the mine. "You had best do as he says, Jack. Satan has taken over Anson's soul. He'll kill you if you harm the harlot."

Thacker's beady eyes bounced from the gun barrel to Moira and back. After a few seconds, his mouth sagged. He gave a resigned grunt and dropped the knife with a dramatic flourish. It clattered to the rocky floor and stilled.

Smart man, for once. "Now kick it over here."

Thacker toed the knife. It bounced across the uneven rock floor and came to a stop near Anson's feet.

"Good. Now release Moira and then move over to the ledge with Mrs. Wentworth. Slowly, no quick moves."

Thacker dropped his hands to his sides and stepped back. Moira pushed away from the wall and sprinted toward him. She molded against his side, body quivering. The tension went out of him. She was safe. She was his. He wouldn't be spending his days in an empty room or his nights in a cold bed.

He slung his free arm around her shoulders. "It's all right, darling. I've got you."

Her eyes lifted and raced over him. No words were

necessary. But he wanted to hear her voice. Wanted to know she was unharmed.

He tugged the gag out of her mouth. A pink tongue swept across rosy lips. He couldn't wait to taste her again. A movement caught his eye. Thacker. He'd best keep his focus on the present, or his future would come crashing down around him.

He steadied his aim on the thug. "Don't even think about doing anything stupid, Thacker. I learned at an early age how to shoot, and I do it well."

Thacker thrust his hands in the air. "Fine. Fine. I was just moving over to the ledge like you told me to."

The man sidled sideways and settled beside Mrs. Wentworth. His words might be conciliatory, but that rigid stance and fierce expression warned of more to come. He would be ready for it.

"How did you know where to find me, Anson?" Moira asked.

"I rode out to the main mine as your note instructed, but found no sign of a cave-in. The foreman provided directions to this mine, even though he said it was boarded up. I figured it wouldn't hurt to have a look." Telling her about the little voice directing him where to go and to hurry would make him sound as deranged as the two zealots eyeing him with hatred.

"What about the guard? Thacker posted an armed man to watch over the entrance."

He jiggled the gun. "This is his. A rock to the head took care of him. He'll have a nasty headache for a few days, but he'll recover."

"What are you going to do with us?" Thacker demanded. "Bash our heads in, too?"

"I will if you try anything. I plan to turn the two of

you over to the sheriff. Let the law exact justice for what you tried to do to Moira."

"We didn't do anything to the witch," he spat. "She's still alive, even though she should be dancing in the fires of Hell."

Moira stiffened in his grasp. Knowing her past, he could only assume the mere mention of fire filled her with fear. She wouldn't have to fear any more. He would always keep her safe.

He gave Thacker a piercing look. "Shut your mouth, Thacker, and keep it that way. One more peep from you and you'll be the one dancing."

The man snapped his lips shut, but his eyes continued to shoot daggers across the short distance. The man could stew in his hatred for all he cared.

Anson gently pried Moira away from his side. "Let's get those ropes off you."

Keeping one eye and the pistol trained on Thacker, he squatted and retrieved the knife. A quick slice and Moira's bindings fell free. Her wrists were raw and oozing with blood. She'd been trying to free herself. She was so strong and resourceful. Yet another trait he admired.

As he started to rise, Moira's gasp sliced the air. Before he could react, something sharp dug his shoulder, carving a heated path of pain. He staggered with the blow. The knife dropped from his grasp. The pistol bucked in other his hand, blasting a piercing gunshot through the tunnel.

Ears ringing, he swiveled around and faced his attacker. It was the guard. He must not have hit the credent hard enough. Time to remedy that.

Pushing through the burn in his shoulder, he hefted

the pistol. He wasn't quick enough. The guard lunged, knocking the gun from his hand and slashing at him with a knife. The blade bit into his side just below his ribs. Poker hot pain surged around the assault. His vision went dark. His knees buckled, and he fell against the rock wall.

Over the clanging in his ears came the crash of falling rocks and Moira's horrified scream.

Chapter Twenty

The mine shaft shook and grumbled. The guard's attack had caused Anson to pull the trigger on the pistol. The bullet had struck one of the support braces. The rotted wood had collapsed, and other posts were quickly following suit. Rocks and dirt rained down from the ceiling. Moira crouched and covered her head. She had to get everyone to safety before they were buried alive.

A pained scream rolled over her skin and then died just as abruptly. In the spluttering lantern light, she could just make out a large pile of rocks where Mrs. Wentworth and Jack Thacker had been standing. There was no movement or sound. Just a large puddle of blood seeping from under the mound. They were gone. There was nothing she could do for them.

The lantern gave one last gasp and went out. Darkness enveloped the mine. Her heart thudded against her ribs. She had to find Anson. The last she'd seen, he had been leaning against the wall, a spreading circle of red staining his jacket.

"Anson, where are you?" she shouted.

"O-Over here."

She followed the raspy reply, arms stretched out in front of her. Dust clogged her nose and charred her throat, making breathing a struggle. Walking was even more difficult. Rocks littered the floor, threatening to twist her ankle at every step. As much as she wanted to rush toward him, she wouldn't do herself or Anson any good if she turned up lame.

The rumbling slowed. Debris stopped raining down. Thank the Lord. The cave-in was coming to a halt. For now.

Her fingers jabbed something soft and warm. It groaned. Anson. She groped for his arm and shouldered under it. "I've got you. Let's get out of here."

Keeping one hand on the rock wall, she guided him along the path that slanted upward. That was the way to the entrance. That was the way to safety.

The going was slow. Rocks hindered each step. Her foot struck something large and bulky, and she had to pull up to keep from falling. She bent and fumbled to discover what blocked their path. Her fingers pressed into something soft and unmoving. No breaths moved the chest. No heart beat thudded under her fingertips. Death had claimed another victim.

"What…is it?" Anson choked out.

"I think it's the guard." At Anson's stiffening, she added. "It's all right. He's dead. Let's keep going."

She helped him over the body. The farther they traveled through the shaft, the more he seemed to rely on her for support. He sagged against her. His breaths were coming in short shallow bursts. He was fading fast. Her chest tightened. She couldn't let him die. He had saved her. In more ways than one.

Faint light shimmered ahead. She gathered her last bit of strength and pushed forward. A few minutes later, they emerged into the sunlight. She paused a moment to catch her breath and to allow her vision to adjust. Anson coughed and slumped against her. It wouldn't be long before his legs gave out completely.

She managed to get him to the base of a nearby tree. He collapsed against the trunk with a grunt. His eyes were closed, his breaths coming in rattling draws. There was little coloring to his skin. Death was knocking on his door. She had to do something. Fast.

She dropped to her knees and ripped open his jacket. Blood stained his shirt at the shoulder. But the ever-widening circle of red just below his ribs drew her attention. He was bleeding out. She had to stop it. Now. Since her healing gift had abandoned her, she would have to use her normal medical skills.

She ripped off the bottom of her petticoat and rolled it into a ball. A hard compress pressed to a wound usually slowed, if not stopped, any bleed. This one had to work. Anson could not die. He was everything she had ever wanted in life. Everything she had denied herself. She would not lose it.

She stuffed the cloth ball against the wound and pressed hard. Moist warmth seeped around her fingers. She leaned forward and put all her weight into stemming the flow of blood. *Stop. Please stop.*

Anson groaned, and his eyelids flickered open. Bloodshot eyes focused on her. "Moira…?"

She smoothed a rebellious lock off his forehead with her free hand. "Yes, I'm here."

"Thacker was going to…couldn't let him hurt…" His words trailed away on a raspy breath.

"I'm safe, Anson. We both are."

"I couldn't live…if anything happened to you—"

A cough seized his words. Her heart heaved with every pain-wracked spasm. She wanted to help him, wanted to heal him. All she could do was hold onto him until his coughing fit eased.

He lifted a trembling hand and settled it over hers on the bandage pressed to his side. "It's not good…is it."

"You're going to be fine. The bleeding will stop soon."

His grip loosened and fell to the ground. "Can feel…slipping away. Dying."

No. No. No. She would be lost without him.

She pressed harder. "I won't let you die."

"Love you, Moira…with all my heart."

"You're not going to die. You can't. I love you." Tears burned in her eyes. She couldn't lose what she'd only just found. "Please Anson, fight this. Be the strong man I know and adore. Don't leave me."

"Don't…want to. Can't hold on any long…"

His words trailed away on a breathless exhale. He was not going to die. He was not. "I won't let you go. I will do anything to save you."

His lips tried to lift into a smile. "My death…not your fault. Nothing…you can do."

Oh yes there was. Her gift was not going to abandon her when she needed it the most. It had been an albatross around her neck for as long as she could remember. Giving life to others but sucking it from her. It was time she gleaned some reward for her sacrifice.

"I'm going to try something, Anson. You're not going understand what I'm about to do. You may even hate me for keeping it from you. But I have to try."

"Futile…just let me go."

"Do you trust me?"

"More than…anything."

"Then let me do this. Please." At his nod, she

leaned back and closed her eyes. Only his ragged breaths broke the eerie silence. Even the birds were quiet. Were they watching from the treetops, hoping, like her, for a miracle?

She gathered herself with a deep breath. She could do this. She had to. For Anson's sake. For hers.

She rubbed her hands together. Nothing happened. No warmth. No coiling of energy. Her stomach roiled. Images rose up of a cold parlor and a dead hearth. Of silence so loud, it was deafening. That would be her life without Anson.

No, it would not. She wouldn't let that happen. Not while she drew breath.

She scrubbed her hands together until they burned from the friction. Warmth crept into her palms and tingled in her fingers. Yes. Yes. That's it. The heat thickened and intensified. Energy coiled in her core, throbbing to be released. Her heart shouted. Her gift had returned. Anson would not die.

Resting both hands on his bared stomach, she let the pulsing energy flow into him. He gave a soft groan but didn't move. She probed his ribs where the knife had invaded his body. Cold. Wet. Black. Vessels had been nicked. Wind whistled inside her head. The blade had grazed a lung. A lethal injury.

She drew in another fortifying breath and concentrated on sending healing waves into the blackness. The cold warmed. The blackness lightened. The whistling slowed and then stopped. Relief coursed through her. One wound healed, one to go.

She moved her probing to his shoulder and sent a pulse into the damaged area. The angriness abated. The weeping halted. She leaned back, drained. She had done as much as she could. He would require a week or so of recuperation, but he would live.

She opened her eyes and looked straight into a face sagging with disbelief. Eyes of blue drilled into her.

"What did you do?"

His breathing was even and steady. His coloring had pinked up. He was stabilizing. He should be strong enough to handle the truth. It was time she came clean about her healing ability. Let the chips fall where they may. Besides, he wouldn't give up until she answered his questions, no matter how poorly he felt.

"I have a gift, Anson. A very powerful gift." She lifted her hands and twisted them to and fro. Her wrists were smooth and no longer blemished by rope burns. "I can heal myself and others by my touch. Well, not fully heal others. I get the process started. It's up to them to do the rest."

"How is this possible?"

"I don't know. I was born with the ability. My mother had it. So did my Granny Tate."

His brow crumpled. "Why didn't you tell me about this?"

"I was afraid to. You were so rigid and skeptical of my potion-making skills. I couldn't image how you would react to my healing gift."

"Did you use this *gift* on Thacker's son?"

He might be physically drained, but his mental faculties were brimming over. "I tried. But Jimmy was too far gone. Once the body gives up, there is nothing more I can do."

"What about the others? Little Charlie Gunderson?"

He could put two and two together faster than a

drunk downed a glass of whiskey. "Yes, I healed him, too. And the men from the lumber mill who were injured during the earthquake."

"Do your patients suffer any after-effects? Surely something that powerful and abnormal has repercussions. Are you able to revive the dead?"

Her heart sank. He called her gift abnormal. He was heading down the path to rejection. She'd seen it before. Many times.

She forced lightness into her tone, even though all she felt was encroaching darkness. "My patients recover from the healing without consequence. I am the one who suffers from the aftereffects. My body's ability to heal itself becomes weakened. I am vulnerable to attack. I have to take extra care with my health. As far as I know, I am unable to revive the dead. The few times I tried were unsuccessful."

"How long does this vulnerable period last?"

"Anywhere from an hour to several days, depending on how much healing I employ."

No frown tipped his lips, but then neither did a smile. Even his eyes were shadowed. "This gift. This healing ability…it's so, so…unnatural. In the wrong hands, it could be deadly."

Deadly. He might as well slice into her heart with a knife. He went silent, his quiet gaze running over her face as if searching for answers. The only thing she could offer was the truth.

She reached out and covered his hand, more to anchor herself than to offer him comfort. "I'm still the same person I have always been, Anson. I care about people. I would never intentionally hurt anyone or use my gift for evil purposes."

His soundless skepticism pealed like a church bell. Loud and papal. How could she fight such disbelief? If he truly loved her, he should be accepting her without question. Perhaps they were not meant to be together.

"I know this is a lot to take in, Anson. Tell me what you're thinking." Anything would be better than nothing.

He pushed out a ragged exhale. "I don't know what to think. I never imagined anything quite so...overwhelming. It's like that voice I heard in my head telling me you were in danger."

"You heard a voice?"

"It's not important." He pulled his hand away, retreating. "I need time to process all this. Alone."

He hadn't denounced her outright. Perhaps she had a chance. A small one, but she would take it. His physical wounds would heal. The mental strain of wrestling with the knowledge of her gift that would be much more difficult to overcome. Hopefully he would remember the good in her, remember how much he loved her. The wait would be painful, but she would give him all the time he required, whatever the outcome.

****

The morning sun filtered through the sheer curtains covering the window. Muted voices and the clatter of wagons rose up from the street below. Anson shifted against the pillows piled at his back. He should be up and about. Not lounging abed like an invalid. It had only been a few days since he'd rescued Moira from Jack Thacker and Edeline Wentworth. Days since he'd been knifed. Days since he'd been healed by an unnatural ability.

His memory after being knifed was wooly at best. He recalled the roar of the collapsing mine. The pain stabbing his side. The feeling of slipping away. Then her hands were on him. Heat and energy pulsed from her fingertips, piercing into him and healing him from within. He'd revisited that invasion over and over in his mind. He still couldn't wrap his mind around what she could do.

She had brought him back to the office and helped him upstairs to her bedroom. Except, it wasn't her bedroom any more. She had packed her things. Said she was moving out. Was giving him the time he'd asked for to think things through.

He still didn't know what he wanted. She wasn't a snake-oil salesman. Wasn't a murderer. Yet, what she could do with her hands went well beyond the ordinary. If used incorrectly or with malice, it could be quite lethal.

With a grunt, he tossed aside the bedsheets and swung his legs over the side of the bed. His ribs screamed in protest. Damned nuisance. He gently peeled back the bandage. The gash puckered and oozed, but not nearly as badly as it had days ago. He was on the mend. Good. He needed to get on with his life…whatever that entailed.

He found his trousers at the foot of the bed and managed to pull them on with much effort and grunting. His shirt was another obstacle altogether. He got one sleeve on, but the other eluded him. Sweat beaded on his forehead and dribbled down to sting his eyes. Why did everything in his life have to be so damned complicated?

Footfalls sounded in the hall, and then the door

swung open. Moira's friend from the orphanage strode into the bedroom, toting a breakfast tray. Mrs. Reese caught sight of him, and her mouth turned down in a disapproving frown.

"You shouldn't be up, Dr. Locke. It's too soon."

"It's mid-morning. Not too soon at all."

"You know what I mean." She set the tray on the bureau. "Let me help you with that shirt. And then back to bed with you."

He pushed to his feet, ignoring the swimming in his head. "It's not healthy to be such a sluggard. It's time for me to get up and move about. Surely there are patients to be seen."

"There are no patients here except for you." She marched across the floor and stopped in front of him, hands hooked on her hips. "And you're not a very cooperative one at that. Now sit and let me help you."

"I'm not a child. I can dress myself." He tried to find the other sleeve, but it dodged his efforts. His breaths were coming in quick draws. His knees were turning to porridge. It wouldn't be long before he made of fool of himself and collapsed.

Mrs. Reese gave him a look that said he was every bit the child he was acting like. She snagged the shirt sleeve and pulled it over his arm. Her exaggerated clucking would make a peahen proud.

"Moira left strict instructions that you are to stay in bed until your wound is healed enough that it won't break open. I won't have you relapsing on my watch. I promised to look after you, and I will, whether you like it or not."

The Seaton House orphans were certainly made of iron. Bull-headed came to mind. As did kind-hearted and full of life. Like Moira. Was she suffering with their separation? He didn't want to cause her pain. But he had to draw his own conclusions. Without distractions.

He sank to the bed. "Fine. But I will fasten my own buttons." Even if it took all day.

Her gruff expression softened. She reached behind him and fluffed the pillows. "There. Just a few more days of being abed, and you should be able get up. I made your favorite. Eggs scrambled hard and coated with pepper, just the way Moira said you liked them."

Buttons evaded him. His fingers cramped. He gave up and plopped back against the pillows, drained. "I'm not hungry." He was being petulant. But this weakness of mind and body was maddening.

Mrs. Reese gathered the tray and brought it to the bed. Was she deaf?

"I said I wasn't hungry."

"You have to eat, Doctor. Or you'll never regain your strength."

She set the tray on his lap. The aroma of coffee assailed him. Thoughts of Moira surfaced, of her sitting across from him at the table, of her pretty lips puckering as she blew across a steaming mug…of hands that could do wondrous things – in and out of the bed. She was definitely a distraction.

"How do you deal with what Moira can do?"

Mrs. Reese shook out a crisp napkin and set it across his chest. "She only does good with her gift."

"How do you know this? Something that powerful could just as easily be turned to evil."

"Moira wouldn't do that. She's good through and through. You've been around her for nearly a month.

You've seen her at work. No one is more devoted to helping those in need than her. In your heart, you know this is true."

His heart, yes. His head? Not so much. It spun with warring thoughts. Part of him wanted a life with Moira. To love and be loved. The other part, the part that wouldn't let him be, screeched that he'd botched one marriage. His life with Alice hadn't been nearly as complicated as one with Moira would be. How could he expect everything to be sweet cakes and roses?

"What if I am able to accept her gift? It may not be enough. I couldn't save my first wife. What if the same happened to Moira? I wouldn't be able to live with myself."

Mrs. Reese went to the bureau and poured water from a pitcher into a basin. "Your wife doesn't blame you. Alice says her death was not your fault, and she wants you to move on with your life."

"How do you know what Alice would want?"

Mrs. Reese arranged soap and a razor beside the basin. "Because she's standing right here telling me."

What the hell? He tossed a glance around the room. "Right where? Here? In this bedroom?"

"Yes, beside your bed, hovering off the floor a bit, but still there." She turned to face him, her expression resigned. "Moira and I are...special. She can heal with her hands. I can see and speak with those who have passed on."

God-almighty. "You talk with spirits?" At her nod, he leaned forward waved a hand through air. He felt nothing. "You say Alice is here? At my bedside?"

"Not that side, the other. But yes, she's wearing the pale blue dress you had her buried in. Her favorite. And the gold locket you secretly stowed into her palm before they nailed the coffin shut."

Mrs. Reese could not know such things. Was he still asleep and in the throes of a nightmare? He pinched his arm and winced at the pain. Nope. Wide awake.

"Why is Alice here? What does she want?"

"She came to tell you that it's all right to love another woman. That it will not besmirch her memory. What the two of you had was wonderful, and she will always treasure your time together."

Sorrow tugged at his heart. He hadn't loved her nearly as much as he should have. She was so young and beautiful. She deserved better than him. Better than death.

"She says there are no regrets. She wants you to start looking to the future, to be happy. She believes you can have that with Moira. She says you can trust Moira. That she's good and kind and will make a wonderful wife."

The weight sitting on his shoulders lifted. For the first time in days, he had hope. Hope for himself. Hope for Moira. "Tell Alice I will always hold a special place in my heart for her."

Mrs. Reese smiled. "She knows that. She feels the same for you."

"Tell her I appreciate her coming here to help me understand."

"She's gone."

"Gone? Where?"

"To be with the rest of her departed family. She was waiting for this moment before moving on."

Moving on. Alice urged him to do that. With Moira. He smiled. He knew exactly what he needed to do.

He picked up the fork. "Mrs. Reese, would you be so kind as to scramble another batch of eggs? I find my appetite has returned."

Chapter Twenty-One

Moira sat on the tree swing, idly swaying while a group of children played nearby. It had been over a week since she'd returned to Seaton House. As much as she wanted to stay at the office and tend to Anson, she had honored his request for time alone to think. It helped knowing that he was well cared for. Nel had agreed to bring him meals and look after him until he could get back on his feet. Her friend's daily messages reported a slow recovery, both mentally and physically.

He'd languished at first, refusing to eat or engage in any type of conversation other than what was required. However, in the past few days, he had brightened and was regaining his strength and his outlook. He appeared to have found something compelling him to get better. Was it the desire to return to his beloved medicine…or to her?

A child's trilling laugh pierced into her gloomy thoughts. She looked up as a young boy darted from behind a bush and chased after two of his playmates. A few yards away, Sophia and another girl were playing in the grass with their dolls, smiling and chatting like little magpies. She heaved a heavy sigh. The happiness that surrounded Seaton House failed to cheer her. Everything felt bleak and empty.

A movement caught her eye, and she turned to find Meredith lumbering across the yard, her bulging stomach leading the charge. She was due any day now. The babe was head down and seated at the birthing canal.

"He's coming, Moira," Meredith called out.

Moira shot off the swing and rushed to Meredith's side, grasping an elbow. "The baby is coming? Did your water break? Why aren't you in bed?"

Meredith smiled and shook her head. "Not the baby. He won't be here for a few more days. It's your Dr. Locke. He's on his way to visit."

"You saw him?"

Meredith had the ability to conjure visions of the near future, though she usually scried for children with special gifts who needed help. Her friend had saved many a child from torture and worse. She knew that first hand.

"I was at my vision tree when the image jumped to Doctor Locke on horseback. I recognized Mr. Tyson's farm in the background. Your good doctor will be here in less than an hour."

That wasn't a lot of time to prepare. She gathered a handful of skirt. "Thank you, Meredith. Wish me luck."

She fled into the house and up the stairs to her bedroom. Her head swam with conflicting thoughts. Was he coming to officially relieve her of her position at the office? Or was he going to ask her to stay? And if he wanted her to stay, what kind of relationship did he want? She knew what kind she wanted.

She peeled off her simple day dress and donned her Sunday best – a yellow muslin gown that Anson had once remarked made her look like a songbird. She hoped she trilled the words he wanted to hear.

The image in the mirror stared back. Circles ringed

her eyes. Her skin was pale and a bit dry. She scrubbed a smudge from her cheek. Not much she could do about an appearance sapped by little sleep and a poor appetite. Anson would just have to accept her for who she was. In more ways than one.

She clattered down the stairs, through the foyer, and down the hall to the kitchen. As she pushed through the door, Mrs. Clement started and tossed her hands in the air. Flour dust billowed around her.

"What the devil, Miss Moira? You scared the verra life out of me."

The woman's Scottish burr rained over her, a pleasant sound that brightened many a gloomy heart. Hers was feeling lighter already. "My apologies, Mrs. Clement. I shouldn't have rushed in like that. But I need the picnic blanket and a jar of lemonade, right away. Oh, and two of those delicious scones from breakfast, if there are any left."

"Are ye having a picnic, then?"

"I hope so. Meredith said Dr. Locke is on his way to visit."

"Is he now?" The housekeeper wiped her hands on a rag, a smile ploughing into rounded cheeks. "The blanket is on the top shelf in the pantry. And you're in luck; there were two scones left from breakfast. I'll put those, the lemonade, and some glasses in a basket for you."

"Thank you, Mrs. Clement. You're a dear."

She scurried to the pantry and gathered the blanket and two cloth napkins. Once Mrs. Clement packed the food, she snagged the basket and rushed through the door. She nearly collided with the brick wall on the other side.

Strong hands reached out to steady her. She found her balance and looked up into tawny eyes. Gabe. In the gloom of the hallway, it was hard to tell if he had gotten over his anger with her or not.

"I'm glad I caught you, Moira."

His tone held a quiet eagerness as if he'd been waiting on something and had found it. She heaved a soft sigh. She didn't have time to dance around his tender ego.

"Not now, Gabe." She jiggled the basket hanging on her arm. "I'm in a bit of a hurry."

"To meet Dr. Locke. Yes, Meredith told me."

Oh dear. He knew. Would he try to inflict another magical casualty on Anson? She sugared her tone. "Perhaps we can talk later? I promise to give you my undivided attention."

"That won't be necessary. What I have to say won't take long." He dropped his hands to his sides and squared himself. "I just wanted to apologize for my behavior at Nel's wedding. It was childish of me to take my anger out on your beau. It's clear how taken you are with him."

Not what she was expecting at all. "That's very mature of you, Gabe."

"I hope you find all the happiness you deserve with the good doctor. He's a lucky man."

"Thank you. But I'm the lucky one. I have kind and thoughtful friends like you supporting me. That means more than you know."

"I'm happy to call you friend as well." He waved a hand. "Go. Get ready for your picnic. If Dr. Locke is half as smart as he looks, he'll grab onto you and never let go."

From his amusing mouth to God's ears. She smiled and clicked her way down the hall and out the rear door. All was quiet and still in the yard and nearby barns. Meredith had taken the children to another location to play. So thoughtful of her to give them some privacy.

Moira unfurled the blanket beneath the big oak tree shadowing the yard. It was one of the spots where Meredith summoned her visions. A charmed place. Hopefully, it would be just the magic she and Anson needed.

She set the scones on the napkins and poured lemonade into the glasses. Thoughts surfaced of the picnic they'd shared on the banks of Dancer's Creek. Anson had been giddy with visions of their future. Of working together, of seeing the practice expand and grow. Did he still want that? Did he still want her? He cared for her. Said he loved her. She sank onto the blanket. Would that be enough to overcome what he knew about her?

After what seemed like hours, a shadow pushed around the side of the house and then Anson was there. Her heart fluttered like butterflies flocking on a hot summer day. Oh how she loved this man. Every ornery inch of him.

He approached, his gait a bit hitchy. He was still on the mend. But his pink coloring indicated he was well on the way to recovery.

"Mrs. Booth said you were around back." He pulled to a stop and cocked his head, his expression giving no hint as to his mood. "A picnic for two? Are you expecting someone to join you?"

"Yes, you. Please, have a seat, Anson."

He dropped to his knees and grunted to a sitting position on the blanket. His face was freshly barbered, and he'd slicked his hair with tonic. The smell of bay rum washed over her, bringing with it the memories of their one night together. She hoped with all her heart there would be many, many more.

"How are you doing? I assume your wounds are healing without issue. You look much better than the last time I saw you." She was rambling. But she didn't know what else to say. The deeper conversation was his to carry.

"I'm feeling much better, thanks to Mrs. Reese. She's quite the task-master." His face scrunched like an old rag. "How did you know I was coming? I wasn't sure myself until a couple of hours ago."

She had trusted him with her secret. The secrets of Seaton House would be safe with him as well. "I told you about my healing ability. Well, everyone here at Seaton House is gifted in one manner or another. Mrs. Booth can summon visions of the near future. She saw me in the mine with Thacker and Mrs. Wentworth, and just now, saw you riding toward the orphanage."

"I see."

"Remember that voice you heard in your head telling you I was in danger? That was Sally. She's the young girl who borrowed your handkerchief at Nel's wedding. She uses personal objects to connect with people and send them mental messages. She did that with you after Meredith saw her vision of my abduction."

"I see."

"Sally's older brother knocked over Nel's wedding placard, not you. Gabe can move objects with his mind.

He thought there was something between us and became jealous. He pushed the placard over, trying to stop you."

"I see."

Was that all he was going to say? Shouting or scathing remarks would be preferable to the blandness. At least she would know which side of the fence he stood on.

He picked up the glass of lemonade and took a sip. "Quite the eclectic mix of orphans you have here at Seaton House."

Was that a good thing or bad? His expression remained as unremarkable as day old porridge. She nibbled on her scone. She was stalling, but she couldn't bring herself to broach the subject that sat like a boulder between them.

"I appreciate you telling me about everyone's *gifts*." Hurt whispered across his face, a hummingbird darting from danger. "But it's a little too late for confessions, don't you think? If you loved me half as much as you claim, you would have revealed all of this sooner. Your distrust cuts far deeper than any knife wound, Moira."

He never was one to mince words, even if they bit. She pinched off a corner of scone. "I'm sorry, Anson. I wanted to tell you. I just didn't know how. You accused me of peddling snake-oil and poisons. I had no idea how you would react if you found out what I could really do."

"I admit, if I had known about your talent when we first met, I would have banished you from the office immediately. This gift of yours is quite…peculiar. I have never believed in or trusted the miraculous."

He didn't believe in her. Maybe never would. "That is who you are, Anson. The man I have come to love. The last thing I want is to cause you pain. Yet my unwillingness to trust you has done just that. I'm sorry for hurting you. I understand if you no longer want me at the office or in your life."

She dropped her head and studied the scone. The humps and bumps on the biscuit were much easier to look at than pain-filled eyes.

"Moira."

When she didn't look up, he grasped her chin and lifted. She met a gentle, loving gaze. Her pulse skipped a beat.

"I have discovered that there are things beyond what can be seen and heard and touched. Wonderful, miraculous things." He thumbed her cheek. "I love you, Moira Devlin. And I *do* want you by my side, at the office and in my life. Will you make me the happiest man on this earth and beyond and become my wife?"

"Y-you want to marry me. After all you have learned?"

"I want every particle of you. I can't imagine my life without you in it."

Her insides bloomed with joy. She dove into his arms. "Yes, Yes. Oh, Anson. A thousand times, yes. I will be your wife."

****

Moira went up on tip-toe and shoved the last of her potions onto the storage shelf. From top to bottom, the pantry bulged with colorful bottles filled with a myriad of potions. A good thing. There would be no more harvesting of herbs. Winter had charged in, dumping snow and chilly temperatures over the town. All her plants had wilted into dormancy.

There was a silver lining to winter. Now she had more time to spend with her husband. More time to wallow in bed with his arms cradling her. More time to indulge in pleasant lovemaking.

Arms trapped her waist in a loving grip. She smiled and melted into the body pressed against her.

"Good morning, Mrs. Locke." He nuzzled her neck. "You smell delicious. Like a sweet treat just for my enjoyment."

She turned and cuddled against him, rubbing her cheek over his cotton shirt. "You are my appetizer, main course, and dessert, all rolled into one."

He planted a kiss on the top of her head. "Why don't we go upstairs and sate that hunger?"

The front doorbell dinged, announcing a visitor. She leaned back and smiled. "Duty calls, Dr. Locke."

He groaned. "Some days, I wonder why I chose this profession. Little sleep and even less time for enjoyment."

"You don't wonder why at all."

He smiled and took her hand. "No, I don't. Let's go see who needs our help."

Our help. Her life couldn't get any more complete.

A girl just budding into womanhood stood in the foyer. Red curls rebelled against hairpins and ribbons. Her skirt buckled, wrinkling like waves in a gale. Even her boots were gray with dust. Had she ridden hell-bent for medical assistance or was this just Madelene Fontaine at her best? Either was possible.

Moira hurried down the hallway. Sally hadn't sent any mental warnings. Yet why else would an orphan from Seaton House come calling?

"Maddie. What are you doing here? Is there a problem at the orphanage? Is anyone hurt?"

"Everyone is fine. I came to talk with you. I have a proposal I want to present."

The gleam in Maddie's eyes warned this proposal could have tricky edges. Moira glanced at Anson who had joined them in the foyer. Other than head cocked and eyebrows raised, he remained silent.

"What kind of proposal?" she asked.

"I'll show you. Is there somewhere we can talk?"

Anson pointed down the hall. "You can use the office, if you'd like. I have some equipment that needs cleaning."

Red curls whipped around a puckered brow. "I'd like you to hear this too, Dr. Locke."

One eyebrow lifted farther than the other. "Very well. Come this way."

Once in the office, Moira settled on the spare chair while Anson took the desk chair. Maddie stood before them, hands balled in front of her. She was uneasy. Quite unusual for a girl who charged through life as if she owned it. This proposal meant a lot to her.

"Go on, Maddie," she urged.

The fourteen-year-old swiped a tongue across her lips and focused on Anson. "I understand from Meredith that your medical practice is doing quite well. Your medical skills along with Moira's potions and healing ability are a great benefit to the people of Mineral. I want to offer them more."

Anson leaned forward. "More what?"

"More options. I can provide solutions to problems that you might not be able to help them with."

"Such as?"

Maddie pointed to his head. "Receding hairlines, for one."

Anson scrubbed a finger over his temple where the hair was retreating faster than ants scurrying away from peppermint oil. "How would you do that?"

"With this." Maddie pulled a small vial from her pocket and held it out in her palm. "One drop massaged into your scalp every morning will prod your hair to start growing back."

He turned, his expression puzzled. "Are you able to make such a potion, Moira?"

She wagged her head. "No. I don't have the power or the knowledge."

He frowned and looked back at Maddie. "What makes this potion so special?"

Maddie hefted her chin. "Me."

"You? How so?"

Green cat-eyes shifted from her to Anson and back. Moira nodded. "Go on, Maddie. Tell him. Anson knows all about Seaton House and our special abilities. This shouldn't be too overwhelming for him."

Maddie moved to the desk and set the vial on top. "This is more of a charm than a potion. I learned how to make such things from the Creoles who worked at my family's estate in New Orleans. My ability expanded when I lived with the Choctaw Indians. Their medicine man recognized my skills and took me under his wing."

"You lived with the Indians?"

Maddie smiled. "That's a story for another day. What say you? Are you interested in having me provide remedies for your patients? My charms can cure warts, reduce wrinkles, and even increase fertility. I have amulets that can ward off evil, bring good luck, or encourage romance."

Anson coughed. "Let's stick to the healthful remedies. The townsfolk might not be ready for those other nebulous ones."

Moira chuckled. He tried so hard to be accepting of their gifts, even if they baffled the life out of him. "If we agree to this venture, what would you get out of it?"

"Money. Lily and I want to open our own restaurant in town...when we're old enough, that is. We'll provide people with the things they love...food and entertainment, sprinkled with just a touch of magic. We'll know what they want."

Of course, they would. "Anson?"

He studied Maddie. She held her ground, no fidgeting, no averting of the eyes. A strong girl, that one.

Anson leaned back in his chair. "This sounds like it could be a promising business endeavor. If Moira is agreeable, we will stock and sell your remedies."

"I'm agreeable," she answered.

Maddie's smile blossomed into a full out grin. "Thank you, Dr. Locke. Moira. You won't regret this. We'll make lots of money. You'll see."

Anson crossed arms over his chest. "Since we're supplying the warehouse and doing the selling, we'll take twenty percent of the price."

Maddie mimicked his stance. "Fifteen. And I'll throw in that hair growth charm for free."

Anson wagged his head. He knew when he'd been had. He stood and held out his hand. "It's a deal."

Maddie took Anson's hand, her face as radiant as the morning sun. "Thank you, thank you, thank you." She whirled around and skipped for the door. "I can't wait to tell Lily. She'll be so excited."

As the red-headed whirlwind disappeared into the hallway, Moira rose and skirted the desk. She snuggled in Anson's arms. "Thank you for agreeing to sponsor Maddie. I've never seen her so excited."

"She's quite the negotiator. She knows what she wants and goes after it." A steady blue gaze poured over her. "Just like another Seaton House orphan I know. Am I still a stepping-stone for your career, my darling?"

"Stepping-stone? Oh no. You are my rock and the love of my life."

Magic in Her Touch

A word about the author...

Donna Dalton lives in central Virginia with her husband, two sons, and a grandson. An avid reader of historical romances, Donna uses the rich history of the "Old Dominion" State for many of her story settings. You can visit her on her website at www.donndalton.net or on facebook at DonnaDaltonbooks.